A BUMPY YEAR

ALSO BY OLIVIA SPOONER

A Way Back to Happy

A BUMPY YEAR

Olivia Spooner

An Aria Book

First published in the UK in 2022 by Head of Zeus Ltd,
part of Bloomsbury Publishing Plc

9 7 5 3 1 2 4 6 8

A catalogue record for this book is available from the British Library.

ISBN (PB): 9781800249516
ISBN (E): 9781800249493

Cover design: Beth Yirtaw

Typeset by Siliconchips Services Ltd UK

Printed and bound in Great Britain by
CPI Group (UK) Ltd, Croydon CRO 4YY

Head of Zeus Ltd
First Floor East
5–8 Hardwick Street
London ECIR 4RG

WWW.HEADOFZEUS.COM

To Mike

I

My heels dig into the earth as I step across the neatly clipped grass towards my friend. "Boss suspects something," I rasp, arriving at the park bench. It's like I've been holding my breath all day and need to get air flowing into my lungs again.

Emma frowns. She looks so comfortable sitting there in her leggings and T-shirt. Hair down. Face make-up free.

"I thought you were going to tell her last week?" she says.

Tugging the waistband of my work trousers higher, I sit next to my friend, kick off my shoes and immediately compare our stomachs. Em must be twice the size and she's only a month further along. Not that I'm jealous or anything. The longer I can pretend I'm not up the duff, the better.

"She's in a bad mood about this big project we're working on," I mutter. "Our client in Tokyo is threatening to pull out and I have to fly over there next week to 'stroke his ego', as Tash puts it." I pause for breath. "Bloody Tokyo."

"I've always wanted to go to Japan," Emma murmurs. She stares at her son, Freddie, who clambers up the slide in the playground, sits down on the platform, places his feet on the top rail of the ladder and leaps off, landing on the ground with a thump. It strikes me as a large and fairly terrifying jump for a recently turned five-year-old.

"Isn't he supposed to do that the other way around?" I ask.

Em shakes her head. "Apparently it's too boring going *down* the slide. You should see him on the seesaw."

As if he's heard, Freddie runs to the seesaw, squeezes his two feet onto the narrow seat at one end, grips the handle, and bounces up and down with such force I'm sure he's going to fly into the air and land on his head like some animated cartoon character.

"How can you watch?" I ask, picturing Freddie's skull cracking open.

Emma sighs. "It's a mother's prerogative to stand by and watch helplessly as their child tries to find new and improved ways to injure themselves."

"Great."

She pats my knee, smiling. "It's not *all* bad, Trish."

I try to block the fact I'm nearly five months pregnant from my mind. Again. Denial has worked well so far and I'm determined to cling to it as long as I can.

"So, why is your boss suspicious?" Emma asks.

Damn. Now I have to face facts.

"She saw me undo the button of my trousers when we were in a meeting. I was trying to be discreet about it, but they were digging into me and I couldn't get comfortable."

"You could have just gained a few pounds."

I lift an eyebrow. "As if she'd believe that."

"True."

I go to the gym five days a week and check calories on

food labels the way others check Instagram. Emma would be horrified to learn I've already weighed myself three times today and each time I stepped off the scales, I had a ridiculous urge to burst into tears.

"It's a good thing, Trish." Emma eyes me with concern. "You're supposed to gain weight when you're pregnant. I was worried when you were throwing up all the time."

"Thank God that's over." I quickly put a hand on the seat beside me. "Touch wood." All this pregnancy talk is not what I need right now. "Have you heard from Mags since she got back?"

"Nope. She's coming tonight, though. We can grill her then."

"Excellent. I thought she might be too jet-lagged."

Emma grins. "Mags says she's too high on life to be jet-lagged."

I raise my eyebrows. "Reading between the lines, would you say that means she's been getting some action?"

"Definitely."

"Wow." I consider what this means for a moment. "Just between you and me, it's going to feel a little weird talking about... well... her sex life."

Emma laughs and I'm reminded of the years I spent at university with my three closest friends: Emma, Mags and Lily. Not only were we inseparable, but we were also powerful. Nothing fazed us. Obviously we grew up and realized the power was a smokescreen over our naivety; a smokescreen eventually destroyed by the harsh realities of adulthood, but I sometimes miss the Emma who refused to take life seriously and was game to try everything. I admired her for it. Was jealous even, since I've never been one to leap into any situation without considering all the facts first. Except for five months ago, when I leapt and will have to live with the consequences for the rest of my life.

Stop it, I tell myself.

"Freddie," Emma calls out. "Time to go home and get ready. Daddy will be here soon."

Ah, *daddy* – such an innocuous little word with so much hell wrapped up in it.

"How's it going with the new arrangement?" I ask softly.

Emma frowns. "OK, I guess." She rolls her eyes. "I'm trying to accept this new Paul, but it's challenging. He's taking Freddie to church on Sunday, for God's sake."

Emma has only recently finalized a custody arrangement whereby her ex-husband has Freddie from 5 p.m. Friday to 3 p.m. Sunday on alternate weekends. At least this gives Emma a little time to herself, or some alone time with her new and improved boyfriend, Finn. Emma leads a hectic life. If she's not trying to be the world's best mum, she's busting a gut running her own café. To think in a few months, she'll be throwing another child into the mix...

"How do you feel about the whole worshiping God thing?" I ask.

"I don't mind Freddie learning about Christianity – I just don't want him going all religious on me."

"Fair enough."

An image flashes into my head of my family groomed and impeccably dressed, sitting to attention in the front row of St Joseph's Church. My father, dressed in full military uniform, is at the end of the pew next to the aisle. He's watching us without turning his eyes in our direction – a skill he excelled at. Once I had to scratch an itch behind my knee. The way my father went on about it when we got home, you'd think I'd picked my nose and flicked the snot at the minister's face. There was no chance Mum was coming to my defence – she'd already returned to bed. And, of course, my two older brothers had disappeared to their room the second Dad raised his voice.

Resting a hand on my belly, I take another deep breath, but it's harder this time. My chest is too tight and I can't get the air down past my ribs.

We stand as Freddie runs over.

"You don't have to come to the scan with me next week, Em," I murmur.

"But I want to be there."

Emma gives my hand a quick squeeze and I force a smile. No one – not even my closest friends – knows how much effort smiling can sometimes take. How many years I've practised, determined to hide the hollow void I carry around inside my chest. Truth is, I've been making myself smile for most of my life.

2

"She has the most beautiful skin. It's soft and velvety and when she rubs against me in the shower, I feel like she's made of silk."

Mags can't even sit like the rest of us. She's pacing about Emma's living room with a crazed look in her eye. I love seeing her so passionate. It makes a change from her usual even-keeled self. Mags is tall, solid, dependable. The one who checks you've got your keys and puts reminders in her phone of everyone's birthdays. She's close to saint-like, especially when it comes to looking out for others. As for her cats – I've lost count of how many – if Mags ever ends up having children of her own, they're going to be thoroughly indulged judging by the way she pampers her feline friends. I wonder how the new girlfriend feels about Mags' precious furballs.

"Did you actually leave your little love nest at any point?" Lily asks, pouring herself another glass of wine.

Emma and I exchange a sympathetic look. It's not easy giving up on the booze, especially when the four of us are together.

Lily's wearing one of her standard-issue work outfits: black trousers, black sleeveless turtleneck and black sandals.

They tone in well with her cropped black hair and eyes heavily accentuated with black eyeliner and thick mascara. She's not quite at the goth level she used to be at university, but she's not far off. I avoid wearing black at all costs. It makes me look like a ghost.

"Of course we did," gushes Mags. "We walked to the local village, and we hired bikes and rode to this amazing waterfall, and we visited an ancient temple, and…" Mags throws her hands in the air. "And lots of other stuff."

"How exactly do you have sex?" Lily demands, blunt as always.

Em chokes on her ginger beer. "Lily!"

"What? I mean we're all thinking it, aren't we?"

"Not really," I say. "I'm not sure that I want to know."

Mags laughs. "Trish, you can take the girl out of the army but you can't take the army out of the girl."

I force myself to keep a relaxed smile on my face, even as my legs start to shake. Any reference to my family makes me raise an invisible shield around me. Impossible to penetrate. My friends had better not take this army reference any further.

"So?" prompts Lily. "The sex?"

Mags flops onto the couch next to me and I sag with relief as the conversation moves on to safer ground.

"It's better than anything you boring heterosexuals will ever experience. Even you, Lily."

Mags has only been openly gay for three months. For the thirty-three years prior she's been a boring heterosexual like the rest of us. Outwardly at least. It's good to know I'm not the only one in our group who's been hiding who they really are.

"I might just have to take your word on that," says Lily.

"Speaking of sex, Lils, how's it going shacked up with lover boy?" Mags asks, taking a huge gulp of her wine.

I've never seen Mags so radiant. She deserves to be happy, but I worry this woman Mags is currently hung up on will break her heart. I've always found my friend's utter faith and trust in people alarming.

Lily makes a face. "Terrible."

"Why?" Em asks.

"He irons his bloody underwear," she murmurs, slouching lower in her chair.

"He what?" Mags yells, with a huge grin "That's appalling!"

"Disgraceful," Em says.

"Unforgivable," I add, smiling despite myself.

My friends can always make me feel better. Their friendship is more precious than they'll ever know.

"Yesterday, I got home late from work and he'd not only cooked a proper meal, but he'd also left mine in the oven to keep warm," says Lily.

"Outrageous." Em's face is one of mock horror. "What did he cook?"

Lily scowls. "You'd have loved it. There was salmon with some kind of fancy stuff on the skin, and that dish with thin layers of potato—"

"Dauphinoise," says Emma.

"No, that stuff you get in fancy pubs… You know, with the creamy sauce."

"Gratin."

Lily points her finger at Mags. "That's it. A bloody potato gratin."

I raise my eyebrows at Emma. "Or, as the French would say, dauphinoise."

"All right, you two with your fancy food terms. I bet you can't tell me what the vegetable was?"

"Charred broccoli and leeks," I state.

Lily stares at me. "How did you—"

"The recipe was in the pull-out food guide in the paper last weekend."

Lily drops her head in her hands. "Well that just makes it even worse," she mutters.

We all laugh and I enjoy the sensation. I've been working on finding more joy. It's the topic of a book I've been reading called *Find Your Bliss*. I hate the title, but the author makes some interesting suggestions. Every night before I go to sleep, I write down three things during that day I was grateful for. It's supposed to make me focus on the wonderful gifts already present in my life and shift my thoughts away from the negative. It can be the smallest of things: the way light filters through the trees, the earthy smell after rain, a smile from a stranger. Mentally, I've added this moment to my list.

"How about you, Trish? Seen pie-boy lately?" Mags asks. "Or Pete," she adds warily.

I exhale and feel the fleeting moment of happiness disappear with my breath. The mere mention of Pete has me gulping for air.

"I've been avoiding both of them as much as possible," I say. "Elliot phoned me on Wednesday night and asked if he could come over."

"And did he?" says Lily.

"No way. That's done and dusted. Even if I did want him

9

to come round, nothing would have happened. My boobs are way too sensitive. Even in the shower, I can't face the nozzle. If the water hits them full on, it's like a thousand tiny needles poking me. Just the thought of someone trying to touch these guys makes me shudder."

I glance down at my large breasts. Boulders more like. The girls have all said to me at various times over the years how they wish they had big boobs like me. They have no idea. If there was one part of my body I could change – and believe me, there are a number of less-than-ideal areas to choose from – I'd shrink these two giant lugs to a quarter their size. Especially now. I remember Emma boasting about her bigger breasts when she was pregnant with Freddie, but I thought it wouldn't happen to me, for some reason. I mean, she had room to grow. I was already at maximum capacity.

"Probably for the best, Trish." Mags gives my hand a sympathetic squeeze. "At least until you find out who the father is."

And there it is.

Sensible, ambitious Trish is not only pregnant, but she also has no idea who the bloody dad is. Well, she can narrow it down to two and she oscillates daily on who she'd prefer the father to be, but this wasn't part of her plan. Wasn't even on the radar.

If Pete hadn't turned up again after two long years to try to break my heart all over again, and if I hadn't had a moment of stupid weakness and fallen into the eager arms of pie-guy, I wouldn't be stuck in this hellish situation to begin with.

I put a hand on my stomach and silently apologize to the

foetus lumped with me for a mother. *It's not that I won't love you or take care of you – I'm just not sure I'm ready for this.*

I wonder how my mother felt when she discovered she was pregnant with me. Was she happy to be having another baby? Excited? Terrified? As a child I'd often catch Mum looking at me with eyes so full of despair that I thought she was silently wishing I'd never been born.

Lily claps her hands together and springs to her feet.

"Now, let's stop talking about sex, guys and babies, and turn our attention to something far more important." She strides into the kitchen. "What delicious morsel have you got waiting for us in here, Em?" she calls. "You realize we only come here for the food."

Mags starts laughing and Emma joins in. I attempt to laugh, too, but I'm distracted by this strange sensation in my lower stomach. It's like there's a silent mobile phone ringing inside me. It's vibrating and leaping about, trying to get my attention. I slide one hand over my stomach and there are little flutters beneath my hand.

My heart begins to beat fast and hard and I feel light-headed. It's real. This baby thing is really happening. Patricia Kirkpatrick, only daughter of Colonel Reynold Kirkpatrick, is having a child out of wedlock to a father who is yet to be identified. It's laughable really, considering my upbringing. There's no way in hell I'm telling Mum and Dad, or my older brothers. Not that it'll be hard. I haven't spoken to any of them in years.

3

The only direct flight to Tokyo leaves Auckland at 8 a.m., which means I've been up since four. I feel jet-lagged already and we haven't even taken off. Unfortunately, the plane is full, meaning the likelihood of getting any sleep during the eleven-hour flight is looking increasingly slim. The problem with living on an island in the Pacific is that I live on an island in the Pacific: New Zealand is a great place, but it's bloody miles from the rest of the world.

I'm wedged between a man around my age with dark shoulder-length curls who smells intensely of lavender, and an elderly lady who hasn't stopped sniffing since we boarded and who wears incontinence pads that need replacing, judging by the smell of stale wee emanating from her body. Needless to say, I'm leaning in lavender guy's direction.

"Heading to Tokyo for work?" he asks as I click my seat belt.

Knowing my luck, he's going to be a talker. Better shut him down early.

"Yes," I say, extending a half-hearted glance in his direction before staring intently at my phone and pretending to be engrossed in an email I've already read twice.

It's from my boss, outlining her suggestions for how

best to tackle my meeting tomorrow. She raises some valid points, but nothing I haven't thought of already.

"What do you do?"

Lavender guy obviously hasn't got the hint.

"I'm in IT," I say, my head down, eyes fixed on my phone.

"Computers?"

"Sort of."

"Isn't that what IT is?"

Accepting defeat, I place my phone face down on my lap. Hopefully, we'll talk for five minutes and he'll get this "be friendly to thy neighbour" out of his system and leave me alone.

"I work for a company that presents clients with algorithms to help grow their business."

"Right."

He looks at me with such pity you'd think I'd announced I worked for an oil company.

"That explains it," he continues.

"Explains what?"

"Your aura."

Oh, Jesus, he's one of those. I should smile politely and get my headphones on, but seriously? I can't let this go.

"My aura?" Surely he can hear the sarcasm in my voice.

"Sorry, that was rude."

"Oh no, tell me more about my aura. What do you see?"

He can tell I'm goading him now. That I think he's some kind of weirdo. A cute weirdo, I'll admit, but a weirdo all the same.

The guy brushes his shiny curls back from his face only for them to flop back down again

"Look, I was kind of joking. I've been reading about

auras lately. Don't ask me why – I just tend to go down little rabbit holes – and I'm not sure they're real, but at the same time... well, there's this sense I get around people. I think we all get it."

"A sense?"

He swivels around to face me fully and uses both of his hands to tuck his thick black hair behind his ears. It should be effeminate, but I find the move strangely sexy.

"Have you ever been in a roomful of people and someone else walks in and suddenly the atmosphere changes?" he asks.

"You mean when my boss walks into the conference room and—"

"I'm not talking about that sort of thing. If your boss walks in, of course the atmosphere is going to be altered. I'm talking more about..."

He pauses and I can see his mind ticking over.

"OK, say you're at home having dinner with you family." He pauses again. "Who is in your family, by the way? Mum? Dad? Brothers? Sisters? Crazy aunts?"

I don't like where this conversation is going. In fact, I'm cursing ever putting down my phone.

"Mum and Dad. Two brothers," I mutter.

He gives me a quizzical look and I notice his penetrating deep brown eyes. They're searching for something inside me and I quickly look away.

"Right," he says. "OK, so imagine you're all sitting at home eating, but one of you is missing—"

"Mum." It slips out so fast I don't have time to stop the word from leaving my lips.

Again, I get the questioning eyes. They're unnerving.

Though not as terrifying as this conversation. I need it to stop.

"So you're sitting there eating," he says quietly. "And your mum enters the room. There's a subtle shift in the air. Now it could be because you've been waiting for her and you're all pleased she's arrived, but maybe it's because whatever she's feeling, whatever emotional state she brings into the room changes the atmosphere. When you look at her you see your mum, but you also have a sense of her internal essence and it's somehow emanating from her. Maybe that's her aura."

My body has started shaking and I can feel sweat dripping between my breasts. I'm gripping the armrests so tightly my fingers are cramping, but I have to act normal.

"Interesting," I croak, my gaze dropping to his shoes.

Nike sports shoes. Black with grey stripes. Very strait-laced for a guy who says things like "internal essence" and "emotional state" as if they're terms used to describe a rugby game.

The man gently begins to pry my fingers loose from the armrest closest to him, his touch so tender it makes my skin tingle. In horror, I glare at the caramel-coloured skin on the back of his hand. Fleetingly, I wonder about his ethnicity – is he part Maori? Samoan?

He wraps my hand in his and squeezes.

"I'm sorry," he whispers.

Damn him. Tears flood my eyes. What the hell is going on? Then I'm suddenly crying and he's got an arm around me and I'm lying heavily against his chest. And it's completely bonkers that I'm crying – which I never do, by the way – in the arms of some stranger who smells not only of lavender, but also something muskier, like cloves. I can't believe I'm noticing the scent of this guy. I feel like I'm outside my body, looking down at the freak who is me, and I'm shaking my head and saying to my other blubbering self: *Stop this, Trish. Snap out of it. This isn't who you are.* People in the aisle across from us are asking if I'm all right and the strange man stroking my hair is telling everyone I'm fine, and I'm sure he genuinely believes it.

But it's not how real life works.

Eventually, I calm down enough to sit up and take the tissue from the incontinent woman smiling hesitantly beside me. Slowly, I wipe my eyes and blow my nose. My make-up must be a disaster, but I don't care. Which is saying something.

I glance at lavender guy, who's still got the palm of his hand on my back. There's a big wet patch on the front of his T-shirt.

"Sorry," I mutter, waving at his chest.

"Forget about it. It'll dry."

I'm not embarrassed by my crazy outburst, even though I should be. Instead, I feel drained. Completely and utterly drained.

"Here." The man lifts his hand off me and leans forwards to rummage in his bag under the seat in front. He pulls out a bottle, opens the lid and holds it out. "Coconut water. Very hydrating."

My hand shakes as I take a sip. I've never been sure about coconut water, even though it's become popular, especially with everyone at the gym. The few times I tried it, I'd stop after a few gulps because it left a sickly-sweet and slimy taste in my mouth. But this coconut water tastes magnificent. I have another sip and another. Then I gulp down half the bottle and hand it back.

"Thanks."

"My name's Scott."

"Trish."

"Pleased to meet you, Trish."

I raise an eyebrow at him. "You sure about that?"

Scott laughs and I can't help but smile.

"It's certainly a memorable first meeting," he says.

"Just so you know, that's only the third time I've cried in twenty years."

Scott puts a hand over his heart. "Well if that's the case, I not only feel honoured but also slightly disturbed."

"Why?"

"I cry at least once a month."

"Don't be ridiculous."

He tips his head to one side, his expression serious. "What is ridiculous is that you haven't cried more. You take suppressed emotions to a whole new level."

I know he's teasing me, but at the same time he's probing and I don't like it.

"I've got a lot of work to do."

I start to lower my tray table, but Scott's hand shoots out and stops it.

"We're about to take off," he says firmly.

"Oh."

I let him clip my tray back into the closed position and glance past the lady, who's pretending she's not listening to our conversation but is clearly lapping up every word. Runway and grass whip past the window as we pick up speed. I can't believe we haven't even made it off the ground yet. I feel like I've been on the plane for hours.

I want to leap out of my seat, run to the exit doors, fling them open and jump. Not because I want to kill myself – I simply need to escape Scott. He's witnessed a side of me not even my closest friends have seen. I'm surprised I'm capable of such an outpouring. I thought I was more like Dad. Stiff upper lip and all that crap. But my recent outburst means there might be more of Mum in me than I realized: and that's a truly terrifying prospect. My only hope is that pregnancy hormones are making me an emotional basket case.

Oh, shit, I'm pregnant!

I'd forgotten all about the orange-sized foetus in my belly. Every time I remember, it comes as a shock. A shock that I'm pregnant and a shock that I'd forgotten I was pregnant. Does that mean I'll be a forgetful mother, too?

Agitated, I flick my thumbnail over and over against my forefinger and stare straight ahead as the plane lifts off the ground. The roar of the engine fills my ears. As soon as we level out, I'll put on my headphones, crank up my playlist and get to work.

Once I get off this plane, I won't have to see Scott again. I can pretend my outburst never happened. It's one moment I'll be delighted to forget.

4

I'm eating eel sushi. Emma – ever the foodie – would be proud of me for trying something so adventurous. Truth is, I didn't realize what unagi was until I'd googled it. I was trying to find something on the menu that was cooked, since raw fish is fourth on the list on my phone entitled *Don't Eat – Might Kill Baby*, and the menu said this unagi stuff was not only grilled, but also teriyaki-flavoured. I love a good bit of teriyaki chicken back home so confidently placed my order with the impeccably groomed waitress before Google informed me unagi was in fact a slimy, hideous eel that lurks in shadowed, murky streams. It's not too bad taste-wise; especially with a good amount of soy sauce on top. Being starving helps. I wonder if there's a boy incubating inside me – my appetite is insatiable. If I don't eat something every couple of hours, the foetus starts grumbling.

The hotel restaurant is surprisingly full at 9 p.m. I had hoped by coming down so late in the evening there would be fewer diners glancing in my direction wondering why the girl with giant boobs (if you ever want to go to a country where a white girl with big tits is going to stand out, Japan is your place) was hunched on her own in the corner. But it must be tradition to eat late. That or the other singletons in the room, of which there are many, all had the same idea as me.

"Trish?"

I glance up with my food halfway to my mouth and when I see who it is, the sushi falls from my chopsticks and lands with a dull thud on my plate.

"Scott?" Dear God, it's him. How can this be happening?

"Hey, this is crazy. You staying here, too?"

I nod, unable to speak.

He tips his head at my plate. "I see you went with the unagi. Well done. It's a little like having the compulsory snails in France – cover the critters in sauce and they're pretty tasty."

I want to bring up the critters and puke them over the starched white tablecloth. Since retrieving my suitcase from the carousel and hightailing it to a taxi, I'd successfully wiped my unusual episode on the plane from my mind. Now, it's back with a vengeance. I'm embarrassed: raging-hot face and cheeks mortified. It doesn't help that Scott's looking all suave and sexy and not the least bit hippy-dippy He's wearing a pale blue shirt – probably had to stuff the T-shirt I soiled with tears in his bag till it could be washed – and dark jeans. His damp hair is tied back in a low ponytail, which somehow he carries off without looking like a woman trapped inside a male body, or a sleazy jewellery salesperson.

"Sorry, Trish." Scott crosses his arms, clearly aware of my discomfort. "I'll leave you in peace."

I nod, hoping he'll run away quickly while I wallow in silent shame, but the waitress arrives and asks in stilted English, "Would the gentleman like to sit? I bring menu?"

Then she waves her hand at the table before pulling out a chair and nodding encouragingly.

I refrain from stabbing her with my chopsticks.

"You can," I say, half choking. "If you want."

Scott smiles uneasily, uncrosses his arms and sits. I stare at my plate as the waitress fusses about pouring some water in his glass and asking if he'd like to order. I do look up, though, when he replies in fluent Japanese.

We both silently watch the waitress glide to another table.

"I've already eaten," Scott says. "There's this alley not far from here where little huts with tiny tables and stools open onto the street. It's loud and busy and the smells as you wander down looking at all the dishes being whipped up – it's incredible. I wish I could show you."

For a second I'd like him to show me, too. "Sounds a tad more exciting than here."

Scott laughs. "That wouldn't be hard."

"You speak Japanese," I state.

"Enough to get by. I've got a mate who's lived in Kyoto for ten years and he still reckons he doesn't fully have a handle on the language."

I appreciate what he's doing – trying to make me relax and give my glowing cheeks a chance to cool.

"I wasn't expecting to see you again," I blurt.

"Yeah, I picked up on that one."

"Sorry, it's just…" I pause. No man has ever looked at me so intently in the face without his eyes drifting to my breasts. It's disconcerting. "I was hoping I could pretend it never happened."

"Do you think that's wise?"

"Yes, I think it's extremely wise."

His eyes still haven't wandered. What's wrong with the guy? Is he gay? Married? Not that being married makes any difference. Or gay, for that matter.

"You don't think I might have stirred up something you've kept bottled inside?"

Unlike most males... actually, scrap that. Unlike *all* males I've ever met, Scott doesn't steer clear of talking about emotions.

"Of course you did, and I intend to ram it straight back into that bottle and screw the lid on extra tight."

I lean forwards in an effort to expose more cleavage. It's not that I want him to be attracted to me – well, OK, maybe – but come on. Is he a man or a mouse?

His gaze drops from my face to my chest and then he quickly averts his eyes to look across the room. Thank God. I was seriously getting worried.

Scott pushes back his chair and stands, his face pale.

"Sorry, Trish. I'd better get going. Enjoy the rest of your unagi."

It comes out in such a rush you'd think he had a bad case of the runs and needed to dash to the loo.

"OK," I say. "Bye."

But he's already halfway to the exit.

It wasn't quite the reaction to my boobs I was expecting. Though, he's not the first guy to be intimidated. I stare at the seat he so abruptly vacated and my heart contracts.

5

It's 5:45 a.m. and I'm eight minutes into my five-kilometre row in the hotel gym, when Scott enters.

"You're fucking kidding me," I mutter, pretending I haven't seen him.

With luck, we'll both ignore each other – which might prove challenging, since we're the only two people in the windowless mirrored room, but not impossible.

He walks right past me and steps onto one of the running machines. Within seconds he's running fast and think I might actually have escaped his notice until he makes eye contact with me in one of the mirrors.

"Morning," he says gruffly.

"Hi," I puff.

And that's it. He looks away to stare at the TV screen in front of him and I'm off the hook. Only I kind of feel let down. Well, more than let down. Rejected. Which isn't the nicest feeling in the world.

I complete my 5k row, periodically glancing at Scott's butt and legs, which are in excellent shape – merely a factual observation, nothing more. Then I wipe my face with my towel and get a drink from the water fountain. Scott continues to run with vigour.

Usually I'd do some upper body exercises next, but I'm keen to hightail it out of here. The problem is, then I'll be in deficit. I won't have completed my usual morning exercise routine and my whole day will be out of whack. While I have another drink and try to decide what to do, a young couple enter the gym. The man leans in to give the woman a kiss on the cheek and she giggles. I dislike them immediately, but they also serve to bolster my courage. Now that Scott and I aren't the only two in the gym, I can carry on with my workout without feeling like a complete lemon or, more accurately, like a pregnant cow with engorged udders. I shudder at my own mental image and head to the assisted chin-up machine.

As I heave myself up and down and the machine grunts and groans, I pretend to look at myself in the mirror, but instead I study Scott's face. I don't think he's watching the TV. He's staring at it with intensity, but his mind is elsewhere. His shoulders are tight and his jaw is clenched. Maybe he always looks like that when he's running, but I sense he's upset, angry even. Oh, shit, I'm one slippery step away from talking about his aura, for fuck's sake. What the hell has got into me?

After four machines, three reps of ten on each, and zero glances in Scott's direction, I'm content to call it quits. Not a great day in terms of my usual workouts, but it'll do. I can always come back to the gym later tonight.

I'm stretching my hamstrings on the mat in the corner, when I hear Scott's machine start to decelerate. I wondered how long he was going to keep up that pace. Panting heavily, he slows to a walk until the machine stops altogether. Would he be offended if I made a run for the door now?

He's clearly no longer the chatty guy from the plane, but he might still feel obliged to come over and speak to me.

I scramble to my feet and head to the exit.

"Trish."

Damn it. Turning, I fix a smile on my face.

"Good run?"

He grimaces and wipes the sweat from his forehead.

"Not really," he mutters into his towel.

Suddenly I wish I hadn't worn my favourite singlet. It's firm-fitting, especially around the midriff area. I put it on because I was standing in front of the mirror at 5 a.m. and there was a definite bump happening. I felt proud of it, to be honest – my baby-in-production body. I was starting to wonder if I was ever going to show.

Now, Scott is either going to think I'm pregnant or fat, and I'm not sure which is worse.

"Look, I'm sorry I took off last night in such a rush."

"It's fine."

"No, it was rude."

"Honestly, Scott. I wasn't in the least offended by your abrupt departure."

He gives me a small, fragile smile and lets out his breath.

"I saw something that upset me and I had to leave."

God, he's referring to my breasts...

"It was my ex-wife."

"Oh." What I really want to say is "Thank God – I thought you were offended by my giant knockers."

"She was with her new husband."

"Oh."

"Anyway, it's still at the raw stage." Scott wipes his face again. "For me, at least," he mumbles.

Poor bugger. He's heartbroken. I know how that feels.

"Did you know they were going to be here in Tokyo?"

"Yes. But I figured they wouldn't stay in this hotel. Harumi used to complain about the rooms when we stayed here while visiting her relatives. I thought she'd steer clear."

"Your ex-wife is Japanese?"

"Yes. Though she's lived in New Zealand for a long time"

"How come you knew they were going to be here?"

"We're going to the same wedding tomorrow."

"Oh. That could be awkward."

"Yep. Neither of us would back down, even though the groom has been my friend since we were at primary school and Harumi knew him for less than a year. She told me she had just as much right to be at the wedding."

"Bitch."

Scott's smile is far more genuine now.

"Thanks."

I'd forgotten about the loved-up couple in the gym with us. They must have decided Scott and I were suitably engrossed in conversation that we wouldn't notice her hand on his crotch and his hand kneading her left breast.

If Lily were here, she'd have yelled, "Get a room," but I don't have the same gumption.

Scott glances in their direction and raises his eyebrows. "Should we get out of here before things go any further?"

"Yes, please," I say, grinning.

Scott opens the door. "Congratulations, by the way."

"For what?"

He looks at my stomach. "How far along are you?"

I stare at my bump for a moment with a mix of pride and guilt. "Five months."

"Is it your first?" he asks as we walk towards the lift.

"Yes."

"Exciting."

I push the up arrow. "Terrifying, more like."

The lift doors open and we step inside.

"How's the dad-to-be taking it? Did he give you strict instructions to avoid all raw fish and meat of any kind in Tokyo?"

I press the number for my floor and Scott presses the button for the floor above mine. Then silently, we watch the lift doors close.

"The dad doesn't know," I say quietly.

"Oh."

"It's complicated."

"Sounds like it."

What the hell – once I step out of this lift, I doubt I'll be seeing Scott again.

"I can't really tell the dad when I don't know who he is," I say, watching the number for my floor light up.

The doors ping and glide open.

"Are there a number to choose from?" Scott asks.

I step out of the lift and turn to face him.

"I've narrowed it down to two," I say, smiling, though why this should be amusing is a mystery.

Scott smiles back and shakes his head as the doors close.

"Good luck," I hear him call.

"Thanks," I mutter, heading to my room. "I'm going to need it."

6

The meeting goes reasonably well. I manage to placate my client with impressive-looking bar charts, graphs and technical jargon. Plus, I assure him his current stagnant period is normal (which isn't a lie, though of more concern than I let on). In a couple of months, I tell him, his business will start reaping the benefits of our tailor-made services.

By the time the meeting is over and I exit the large marbled foyer, my stomach is grumbling so loudly the doorman turns to look at me. My baby wants food and it wants it now.

I merge with the swarm of immaculate Japanese women and men in suits, and keep my eyes peeled for something that looks vaguely European. A bakery or a burger joint. Anything that doesn't involve rice or fish. Not that I don't enjoy Japanese food, but my baby is telling me it needs stodgy carbs right now. Sugary would be a bonus.

Finally, I spy what looks to be a cake shop and push my way through the masses to the revolving door. Inside, it's hot and smells so sweet, I'm sure the air is 50 per cent icing sugar. The cakes all look the same – like boring old vanilla cake with no icing. I point to one then carry the cake outside, open the box, tear off a hunk and take a bite.

It tastes very sweet and extremely dry. Emma would be horrified. Right now, I'd do anything to be sitting in my friend's café eating a slice of her carrot cake or a freshly baked muffin.

Forcing down a few more mouthfuls, I continue my walk towards the hotel. I used to love taking business trips, but they're less enjoyable now, more effortful. For years I revelled in the feeling of importance as I boarded the plane, pulled out my laptop and ordered a glass of champagne. I'd delight in staying in fancy hotels in different cities surrounded by complete strangers. My friends were jealous – they said it often enough – and I was pleased because I wanted them to envy me a little. The way I envied them.

Mags who wears her uncomplicated heart on her sleeve. She's convinced all human beings have the ability to be kind and compassionate, and she'll look for the positive in anyone. If I could have even half of her belief in love and goodness, I'd be content.

Lily knows who she is. No questions, no blurry areas. She says to the world, "This is me and I like who I am, and I'm not going to change for anyone, so fuck you." God, to feel like that for a few moments... Not to question everything about myself on a daily basis.

And Emma is the fearless one, the one who will take risks. Maybe she'll fail, but she'll keep going. And she has parents who would do anything for her, a child to bring joy to her life and a boyfriend who adores her.

Then there's me. The jet-setter. The blonde with the big tits. The smart one. The one who plays the field and never lets her feelings get the better of her.

Before I realize what I've done, the entire cake has

disappeared down my gullet. I feel gross. Utterly gross and utterly alone in a city packed with petite people.

I slam the offending empty box into a rubbish bin outside my hotel, ignore the doorman, stride across the foyer and punch the button on the lift in an unladylike and undignified manner. It helps a little.

On reaching my floor, I scowl at the slim, flat-chested young maid folding towels on a trolley in the hallway and charge past her to my room.

"Trish."

I turn to see Scott walking towards me and fold my arms. I haven't got time for him today. Him or anyone else.

"How was the meeting?" he asks.

I know I should return his smile, but I can't. "Fine."

His smile falls away. "Everything all right?"

"Were you looking for me or did you just happen to be walking on my floor?" Jesus, can't the man leave me alone?

Scott hesitates, opens his mouth and closes it again.

"I saw you getting into the lift and... I was going to ask you something, but I'm pretty confident now isn't a good time. Sorry to bother you."

He backs up a couple of steps.

"What?" I blurt.

He studies me for a second, then sighs loudly.

"I was going to beg you to come to this bloody wedding with me. I thought I'd be fine going on my own. In fact, I think I wanted to be the poor jilted Scott all alone while his ex-wife clings to the arm of another man. But I don't want to be that guy. That guy is a miserable fuck."

He looks fairly miserable already, not that I'd tell him. And I know where he's coming from. When Pete left me,

I spent months going to all these events without him, knowing everyone was looking at me and feeling sorry for me, and it was the worst.

"OK," I say, wishing instantly I hadn't opened my mouth.

Scott's expression changes to one of wonder.

"Really? You'd do that?"

What the hell am I doing?

"What time does it start? I'd need to get myself sorted."

In other words, go to the gym downstairs for an hour, have a long shower and try to figure out what I've let myself in for.

"It's not till 6 p.m. I could come get you at five thirty? Are you sure, Trish? It's a big ask."

"Yes, it is a big ask, and no, I'm not entirely sure, but the alternative is watching an in-room movie and eating too much, so as it stands, there are pros and cons either way."

"Have you… Do you have a dress or something to wear?"

His genuine concern for the state of my wardrobe makes me smile.

"Yes, Scott, I have something to wear, unless this is a themed wedding. If it's country and western or Hollywood, then I might struggle."

Scott laughs. "It's just your regular strait-laced, run-of-the-mill wedding."

"OK then." I hold my card over the sensor pad and my door clicks open. "See you at five thirty."

Scott grabs my hand and pulls me into a hug.

"You're amazing, Trish," he says into my hair.

I choke, pretending he's strangling me. "OK."

He's not far off – his arms are tightly wrapped around me.

Letting me go, Scott pushes my door open.

"See you later," he says.

"Bye."

I brush past him and close the door. Then I lean against it and let my breath out. What have I done?

7

Having travelled so often for work, I have a staple list of items I always pack. Exercise gear (including running shoes), a universal adapter plug, tweezers, comfy socks, a pair of equally comfy trackpants, Marmite (for emergencies) and a dress. A dress that I can wear to a last-minute dinner invite or cocktail party. A dress that can be folded into a suitcase and not need an iron. It took me a while, but I have said dress on my body and I'm extremely grateful I found it on my shopping expedition last week. I was looking for several items that I could wear to work and that would disguise my growing belly. When I tried this dress on, I knew it was a winner.

The wide shoulder straps mean I can wear a good supportive bra and the smoky-blue fabric falls in neat, gathered folds from the straight-across neckline to my thighs. It not only makes my boobs look less obvious, but it also disguises my belly and accentuates my toned arms and legs. With the strappy silver sandals, a good application of make-up and my long blonde hair swept into a loose bun, I look OK.

I'm putting on delicate leaf-shaped earrings when Scott knocks. It's ridiculous how nervous I'm feeling. I know this isn't a date in the usual sense, but it's still a date, as in, I'm Scott's date for the night. Plus, I won't know anyone. Chances are we'll arrive and then Scott will walk off and spend the night talking to his mates, leaving me to fend for myself. It's something I should be used to. Pete was a master at it – though he always sought me out towards the end of the night, drunk and horny. At least I won't have that part to worry about. I'm confident Scott won't make any amorous move on me.

"Wow," Scott says as I open the door. He gives a low whistle. "You look stunning."

"Thanks, you're not too shabby yourself."

I've always had a soft spot for a man in a suit and Scott's tailored striped suit and white shirt with the top button undone is quite something.

"It's uncomfortable as hell," he says, wriggling and grimacing. "Give me shorts and a T-shirt any day."

I think of the trackpants I reluctantly removed when I had to get ready. I'd never considered it till now, but dressing up has lost its lustre. For years it's been vital for me to look smart and well groomed – not just for the sake of my job, but so that people would glance at me and go "Wow! She must be successful." I hate leaving the house without make-up and I never miss my weekly hair appointment. But since I fell pregnant, there's been several occasions – OK, only two so far – when I've dashed down the road for milk or bread and all I've done is put my hair in a rough ponytail. No make-up. No changing into something smart yet casual. The first time I did it, I felt like I was walking down the street topless. Surely everyone was going to stare at me in horror. But no one did. No one noticed me at all.

Scott holds something out.

"I wasn't sure how to say thanks or what I was supposed to do in these circumstances."

It's a clear box containing a tiny spray of exquisite ivory-white flowers attached to a hairpin. I lift the pin out and inhale a scent similar to jasmine, only muskier.

"They're real," I whisper.

"You don't have to wear it," Scott says quietly.

"I'd love to. It's very thoughtful." I'm pretty sure it's the most thoughtful thing a guy has ever done for me. Ever. "Can you…?" Turning, I hold the pin at the top edge of my bun. "About here."

Scott attaches the pin carefully and my scalp prickles at his touch.

"Right," he says as I turn to face him. "Ready?"

Our eyes meet and I feel as if Scott is no longer a stranger. There's a connection between us that I can't describe.

"As I'll ever be," I say, my heart beating faster.

"I'd suggest a stiff drink beforehand, but…" He raises his eyebrows. "Baby wouldn't approve."

Once again, it hits me. For all of ten minutes, I'd forgotten I was pregnant.

"Sadly, I'm unable to partake. But we could always stop at the bar if you need some liquid courage."

Scott frowns and shakes his head. "Only a dickhead would do that, Trish. Besides, I'm feeling pretty good about it all right now. You must have a calming effect on me."

I laugh. "Usually, I have the opposite effect. My friends are always telling me I can't relax. Lily says being beside me is like standing next to a gagged and bound gorilla itching to break free and attack."

We enter the lift and Scott presses the button for the ground floor.

"This Lily sounds interesting."

"She's brilliant. I love her to bits. And Emma and Mags. The four of us have been close since university. I couldn't imagine not living in the same city as them."

Scott nods. "They sound like your family."

I know he's remembering my outburst on the plane. If he brings up my parents now, I'll throttle him.

"They're better than family," I mutter. "Mine, anyway."

8

Arriving at the wedding venue is like stepping onto a movie set. The scene seems too gorgeous to be real. Scott and I are directed along a path lined with lanterns glowing faintly in the fading light. Surrounding us on every side is a mass of trees aflame with autumn colours. I've never seen anything like it and for a moment I simply have to stand and stare.

"Wow," I breathe.

"It's pretty impressive," says Scott.

"That doesn't even begin to describe it."

We wander past a still pond reflecting the oranges, reds and yellows of the trees, over a small curved red wooden bridge, to a traditional three-storey Japanese pagoda. Lined up facing the pagoda are rows of seats with starched white covers and lavish crimson bows. Most of the guests have already arrived and we find a seat in the back row. Scott waves to a few people who glance our way and they make little effort to disguise the fact they're checking me out.

"You OK?" asks Scott.

I nod quickly. "This is the most incredible wedding I've ever been to."

He puts a hand on my thigh and squeezes gently, then

quickly lifts his hand away and turns as someone taps him on the shoulder. He leaps to his feet and throws his arms around a slim man in a dark blue suit.

"Harry!"

The two men hug each other enthusiastically.

"Thanks for coming, man," says Harry once the hug is over. "It means a lot."

"Wouldn't miss it," says Scott gruffly. "Shouldn't you be up front?"

Harry screws up his nose. "Suppose." He glances at me and holds out his hand. "Hey, I'm Harry."

"Trish, this is the groom, Harry. Harry, this is Trish."

His palm is clammy as we shake.

"Pleased to meet you, Trish. Thanks for coming."

"Thanks for having me – assuming you even knew I was coming?"

Harry laughs. "Scott did inform me a few hours ago he was bringing someone along. Lizzie had a mild panic, but she's recovered."

"I bet she did," says Scott, and even though he's smiling, I can tell it's forced.

Harry winks at me. "Lizzie will be the one wearing the expensive white dress."

"Right, good tip."

Harry glances towards the pagoda and takes a deep breath.

"Better get on with it." As he adjusts his tie, his hands shake with nerves. "Catch up with you later?" he says to Scott.

"Good luck." Scott slaps his friend on the back.

I'm about to ask Scott what he thinks of Lizzie, when a

young woman in a black satin dress steps out of the pagoda, lifts a violin to her shoulder and begins to play. The guests immediately hush and the ceremony begins.

"What did you think?" asks Scott a short while later as we make our way back around the pond towards the reception venue.

"It was lovely," I say neutrally.

Scott laughs. "It was pretentious as hell."

Grinning, I bite my lip. "It was very…" I search for the word. "Dramatic," I say finally.

"Yeah, well, that's Lizzie to a tee."

"She certainly seemed to enjoy her moment in the spotlight," I state, remembering Lizzie's theatrical arrival in a horse-drawn carriage and her painfully slow walk down the aisle in a dress covered in sequins and with a bridal train so long it needed six bridesmaids to lift it.

We enter the reception room – a large hall with dark wooden beams, huge chandeliers and grand displays of flowers – and line up for the obligatory "congratulate the bride and groom" moment. When we reach the front of the queue, Scott places a hand on my back and guides me forwards.

"Lizzie, this is Trish."

The bride gives me the quick once-over.

"Hi," she says. "I was surprised to hear Scottie was bringing someone. Have you been together long?"

Man, she doesn't muck about. I know a loaded question when I hear one. I'm guessing Lizzie is fairly friendly with Scott's ex-wife.

Scott clears his throat. "Well, she—"

"Not long," I interrupt. "Thank you for letting me come to your wedding at such short notice. You look absolutely stunning."

Lizzie smiles, no doubt pleased with the compliment.

"Enjoy your night," she says brightly.

Harry is a lot more genuine as he hugs us each in turn.

"Glad that part's over," he says with a wink before turning to greet the elderly man behind me.

We head to the bar, where Scott declines the champagne being handed around and orders a beer and a lime and soda for me.

"Thanks for before," he says, handing me my drink. "But I should warn you – if Lizzie thinks you and I are an item, there's going to be a lot of people in this room asking questions."

"You mean checking me out."

Scott chuckles. "That's another way of putting it."

"Would you rather I'd told her I was some random stranger you accosted and begged to come to the wedding so you wouldn't be a sad singleton?"

Now Scott laughs outright.

"This is why I knew it was going to be great having you here, Trish."

Smiling, I sip my ice-cold drink and risk a quick glance around the room. There's a large contingent of family members – I'm picking up that they're on Lizzie's side – taking their seats at the two round tables near the front. They look tense and uncomfortable, as if at any moment, the whole lot of them are going to erupt into a full-blown feud.

Hovering around the windows overlooking the pond

are family members from the other side. There are several pretty little girls in cute linen dresses and a couple of oldies sunk into seats already looking exhausted. Overall, the window group are a more laid-back, relaxed-looking lot. One pimply teenager is even in jeans.

Circling the bar area appear to be friends of the bride and groom. They're possibly my age or younger. Some of the females are in cocktail dresses so short they're going to have serious trouble keeping their arses covered when they sit. I catch a few of them glancing in my direction. One guy isn't even trying to hide his fascination with my chest area. Nothing new there.

I return my gaze to Scott. "Seems strange that hardly anyone here is Japanese."

Scott rolls his eyes. "Harry was keen to have the wedding back in New Zealand, but Lizzie wanted to have it somewhere more exotic."

"She sounds Australian," I state, recalling her accent.

"Yeah, she's from Brisbane originally. I'm surprised how many people have made the effort to come. It's not a cheap place to fly to."

We're interrupted by an attractive woman who throws her arms around Scott and gives him a loud smacking kiss on the cheek.

"Scott! You look completely gorgeous, as always."

For a split second I feel a flare of jealousy.

Scott smiles. "Hey, Annie, you're looking pretty nice yourself."

Annie punches him on the arm. "I look *hot*, Scott, and I have every intention of finding myself a man tonight. Any ideas?"

Scott shakes his head. "None whatsoever. Annie, this is Trish. Trish, this is Harry's little sister, Annie."

Annie pulls me into a hug. "Aren't you stunning," she shouts. Lowering her voice, she tries to look menacing. "You'd better not go breaking our Scottie's heart. If you do, I'll be—"

"All right," Scott says, pulling her away. "Leave her alone."

I'm saved from saying anything, as Annie spots someone across the room, calls out to them and charges off.

"I think she may have knocked back a few already," I murmur.

Scott grins. "You think?"

We both pause to sip our drinks. I wish I could be having a glass of champagne like nearly everyone else in the room. I could do with the Dutch courage.

"This is going to sound weird, Scott, but I've been curious about something since I dribbled all over your T-shirt on the plane."

Scott raises his eyebrows. "I was under the impression that incident was never to be mentioned."

"True. It's just I keep being reminded of it because of your smell."

Scott snorts into his beer. "Sorry?"

"Please don't take this badly, but I've never met a person – especially a male – who smelt so strongly of lavender in my life."

Scott erupts with laughter. I try to look cool, calm and collected, but seriously, he needs to stop. Half the room is bound to be staring at us right now – not that I dare look.

Once Scott is breathing normally again, he speaks.

"My sister knows I'm struggling to sleep at the moment and she's been getting into essential oils lately. She made me a special dropper bottle of her 'sleep potion', as she called it, which contains lavender along with some other oils I can't remember the name of."

"That was thoughtful of her," I say.

Whenever anyone talks about a sibling doing something nice, it comes as a shock.

Scott grimaces. "Only the damn bottle leaked in my bag just before I boarded the plane. I tried to clean it up, but... well... as you've borne witness, it's a hard smell to remove."

I'm enjoying having a normal conversation. I haven't felt this relaxed with a guy in a long time.

"Mystery solved," I say.

Scott glances behind me and I know from his frozen expression of confusion and pain he must have spotted his ex-wife.

"Should we go and find our table?" I ask.

He blinks and musters a weak smile. "Let's go," he says, slipping an arm through mine.

We wander over to the seating plan displayed on a stand and find our names. I've been a last-minute addition, judging by the hand-written "Trish" as opposed to everyone else with their name neatly printed in an old-fashioned font.

"At least I made it on there," I say, pointing.

Then Scott takes my hand and leads me towards table 11.

9

We're the first guests to take our seats at our designated table and I'm relieved to see it's not quite the loser's table – that's obviously table 12, where a motley bunch sit in wide-eyed, uncomfortable silence. No doubt they'll be the loudest, most boisterous table here once they've had a few drinks.

"It's all very grand, isn't it?" I say, hoping to continue our easy conversation.

"And regimented. All the guests are probably worried they'll get told off by the bride if they do anything untoward."

I think of my father's rigid, unbending rules and permanently stern expression. The way I'd quickly check the house was tidy and my outfit respectable every time I heard him put his keys in the front door. *Stop, don't think about him.* I refocus on our conversation.

"I take it you're not so keen on her."

"Lizzie's a nice enough girl, but she likes to keep on top of everyone's business."

"So she's a tad high maintenance." I lean one elbow on the table and watch Lizzie rip into some waiter as she inspects the top table.

Scott nods. "Good description."

I catch him glancing quickly behind my left shoulder and a shadow passes over his face. Assuming he's caught sight of his ex-wife again, I casually shuffle around for a look.

"Which one is she?" I ask quietly.

Scott sighs. "Tight cream dress," he mutters.

I hate to admit it, but Harumi looks incredible in a figure-hugging ivory silk dress and sleek dark hair to her waist. I wonder if Lizzie is pissed at her – talk about upstaging the bride. She's grasping the arm of a tall blond guy who looks at least ten years older than her and he's attractive, I'll give him that, but not a patch on Scott.

I swivel away. "So," I say forcefully. "How did Harry and Lizzie meet?"

Scott sighs and looks at me, a haunted look still in his eyes.

"Harry has been living in Japan for years – he got a job out here shortly after graduation. We were best mates in school but kind of lost touch. Then when Harumi and I got together, we started making regular trips—"

"So you didn't meet Harumi here?"

Scott shakes his head. "Harumi swears she'll never live in the same country as her family ever again. She was sent to a fancy university in the UK and hasn't lived in Japan since. We worked at the same company in London for two years – that's where we got together – before I got a transfer back to Auckland."

"And Lizzie? Where does she come in?"

"I started to catch up with Harry when we came to Tokyo, which was about four times a year. Too many for Harumi, but I enjoy coming here – at least I used to." Scott gives a wry smile. "Anyway, one night Harry and I were at a sake bar and sitting at the table next to us was a group of very loud, drunk tourists. They invited us to join them for a drink and I wasn't that keen, but Harry leapt up and squeezed in next to..." He pauses and raises his eyebrows.

"Lizzie," I state.

"They've been loved up ever since."

The rest of our table guests arrive at once. A swarm of handshakes and polite cheek kisses ensue. They all seem to know Scott and every one of them avoids saying Harumi's name. They're also all in couples – four pairs in all. I'm glad I came now. Scott being on his own would have stuck out as much as my giant breasts regularly do.

The pale Irish man named Alistair sitting beside me puts a hand on my arm and leans closer.

"I have to warn you – I talk complete bollocks most of the time. Especially at events like this. My wife will try to disown me later."

His wife, Shiva, leans across him. "He's right. I will. Just give me the word, Trish, when he gets too much. I'll send him home in a taxi."

I like them already. They appear so mismatched physically – he's pasty white, tall and balding in a crumpled suit, and Shiva's a tiny Indian woman in a bright orange sari. But I can see how connected they are in the way they respond to each other physically. It's like some invisible tie has joined them. Shit. There I go again. I might as well be discussing their aura.

Scott keeps an eye on me throughout the meal and makes sure I'm not left out of the conversation. Once or twice, he leans in and asks if I'm going OK. I assure him I'm enjoying myself, and I am. The only slight disarming part is I keep having to remind myself we're not an actual couple. Every time Scott brushes against me or leans close, I experience a jolt of excitement. I want him to sit beside me all night long. I like that we're here together. I like it way too much.

Once the meal is over, we're encouraged to head onto the dance floor. I'm extremely relieved when Mike from Australia sitting opposite announces there's no way in hell he's dancing and suggests we all stage a sit-in.

By this point, most guests at our table are well oiled, so they cheer loudly and pour themselves another drink. I've been keeping an eye on how many drinks Scott has consumed and he's been very cautious. After his initial beer, he's only had one glass of wine.

"You're welcome to get completely sloshed," I say as I notice him eyeing up the wine bottle sitting beside the flowers.

"Thanks, Trish, but you're doing me a big favour being here and me getting shit-faced is hardly a great way to repay you."

"Scott, believe me when I say this. If I was in your situation right now, I'd be well and truly inebriated. Please don't be sensible on my behalf."

"You sure?"

"Absolutely."

Scott reaches for the bottle. "I'll have one more glass, then."

Just four glasses later, Scott is dragging me to my feet. "One dance, Trish, come on."

The dance floor is no longer heaving. Half the guests have already gone home and I'd quite like to do the same. Last time I checked my watch, it was nearly 1 a.m.

"Just one, Scott, and then I'm going back to the hotel."

"Excellent."

The only remaining couple left at our table shake their heads as we abandon them and their dwindling sit-in. Scott takes my hand and leads me right into the middle of the gyrating, swaying bodies. Then we dance.

It's been a while since I let myself break loose. Dancing used to be my thing prepuberty. Dad often introduced me as the dancer in the family and Mum would occasionally come to watch me at recitals, which is probably half the reason I loved it so much. But once the boobs started to swell and my periods became heavy and painful, I gave it up. Where I used to feel joy and freedom when I danced, I felt awkward and exposed. Dad was relieved when I told him I was stopping dance so I could concentrate on my schoolwork. He felt uncomfortable with my changing body, too.

"You're a good dancer," Scott yells.

"You're pretty good yourself," I call back.

He steps closer, puts his hands on my hips and continues to dance, only there's a look in his eye now, one I know well. A part of me is pleased – thrilled, even – but mostly I'm scared. I stop dancing.

"I'm going to take off."

His hands drop from my body. "Sorry, Trish. That was out of line."

I shrug. "It's fine. I'm tired, though. Think I'll call it a night."

Scott nods rapidly. "Absolutely. I'll come with you."

"I don't need an escort."

"I want to leave. Give me one sec to say bye to Harry, OK?"

Then he weaves off through the other dancers without waiting for my answer.

I retrieve by jacket and say goodbye to an older man standing by the door. I was introduced to him earlier – one of Harry's uncles – but haven't the faintest memory of his name. Then I push through the door and out onto the path lit with lanterns.

Putting a hand on my belly, I take a deep breath, enjoying the quiet. I can't believe I've just spent all night at a complete stranger's wedding half a world away from home. Even more surprising, I agreed to come to this wedding with a complete stranger who I met on a plane by crying all over his T-shirt. What has come over me? I don't do spontaneous things like this. Is it pregnancy hormones making me act out of character? Or did I simply want to spend more time with Scott? I wanted him to kiss me just now on the dance floor. The way he looked at me, it was as if everything around him had ceased to exist and the only thing he wanted was me.

No wonder I made a quick getaway. I've learnt the hard way not to believe in that look. Pete used to gaze at me the same way: make me feel as if I were special. And believing him, I opened up my fragile heart – the one I've guarded so carefully since childhood – and let him tear it apart.

Pete asked me to marry him once after a work party. I never told my friends about his proposal. I never told anyone. Mostly, I'm confident I did the right thing, as he'd been drinking tequila all night, but every now and again I let myself consider what it would have been like to say yes. I loved him enough. I wanted to have his babies and grow old and wrinkly with him by my side. But I couldn't say yes. Not when I knew he didn't mean it.

He'd stopped giving me that special look a few months earlier. About the same time I noticed his eyes seemed to be elsewhere. The day he told me he was moving to Sydney for work was also the day he confessed he'd slept with someone else. He felt he couldn't leave without letting me know the truth. It was no one I knew, he'd said, as if this somehow made things better. And it was only the once, that's all. *That's all*, I'd screamed, the first time in my life I'd let my emotions get the better of me. Then I'd thrown the glass I'd been holding at his head.

It hit him on the cheek and landed on the floor with a smash. Pete held a hand to his bleeding face in shock, but there was also a hint of something else in his expression. Was it smugness? Was he pleased to see the unflappable, in-control Trish snap finally? Is it ironic that he then told me the reason he'd strayed was because he'd grown frustrated with my lack of emotion? I never cried or yelled. Pete said he felt like I was silently judging him, waiting for him to mess things up.

Maybe I did hold back a little. I loved him so much, but it was never a love free of fear. I doubted him because I doubted the whole concept of love.

Slipping off my sandals, I slowly wander down the path, enjoying the sensation of the cold concrete on my hot and swollen feet. Normally I wouldn't be caught dead walking around in bare feet, but right now I can't see anyone and it's liberating to realize how little I care.

"Trish!"

I turn to see Scott running towards me. He stops a good metre away.

"Hey," he murmurs.

"Hi."

I wish there wasn't a great big lock of his hair hanging over his attractive drunken face screaming at me to reach up and brush it back.

"Please can I walk to the hotel with you? I'll try really hard to keep my mouth shut and to keep my distance."

He flicks his head and the lock of hair swings away then flops back down. He smells like a slightly sweaty, drunken male and it should be off-putting, but it's having the opposite effect. I want to throw myself at him. Instead, I shrug.

"If you want."

Scott nods rapidly. "I do want."

We walk silently down the rest of the path and burst out onto a busy, bright street pulsating with flashing lights and noise.

Scott shields his eyes. "You know, this is one of the things I love about Tokyo – the way you can be in some tiny lane where the locals are quietly going about their lives, then you turn the corner and you're back in the mayhem."

"It's incredible," I say.

"Yeah, only I'm not such a fan right now."

I pause to put my shoes back on, laughing at Scott's pained expression. We cross the road and head down the street to our hotel.

"How's the head?" I ask, smiling.

"More like how's my stomach. I'm trying extremely hard not to throw up in front of the most beautiful girl in the world, but it is proving to be a battle."

Sure, he's drunk and probably doesn't mean what he says about me being beautiful, but it's nice to hear. I suspect that makes me a sad, pathetic sap.

We reach the hotel and head across the foyer. Scott puts a hand on the wall beside the lift to steady himself while we wait.

"Trish, that was the most generous thing anyone has ever done for me."

"What was?"

"You, coming with me to the wedding. I'll never forget it."

"It's no big deal, Scott. Anyway, I enjoyed it."

"Yeah, me too."

He turns away, but not before I've seen that look back in his eyes. I shouldn't be pleased he's attracted to me, but I am. Best to move on swiftly.

"I saw you talking to Harumi at one point. How did that go?"

Scott stares intently at his shoes and I think he's not going to answer.

"She wanted to know about you," he said at last.

"Me?"

"She was annoyed I'd brought a date."

"That's ridiculous."

Scott looks up. "I didn't want you there to make her jealous, Trish. I hope you know that."

"It doesn't matter if you did."

"No, it does matter. I wanted you to come because since meeting you, I've… I felt… I enjoyed your company and I was nervous about going on my own. I knew if you were there with me, it was going to be OK."

"That's very kind of you to—"

"I'm actually jealous of whoever the dad is."

"Sorry?"

Scott suddenly looks extremely sober.

"I wish you were my proper date tonight."

I can't speak. I should be angry with him. When the lift doors open and I step inside, Scott stays where he is so long I think the doors are going to close. My heart gives a weird thump and I leap forwards to press the button to keep the doors open.

"Get in, Scott," I snap.

He enters the lift, presses himself into the corner and hangs his head like a disgraced toddler.

I wait for the doors to close.

"That was out of line," I whisper.

"I know."

"You're drunk, Scott. Tomorrow, you'll probably have no memory of this at all."

Scott looks up, his hair once again infuriatingly across his face.

"It's possible," he mutters.

Oh, to hell with it. He's too goddamn cute for his own good.

"So you'll probably forget about this, too."

I cross over to Scott, put a hand on his cheek, lean in and kiss him on the lips. He responds immediately, his hand flying around my waist, pulling me closer, his lips pressing into mine. My heart is pumping so loudly, it pounds in my ears.

The lift pings and I pull away, even though my body is screaming for me to stay.

"Goodnight, Scott."

"Trish, wait—"

"Thanks for a fun night."

Then I race down the hallway. If he follows me, I have no idea what I'll do. Reaching my door, I hold my breath for a few seconds before glancing back towards the lift. There's no one there.

10

"How was Tokyo?" Emma asks, spreading a thick layer of cream cheese icing on the carrot cake before her.

A blob falls off the palate knife onto the bench and I swipe it up with my finger and deposit it in my mouth.

"It was OK," I mutter. "That's damn good icing, by the way."

"Did you manage to do anything other than work? Please tell me you at least ate one meal outside the hotel restaurant."

"Actually, I went to a wedding."

Emma freezes mid-spread. "You *what*?"

"It's a long story."

Emma continues to smooth out the icing.

"Well, since we aren't due at your scan for another half an hour, I'm going to cut you a slice of this beauty and you can sit down and tell me everything."

I'm looking forward to telling Emma about Scott – leaving out the weeping on his chest part. I've wanted to talk to someone about him ever since I got back. Emma's going to think I was doing my usual thing: dipping my toe, as she likes to say. I suppose she's right. Ever since Pete left, I've been enjoying the freedom of casual relationships. Sometimes it might be a night of flirting ending with a snog at the bar, other times passionate sex followed by a fry-up the next morning at some café and a swift goodbye, never to see them again. With Elliot, it was worse: sympathy sex.

He was so earnest about his feelings for me. Always walking past my desk or dropping by with some lunch for us to share. My colleagues thought it was hilarious. As for my friends: ever since Elliot gave me a mince pie and asked if we could have another date – in other words, another round of sex – he's been called "pie-guy". The poor bugger.

"And you didn't see him again?" Emma asks. "After the kiss."

"Nope." I wipe the corner of my mouth with the back of my hand. "Thank God."

"What do you mean? He sounds like a really nice guy and you were obviously attracted to him."

I think about denying the attraction but why bother? I like entertaining the impossible scenario whereby Scott turned up at my hotel door the next morning and insisted he take me out for breakfast.

"Has he tried to call?" Emma asks.

"He doesn't have my number."

"Do you have his?"

I frown. Why is Emma so fixed on me seeing Scott again?

"Of course not."

"It's just…" Emma hesitates.

"Just what?" I push back my chair and stand. "That was delicious, by the way. Almost makes me want to learn how to bake."

"Trish, you haven't been this into a guy in ages."

I force a laugh. "I barely know him, Em. Come on, let's get this scan over with."

Emma shakes her head. "Some days I wonder if you realize how often you do that."

I follow Emma out of the door.

"Do what?"

"Suppress how you feel," she says over her shoulder.

"I blame my upbringing," I say lightly.

We hop into my car and I pull out onto the road, but Emma isn't ready to let it go.

"You joke about that all the time, but I'm starting to wonder if it's actually true."

Of course it's true, I want to yell. *Why do you think I never talk about it?*

"What was it like growing up?" Emma asks. "Honestly."

"Oh, Em, let's not go there now, OK?"

She opens her mouth then closes it again. I think she must be annoyed, as we barely speak again during the twenty minutes it takes to get to the radiology centre. I park, turn off the engine and stare at the double doors.

"What if there's something wrong with the baby?" I whisper.

"There won't be."

I take a deep breath in and let the air out loudly. "Right then, let's go."

We walk into the reception and I fill in a form while Emma sits beside me messaging Finn.

"How's it going with you two?" I ask once I've handed my form back to the receptionist.

Finn is the new love of Emma's life. I'm a tad jealous she's in a stable relationship with him, especially as he's handily the father of her unborn child.

"Great, only…" Emma bites her lip. "He's thinking about moving in, which makes sense, I guess, because with his job he'll be away for several months at a time and there's no point in paying rent for a place when he'll hardly be there. And he's at my place most nights at the moment anyway, so…" She trails off.

"So, what's the problem?"

"I can't help thinking that if I wasn't pregnant with his child, we wouldn't be moving so fast. If I'm honest, I'm still recovering from the whole divorce from Paul and I'm not sure I'm ready to jump straight into living with another guy."

"Fair enough."

"But, Trish, I love Finn – like head-over-heels love him – and Freddie does, too. And I'm sure if he moved in it would be fine."

"Have you talked to Finn about any of this?"

Emma shakes her head. "I don't want to hurt him."

"What would be worse, him moving in and you not feeling comfortable about it, or him possibly feeling a bit put out that you aren't ready to live together yet?"

A man in a white coat appears and calls my name before Emma has a chance to reply. I stand, feeling like I'm being called into the principal's office as we follow him down the corridor and into a room.

"This is my friend, Emma," I say as I lie on the plastic-covered bed.

Emma pulls up a chair beside me. "I'm her support person."

"Glad to hear it," the man says brightly.

He seems kind enough, but I was expecting a female. This guy looks old enough to be my father. Just imagining my father standing next to me makes me roll my eyes. Dad refused even to go into the doctor's room when I was six years old and suffering from an infected cut on my foot. He said it was "too personal" and that he'd stay in the waiting room.

"Right then."

The man squirts gel on my exposed stomach and draws my attention to a screen by his head. As he moves a weird plastic-covered apparatus around on my belly, he points at various grainy shapes on the screen that I recognize – with his guidance – as various parts of my baby.

"Everything looks good. I'll just take a few measurements."

I let my breath out. "There's nothing unusual?"

He shakes his head. "All perfectly normal. Would you like to know the sex?"

"No," I say quickly.

He nods. "Nice to keep as a surprise."

After a few minutes, the man removes the gel with tissues, helps me to sit up and hands me a black-and-white picture of my baby.

"All the very best, Trish," he says, patting me on the arm.

I swallow over the lump in my throat.

Emma grins and wipes her teary eyes. "That was amazing, Trish. I'm so lucky I got to be here with you."

She knows I don't cope well with sentimentality.

"Certainly makes it real," I mutter.

We head outside and I walk ahead of my friend to the car.

"You OK?" Emma asks, getting in the passenger seat.

"Fine." I put on my seat belt.

"You don't look fine."

I grip the steering wheel and stare out the windscreen at nothing.

"I need to find out who the father is," I whisper.

Emma doesn't speak.

"I can't pretend it isn't happening anymore."

Emma leans over and throws her arms around me. "I'll be there while you break the big news if you want?"

"Thanks, Em, but this is something I should do on my own."

11

Pete is fifteen minutes late. I'm sitting at my table nursing a second decaf flat white when he bursts through the door and scans the café. My heart gives a jolt and I want to hold something up in front of me – a book, a plate, a large piece of thick indestructible metal – as a shield. I haven't seen Pete since we had sex five months ago and he left my house yelling. He's different. His blond hair is clipped short and his face is so tanned it's like he's been living in the tropics. His grey T-shirt is tight, showing off his well-defined pectorals and huge biceps.

I'm not the only female in the room with my eyes on him.

When he spots me, his expression doesn't alter. He strides over and sits opposite.

"Morning, Trish."

"Hi," I croak before clearing my throat. "How are you?"

"Good, actually," Pete says in his familiar deep voice. "I've been surfing in Sri Lanka for a month."

"That explains the tan," I say, trying to smile.

Pete narrows his eyes. "I thought you never wanted to see me again. Why did you ask me here?"

Ah, Pete – always straight to the point. One of the many reasons I fell for him.

"Something has happened and I thought you should know."

He leans back and crosses his arms, his biceps threatening to rip a hole in his top.

"What?"

I knew he wouldn't make this easy for me. Maybe I should retreat while I still can. I know an angry Pete when I see one.

"Look, I'm sorry I was so harsh last time we... when we—"

"After we'd made love and I told you I wanted to be with you forever."

I look at my hands clasped on the table rather than the hurt written on his face.

"I wasn't ready to have you back in my life, Pete."

This isn't going the way I'd planned at all.

"If you'd been offered a job like the one I was presented with, tell me honestly, Trish, would you have turned it down? For me?"

"It wasn't just about the job. You slept with someone, remember? And you left without even trying to save our relationship. You could have asked me to go with you to Sydney."

Damn! Why don't I just stop? All this has been said before.

Pete is silent. He stares at me like my sole purpose is to make his life a misery.

"Could you say what you need to so I can leave, please?" he growls.

I sit up straighter and breathe in. "I'm pregnant," I whisper. "And there's a fifty per cent chance you're the dad."

Oh, God. It sounds even worse when I say it out loud.

Pete stays completely still. Apart from a twitching left cheek, his expression is stony.

"You're pregnant," he states loudly. "Well that's fucking perfect."

It's like he's slapped me across the face.

"Sorry?"

Pete uncrosses his arms and leans forwards.

"I came back from Sydney with the sole purpose of getting back together with you, Trish. It was all I wanted and when you made it clear you didn't feel the same, I was devastated. I've spent the last few months doing everything I could to try to get over you. I saw a psychologist, a psychiatrist, I fasted for a week, I gave up alcohol, I climbed a mountain, I even meditated, for fuck's sake. And now you spring this on me."

I can't say a thing over the lump in my throat.

"I'm sorry I can't be more supportive, Trish," he says, his voice low. "I can't throw my arms around you and say how wonderful this news is. I can't tell you that I don't mind at all that you were shagging someone else when I thought we were getting back together. And I definitely can't tell you that I hope I'm the dad."

I start to breathe heavily, in and out, in and out.

Pete watches me, waiting for a reaction. But I won't give him one.

He shakes his head and stands.

"I need you to take a test," I blurt. "To determine if you're the father or not."

Pete's laugh is bitter and fake.

"Can't you ask the other guy to do it?"

"Pete, please."

He lifts his eyes to the ceiling then glares at me.

"I'll think about it," he snaps before striding away.

I put a hand on my stomach and feel the baby nudge me.

"That went well," I mutter.

The baby stops moving and though I sit there for another five minutes without shifting my hand, it doesn't communicate with me again.

12

A full week passes before I can pluck up the courage to talk to Elliot. He hasn't been visiting me at my desk so often lately. I think the fact I keep turning down his invitations out – a movie, dinner, walk in the park at lunchtime – is starting to have its desired effect. With luck, he'll be figuring out our sexual encounter wasn't the start of some loving life-long relationship.

On Tuesday when he walks past my desk, I call his name. He looks startled, as do several others in the open-plan office space.

"Hey, Trish," he says, coming over. "How are you?"

Oh no. He's wearing his violet shirt with the white collar and cuffs I can't stand. Combined with his preppy short back and sides and long on top blond hairstyle, he looks like he should be living in the Nineties. To think this man-child could be my baby's father. I suppress a shudder.

"Not bad. I was wondering if you… if you might be free to grab a quick lunch with me today?"

He frowns for a moment, then his face clears and he grins.

"That would be great."

"I can meet you outside at 1 p.m.?"

"Perfect," he says, still grinning.

I try to smile back. "Thanks."

He carries on his merry way and I close my eyes. I thought telling Elliot couldn't be any worse than telling Pete but I have grave concerns I might be wrong.

"This is a nice surprise," Elliot says, taking another big bite of his wrap.

I stare at my untouched cheese and salad roll, my appetite non-existent.

"I was beginning to think you weren't interested in me," he adds.

Oh wow. If he's only beginning to think I have no interest, I've been subtler than I thought.

"Elliot, I'm pregnant."

There. Might as well jump straight in.

He chokes, chews and swallows.

"Sorry, what?"

"I thought you might have noticed." I pat my stomach briefly. "It's getting harder to keep the fact hidden from the boss. And everyone else at work, for that matter."

Elliot blinks at me rapidly, over and over.

"Is it… I-I mean, am I the father?" he stammers.

"Possibly," I say, wincing at my bluntness.

Why can't I be more gentle and kind and, well, more emotional?

"What does that mean?" Elliot asks, looking confused.

"It means that around five months ago when this baby was conceived, I had sex with you and one other guy. There's a fifty per cent chance you're the dad."

He's still blinking like he's got something stuck in his eye.

"Sorry to spring this on you," I say quietly.

"But we used... I mean..." He drops his head into his hands and groans. "It was the split condom, wasn't it?"

I say nothing.

He lifts his head to look at me. "I should have—"

"We were both to blame."

I don't tell him that I figured I wasn't the fertile type having had a few slip-ups over the years without repercussions. I also don't tell him that his chances of being the father are possibly lower than half. Pete and I had sex twice that one fateful night and we made no effort to use contraception whatsoever, being in the throes of a passionate reunion. Presumably this means he's twice as likely to have planted the seed, so to speak. Or maybe not. I might be great with numbers, but my memory of reproductive science in school is vague.

"I thought we were... I didn't realize you were seeing someone else," Elliot says, his face still in his hands.

"An ex-boyfriend turned up and we ended up having some drinks and sex. It was a one-off thing."

He lifts his head and puts a hand on my thigh.

"I forgive you," he says softly.

I don't think I've done anything that needs forgiving, but I keep quiet. I don't want a repeat of the conversation with Pete.

Elliot lifts his hand off my thigh, shuffles closer and puts his arm around my shoulders. He pulls me towards him so I'm leaning on his chest. For a second I recall crying on Scott's chest, his lavender smell, his hand stroking my hair.

"I'm here for you, Trish," Elliot says. "Whatever you

need. And I really hope the baby is mine, but if it isn't, I'll still be yours, if you want me."

I knew this was going to be worse than telling Pete. What the hell am I going to do now?

I let him hold me for several more seconds then sit up and shift away.

"Elliot, I'm telling you so you can get a genetic test done. I figure the right thing to do here is find out who the biological father is so that in the future, when this baby asks, 'Who's my dad?', I can give him or her an accurate answer."

Elliot nods. "Fair enough."

"I'm not telling you because I need you to help me. I don't want..." How do I put this? "I'm not looking for us to have a relationship, Elliot. I'm intending to go ahead with this pregnancy and raise the child alone."

"But that's crazy, Trish. You don't need to be going it alone. I want to be a part of this." He waves his hand back and forth between us.

God, the man is impossible.

"Elliot, this is going to sound terrible, but..." I pause, wondering if I should stop now. "It wasn't fair of me to sleep with you... for us to have sex."

"Why?"

"Because I wasn't ever going to get together with you. Not properly, as in girlfriend and boyfriend."

He frowns. "That wasn't the impression I was under."

"And I apologize for that, I really do. You're a nice guy—"

"Oh no." Elliot holds up his palm. "Don't start down the 'you're a nice guy' path."

His voice has dropped low and deep. And he's no longer looking at me like I'm the best thing since sliced bread.

Standing abruptly, Elliot takes a couple of paces away, then turns to glare at me.

"So, why did you decide to have sex with me?"

I shrug. It's heartless of me, but the truth is so much worse.

"You felt sorry for me," Elliot states.

Do I tell him yes or do I stay quiet?

He carries on.

"I know everyone in the office thought I was pathetic, the way I kept turning up at your desk with gifts like a besotted teenager."

"It's not—"

"I ignored them because they could think what they wanted. I thought you were beautiful and clever with a tough outer shell. I wanted you to trust me. I wanted you to like me enough to let me in past this shield you have around you."

His voice is high-pitched with anger. Tears threaten to fill my eyes. I can't speak now for the pain in my throat. He knows me far better than I realized.

"I'll take the test, Trish. And since we're being so honest, I'll tell you now – I hope I'm not the father. I hope I can move on with my life and forget all about you."

He takes a deep breath in, then lets it out with a hiss and walks quickly away.

I sit there for a long time staring into space. Eventually, I throw my uneaten roll in the bin and head slowly back to work. Elliot's not the first person to mention my "tough outer shell", as he called it. I know I clam up when people ask me about my childhood and I tend to freeze like a possum in headlights if things get emotional. What no one realizes is how important it's been for me to keep that barrier in place. When you've been through so much pain and hurt as a child, you learn the key to survival is protection. It's the only way to continue

On my ninth birthday, I received an unexpected gift from my parents. They came into my bedroom early and Mum gently shook me awake.

"Happy birthday," she whispered in my ear, her blue eyes clear and bright.

I didn't know how to respond. Especially when I saw Dad smiling at me from the doorway.

"Come on," he whispered, waving me towards him. Then he put a finger to his lips. "Shh."

Still half asleep, I stumbled out of bed, rubbing my eyes and staring at them both, wondering if I was still dreaming.

Mum held out my dressing gown and helped me to put it on before we trailed after Dad. Past the closed doors of my brothers' bedrooms, past the bathroom, past the open door of my parents' bedroom. I was reassured to see that they'd made the bed already – the corners neatly tucked, the covers smooth, the pillows symmetrical.

We crept downstairs, through the laundry and out of the back door.

Mum took my hand, squeezed hard and continued to hold it tightly as Dad led us down the concrete path with the clipped grass on one side and the manicured hedge on the other, to the shed at the rear of our narrow garden. I didn't spend much time in our backyard as too often my brothers were out there; kicking the ball when they were allowed, doing their morning exercises (when Dad was home), lying about on the grass (when Dad was at work). If I tried to join them, they'd yell at me to get back inside where I belonged; to go and check on Mum; to go play with my girly toys. I wanted to lie on the grass with them, to join in with their conversations on football, or what their mates at school were up to. My brother, Will, was particularly fixated on the goings-on of his friends – the parties they went to, the girls they hooked up with, the freedom they had, when he felt like he lived in a prison. Will was the nicer of my two brothers. I think he knew I was lonely and sometimes he'd play cards with me or ask a question about school. Sometimes he'd offer to take Mum her afternoon cup of tea in my place and I always took him up on it. James never offered. In fact, he did his best either to ignore me or boss me around. Nothing in between.

Dad pushed open the shed door and stepped back.

"Happy birthday, Patricia."

His voice was so loud in the still morning air, it made me jump.

Mum let go of my hand, leant down and kissed me on the cheek.

"It's your favourite colour," she said in her quiet, shaky voice.

I stared at my gift, tears immediately springing to my eyes as Mum stroked the top of my head. She hadn't touched my hair in years.

It was a purple bike (which had ceased to be my favourite colour two years earlier – not that it mattered) with colourful streamers on the handlebars and a basket on the front. Too frilly and girly for a nine-year-old, but

I didn't care about that. My parents had given me a bike. They'd given me the one thing I'd asked for. They'd listened to me. It was the first time in my life I'd received a present from my parents that I'd requested. I'd given up hope of ever getting anything I actually wanted. And now this... this miracle had happened.

It was almost too much for me. I wanted to collapse wailing to the ground.

Instead, I smiled and said, "Thank you, Daddy," before giving him a peck on his proffered cheek. Then, "Thank you, Mummy," as I kissed her, too.

I wanted to hug her so tightly both of us would lose our breath, but I knew it would be too much. For both of us. Instead, I stepped into the cool, dark confines of the shed and rested a hand on one of the handlebars.

"It's amazing," I whispered.

Then I turned to look at my parents and they were so bright, standing there in the morning light. Dad had put his arm around Mum and they were looking at me and smiling, like they were the mum and dad of my dreams come to life. I wanted the moment to last forever.

It was the one and only time I saw any sign of affection between my parents. It was also the one and only time I felt noticed. As the sun shone and my parents smiled, I experienced a brief and fleeting moment of love.

13

I call in sick the day after my conversation with Elliot, telling my boss I've got a head cold. If only it were true. I recognize my symptoms for what they are, though I've never allowed myself to put a name to it. Lethargy, excessive sleepiness, lack of appetite, a dullness to my senses. I stay in bed for three days, rising to go to the bathroom, or sit on the couch to watch a movie, or get a handful of biscuits from the pantry. I try to eat an apple, but it tastes acidic and foreign. I throw it in the bin after the first bite.

My phone stays on silent. I look at it once or twice and see the missed calls from my friends, so I send them a quick message:

Snowed under with work. Talk later.

It usually does the trick.

I don't shower or change out of my pyjamas. I don't speak to anyone, especially my growing baby. What can I say to it without sounding weak and pathetic?

On my fourth morning at home, I open my curtains and let the sun warm my face. Although I don't want to, I force myself to have a shower, wash my hair, put on some clothes.

Then I get back into bed in my T-shirt and trackpants, and sleep.

At lunchtime, I drag myself out of bed and make a fried egg on toast. It tastes good, which I take as a reassuring sign. So much so, I venture as far as the back porch. I sit on the top step in the sun and look at my little garden. Weeds have sprouted around my camellias, the roses need deadheading and the trailing rosemary could benefit from a trim. I slip on my wellingtons and walk round to the side of the house to my shed. I collect my gloves, weeding tool and secateurs, and clump across the grass to the roses I planted the week I moved in.

After slipping on my gloves, I begin to assess the bush in front of me. There are no signs of leaf rust or aphids. Even so, I'll give them a feed when I'm done. From my own experience and copious reading on the topic, I know it's better to keep plants healthy than try to treat them once a disease or pest appears. Intervention is never as successful as prevention.

I bought myself this property complete with its blank canvas back garden for my thirtieth birthday. The house ticked all of my boxes for a first-home purchase and was only slightly more than I'd budgeted for. It was close enough to work I could be there in less than twenty minutes, had three bedrooms (one spare, one for an office), was positioned well for sun (the back porch, kitchen and my bedroom receive a great deal – almost too much in the summertime). And it had a garden, or in this case an area I could turn into a garden. It was several months after I'd moved in before I admitted to myself the back garden the previous owners had created was almost identical to the one I'd grown up with: grass and a hedge circumnavigating the boundary. No plants, no colour, no beauty.

A man came with a digger the day after I moved in and tore out the hedge. He also dug up half the grass. My friends were horrified.

"Why do you want to turn all of this into garden? You're creating more work for yourself. Don't you work enough already?"

I told them it had been my dream to have a beautiful garden. I didn't tell them about Grammy Rose, my mother's mother, who I went to stay with for a few weeks while Mum was in hospital. I didn't even know who the elderly woman was when she turned up on our doorstep the day after Mum left in an ambulance. I was fifteen years old; my brothers had grown up and moved out by that point. I was the only one at home when I opened the door and she told me she was my grandmother. She pulled me into a bear hug, cried giant tears and told me how much she'd missed me.

Apparently, Mum and I had spent several months living with Grammy Rose after I was born. Mum needed help and Dad thought we'd be better off there till I was at least sleeping through the night. Who knows what happened to my brothers; I couldn't imagine Dad stayed home to look after them, but William was only five – too young, surely, to fend for himself.

"You were such a contented, happy baby, Trisha," Grammy Rose said as we sat on her back porch sipping our drinks – water with a splash of lime for me, gin and tonic with a splash of lime for her. "I'd take you into the garden and lay you on a rug under that tree"—she pointed to the walnut tree in the corner—"and you'd lie there on your back for hours, kicking your little legs, watching the leaves and the shadows."

"Where was Mum?" I asked.

Grammy Rose gave me a funny look, like I'd asked a stupid question.

"Same place she has been for years, Trisha. Same place she's been since she was twenty years old, though things got a lot worse for her after she married your father."

I wanted to ask what she meant, but I was afraid. I'd already learnt by then it was better to keep emotions locked away.

Grammy Rose and Dad didn't get on. Apparently, shortly after my second birthday, Dad told Mum she wasn't to see her mother anymore. He said he wouldn't have a disapproving mother-in-law questioning the way they raised their children.

Grammy Rose says she was banished from seeing her own daughter. A daughter who she could see was struggling to keep on top of a household and three young children.

Those two months I stayed with Grammy Rose were the happiest of my life. Largely because I convinced my grandmother I didn't need to go to school, claiming I was smarter than everyone else in my year – which I was. I didn't tell Grammy Rose that at fifteen, I'd become a constant source of attraction to all of the boys in the school and that they stared openly at my breasts as if it were their right. Many of the girls taunted me mercilessly – especially in the changing rooms. "Check out the cups on that bra," or "Don't stand too close – she might knock us out with those knockers." I did my best to look frumpy, boring. I kept my straight blonde hair short, I wore oversized shirts, kept the uniform skirt far too long than was considered cool.

There were only two girls in the entire school I considered my friends, though I hardly saw them at all outside school. I was too busy at home to socialize anyway. With Mum nearly always out of commission, I was expected to do all the cooking and cleaning, and there was no way I wasn't going to study hard. By then I knew the best chance of escaping home was to get a good qualification and a well-paid job. I never wanted to depend on anyone, because then no one could let me down.

Grammy Rose let me stay home from school in the same way she let me leave food on my plate. No disapproval, no shaking of the head. Just a smile and a nod. She wrote to the school and informed them I was taking an extended holiday. Surprisingly, the school didn't make a fuss. My English teacher, Mrs Miller, even sent a note to say she thought it was a good idea for me to take a break. She claimed I was too grown up to be healthy, whatever that meant.

When I lived with Grammy Rose, she cooked for me every night. She did my washing, made sure there was always food in the house. She was horrified when I pulled out the vacuum cleaner the day after I moved in.

"You're here for a holiday, Trisha. I'm taking care of *you*, remember."

No one had taken care of me before and no one has taken care of me since.

The one thing Grammy Rose asked me to help her with was the garden. The sprawling quarter-acre of land was proving more difficult to maintain due to her "aches and pains", as she begrudgingly admitted. Every day of those two months we spent time in the garden or the small greenhouse. She taught me to weed and prune, plant and propagate, feed and water. She taught me the names of plants, what position suited them best – too much sun could be worse than too little. Her guiding principle was that the health of all plants began and ended with the soil. Soil was everything to Grammy Rose. I couldn't believe a person could be so enthusiastic about their compost bin – I didn't even know what compost was. As for worms, Grammy Rose would squeal with delight every time she spotted one.

Grammy Rose loved all of her plants, but she had a special affection for her roses, tending to them as if they were pets. She'd talk to them, feed them, make sure they were well looked after. One of my clearest memories is of Grammy Rose wandering around her garden, pausing to smell her roses and smiling as if to say, "life can't get any better than this". She claimed her name had nothing to do with it. She'd have loved roses more than any other plant even if her parents had called her Daisy or Fern. Grammy Rose was always making funny little remarks. Something I took a few days to get used to.

I never made it to Grammy Rose's funeral. She died while I was at university and by the time I found out, it was too late to get a flight home.

Once I've weeded around the camellias and tidied the roses, I'm feeling better. I even say a few words to my baby, who becomes more active as a result, shifting and rolling about as if to say, well about time you remembered I was here.

My stomach growls and I pause to eat sliced banana on toast (something I'd never eaten before I stayed with Grammy Rose and which has now become a staple in my diet). Then I drink a large glass of water and return to my garden until the light fades.

After returning to the house, I run myself a bath, adding rose salts, and lie in the water with my hands on my belly, feeling every ripple, every nudge beneath my fingers.

"Hello, little one. You are having an active day today, aren't you?"

My baby replies enthusiastically by performing what feels like a forward roll. After my bath, I defrost a chicken breast, roast it in the oven, and eat it with grilled tomato and some French beans – the only vegetables I could find in my fridge that hadn't begun to rot.

Then I devour a bowl of vanilla ice cream, change the sheets on my bed and go for a walk.

In the early days, Pete always insisted on coming with me when I headed out on one of my "midnight strolls", as he called them. He was bemused and alarmed I'd want to go walking in the dark on my own. I'd let him come with me on the proviso he wasn't allowed to talk. Talking spoilt the atmosphere. I was relieved when his boredom at the walks overcame his perceived danger of a woman out at night alone.

As I walk, my senses heighten. My footsteps are rhythmical, fast-paced and steady as my shoes land and lift, land and lift. Dew already glistens on the grass running alongside the path and the cool, damp air laced with that familiar scent of wet grass enters my nostrils, travels to my lungs and is absorbed into my cells. A bird makes a muted call as the last of the evening light disappears. Crickets and electricity lines create a background hum. In the shadows between each street lamp, I look up at the few flickering stars. The moon is a thin crescent with a black halo. My tongue is coated with a milky film from the ice cream and it's making me thirsty. Pivoting on my heel, I head for home.

I'll go into work in the morning. Head to my boss' office first thing. Tell her the news I expect she knows already. It's time to pick myself back up. Again.

14

"How far along are you?" snaps my boss, Tash. She wasn't surprised in the slightest when I told her I was pregnant, just resigned.

"A little over five months."

In reality, I'll be into my third trimester in under a week.

"Five months!" Tash shrieks. "Tell me you're joking."

"I'll happily work up to my due date."

Tash rolls her eyes. "You say that now, but you'll be calling me in a month saying there's been some complication, or you're getting too tired. I've seen it before, trust me."

"I'm confident that won't happen."

"Well, you can't do that seminar in Sydney next week," Tash states. "Mark will have to go."

Mark is my nemesis. He's younger, fitter, stronger and faster. I dislike him immensely, even though he acts like we're friends. He knows that I know it's all a big act.

"I've done all the prep for it. Of course I can still go. Look at me – I'm barely even showing." I wave a hand at my tiny bump.

"Hand it over to him this morning," Tash says. "And anything related to Omnus."

Nausea hits and I swallow down the vomit collecting

in my throat. Omnus are the clients I visited in Tokyo – the ones with whom I've been trying so hard to build a relationship.

"That's unfair, Tash. I've been working with them for months."

"They called me yesterday while you were off *sick*."

It's clear she thinks there was nothing wrong with me.

"They want you to go back to Tokyo to run through an alternate solution for migrating data from their new subsidiary."

"Great, I'll get on to it."

"As I said, Trish. Mark will take over Omnus. Get him up to speed."

I stare at her lips pressed together, her narrowed eyes.

"Please, Tash, let me go to Tokyo. Give me the chance to tell them in person that I'll be handing over to Mark. They like for things to be done formally... *respect*fully," I add.

Tash sighs. "I was so sure you wouldn't be the one," she mutters.

"The one to what?"

"Rumours are Elliot's the father," she states, straightening some papers on her desk.

Jesus! Office talk is rampant.

"I don't know who the father is," I reply quickly.

She shakes her head. "I didn't think you had the mother gene. I thought you were going to be a career woman."

I'm so shocked by her words, I'm speechless. To think I've worked with this person for nine years. That I looked up to Tash as some ball-busting feminist. What the hell is the mother gene, anyway?

"My career is very important to me, Tash." I'm finding it

hard to keep my voice low and measured. "I'd like to go to Tokyo next week as I believe it's in the best interests of this business to do so."

Tash throws up her hands. "Fine," she says loudly. "Go." She taps her keypad and scowls at the screen. "Better make the most of it," she mutters. "You won't be going anywhere after that."

I leave her office on wobbly legs, avoid eye contact with anyone, get to the ladies' toilet, shut the door and lean against it.

"Bitch," I whisper, then I scream it again so loudly I'm sure everyone in the building can hear. "Bitch!"

Then I return to my desk, turn on my computer and start an email to Mark. In the subject box I type "Sydney seminar" and in my head I repeat "bitch" over and over.

15

"I've been worried about you," Mags says, following me inside.

She rang last night and asked if she could pop in after work. I reluctantly agreed, then she texted me ten minutes later to say Emma and Lily were coming too. One friend I can handle – all three is going to be a challenge. Especially Lily. She smells evasion the way others smell McDonald's – from a bloody mile away.

"I've been battling some bug and work has been a nightmare."

I'm hoping we can get my issues out of the way before the others get here.

"What sort of bug?" Mags collapses onto the freshly vacuumed couch.

I've spent the last hour tidying in preparation for the arrival of my friends. I also made a stop at the supermarket on the way home so I could have a semi-passable fridge. Emma is bound to open it for inspection.

"Just a bit of a cold." I hold up the bottle of wine I pulled out of my wine cupboard this morning. "Can I get you a glass?"

Mags assesses the bottle then shakes her head. "Too cruel drinking when you can't. I'll wait till Lily gets here."

I place the bottle back on the coffee table and perch on the arm of the couch next to Mags. She looks tired.

"How's it going with the girlfriend – Phoebe, is it?"

Mags nods. "Good, I guess." Mags wrinkles her nose. "She wants to go travelling."

"Where?"

She shrugs. "India, Nepal, Africa."

I can't picture Mags wanting to visit any of those countries. She's a First World, creature comforts kind of girl.

"Has she asked you to go, too?"

"Not exactly."

There's a knock at the door and I let Lily and Emma inside.

"What the fuck is going on?" Lily states, pulling me into a vice-like hug.

I choke. "Nothing."

"We've been seriously worried," Emma says, waiting for her turn.

Lily releases me at last, and Emma and I have a quick hug, smiling as our bellies bump together.

"I'm fine," I say brightly.

"Sure," Lily mutters, heading into the living room.

Mags is stuffing a cracker with cheese into her mouth from the cheese board I rapidly put together.

"Sorry," she says, crumbs flying from her mouth. "I was hungry."

"Eat as much as you want. I've got plenty more."

That's not entirely accurate, but I'm sure there's a packet of nuts I could open.

"So, what gives, Trish? Why have you been hiding from us?" Lily fixes me with her intimidating glare.

"I've just had a cold, that's all."

"Bollocks," says Emma. "Tell us what's going on. You've got your nervous thumb thing happening."

The problem with having friends who know you so well is that you have friends who know you too well. I didn't even realize I was rubbing my thumb against my forefinger – something I do when I'm majorly stressed. I sit next to Mags and take a deep breath.

"I told Elliot and Pete a few days ago."

"How did they take it?" Mags asks.

"Not great."

"Are they going to do the DNA test?" Emma asks.

"I don't know. They *did* both say they hoped they weren't the father, so that was nice."

"Arseholes." Lily leans forwards and picks up the wine bottle. "Is this just for decoration or can I open it?"

"Go ahead."

"I can't believe they weren't more supportive," Emma says, frowning. "Especially Pete. Having never met Elliot, I can't vouch for him, but, well, Pete is... *Pete*."

"Em, that means nothing," says Lily, taking a quick sip of wine. "This is the same guy who decided it was all right to bugger off to the other side of the world so he could advance his career without so much as a goodbye."

"Good point, Lils," pipes Mags.

I never told my friends Pete also had sex with someone else while we were together. It was easier to keep that painful news to myself.

"I also told my boss I was pregnant," I state. "She was a complete bitch."

"Spill," says Mags.

"She basically said she was disappointed I'd chosen to

ruin my career and that I needed to hand over all of my projects, including the one in Tokyo that I've sweated over for months. Oh, and she said she didn't pick me as being someone with the mother gene."

"The mother gene? Is she mental?" Lily demands.

"You should quit," Emma says firmly.

I shake my head. "I don't want to leave my job."

"You'd get another one, Trish," says Mags, cutting herself another slice of brie. "You're the smartest person I know."

"Thanks, Mags."

"She's right." Lily shuffles forwards in her seat, her face fierce. "You've been in that job too long, Trish. Give them the finger and bust a move."

"Who's going to take me on with this?" I point at my bump.

"Do you even like your job?" Emma asks.

I'm about to say yes, when I hesitate. My work has been the biggest, most important part of my life since I left university. Without it, I don't know who I'd be. But I've never stopped to ask myself if I actually *like* what I do. It seems irrelevant.

The others are all staring at me, waiting.

"I can't imagine *not* working there," I say. "And I definitely like it way more than working in a law firm."

I knew before I'd even graduated with a double degree in law and commerce that the law aspect had been a poor choice. I'd chosen it mainly because of the appeal of a hefty pay packet and title of being called a lawyer, but after one year in a fancy law firm, I accepted it wasn't for me and went down the commerce path instead. Law was all about conformity, black and white, right and wrong.

It was about dotting the i's and crossing the t's. I'd had enough of that growing up with my military father.

"Not quite a glowing endorsement," says Lily.

She takes an olive from the small bowl and shoves it in her mouth as if the poor little green thing has offended her and needs to be chewed to smithereens.

"If you can make it through the next couple of months at work, then you'll get maternity leave and you'll be knee-deep in nappies. Your sole thought will be 'when will I ever sleep through the night again?'," Emma says, grinning. "It'll give you a chance to re-assess. You might decide not to go back."

My skin prickles and I get hot and sweaty, like I'm suddenly feverish.

"Is that supposed to make me feel better?" I croak.

They all laugh as if it's funny to see me panicking about becoming a parent with no father on the scene and no parents up the road to help. It's just me. Alone. I should be used to it by now. But I'm not.

Mags puts an arm around me.

"You're going to nail this mother stuff, Trish. And we're going to be around here so often to help you'll be sick of us."

"Exactly," states Lily. "In fact, I'm thinking I might move in once the little critter's born."

We collectively look at Lily like she's grown another head.

"What?" she says. "It's got to be better than living with a guy who irons his undies."

I feel laughter swell inside me like a pocket of air, then I begin to giggle. Emma and Mags join in and soon we're collapsing against each other, breathless, with tears in our eyes. Finally, I have something I can write on my list of three things I'm grateful for tonight. I was worried I'd struggle to find anything again. The past few days the page has remained blank.

"All right, all right," Lily says, smiling. "Have a good laugh, but I was serious, you know. I'll move in, Trish, for the first few weeks at least."

I calm down and wipe my eyes. "That's a wonderful offer, Lils, thanks."

"Me too," says Mags.

I look at her, confused.

"You too what?"

"I'll move in, too. There's no way I'm going to India with Phoebe – not that she's even asked me. I'll tell her I can't go because I'm coming here to help you with the baby. It's the perfect excuse."

"Well, that's not fair. If you three are all living here, I'm going to feel left out," Emma says indignantly.

I shake my head. "You're all mad."

"I'm actually deadly serious." Mags leans her head against my shoulder. "If Phoebe goes, I'll need a major distraction to stop myself from falling into the depths of despair."

"What about your cats?" Lily asks. "Will they be moving in with us, too?"

Mags puts a hand over her mouth. "I hadn't thought of them," she breathes. "Can they come, Trish? I promise they'll be good."

Shaking my head, I get to my feet and put my hands on my hips.

"Who wants a tea or coffee?"

"Have you got herbal?" asks Emma.

"Peppermint and camomile."

"Peppermint, please."

Lily holds up the bottle. "I'll stick with the wine," she says, winking.

Mags considers her options. "I might just have a glass of wine with Lils, thanks, Trish. If that's OK?"

"Of course it's OK. Back in a flash."

I walk to the kitchen, put the kettle on and find the tea. Usually I'd have a coffee; actually, that's a lie. I'd be helping myself to a share of the wine. But baring that, I'd be making coffee. I'm sure drinking coffee has contributed to my problems sleeping over the years, but ever since my final year in school, it's been one of my biggest weapons in the fight to succeed. I'd make a strong coffee when most people were heading to bed, then sit down to study. Then three or four coffees later, I'd realize it was four o'clock in the morning and I'd make myself lie down for a few hours' sleep before my alarm went off. Now, coffee in the evening is a habit. Well, it was until four months ago when I went cold turkey. I still have the cravings, though. Especially when I'm worked up.

My phone rings as I'm pouring water into two mugs. It's still in my handbag hanging on the back of the kitchen door. I dig it out, read "private number" and answer.

"Hello?"

"Hi, Trish, it's William."

There's a long pause where I hold my breath.

"Your brother."

"Hi," I manage.

Holy shit! My brother is calling me. How did he get my number?

"You're not the easiest of people to track down."

I can't tell by his tone if this is an accusation or a mere observation.

It's my turn to speak, but I don't know what to say.

William clears his throat loudly, reminding me of our father. I'm expecting a clipped command.

"Trish, this is going to sound odd, but I'm standing outside your front door."

The phone starts to slip from my hand and I grip it tightly.

"I'm sorry?"

"I'm outside your house. Any chance I could come in?"

My heart is beating so rapidly, I think I'm going to pass out. My brother. Here. It makes no sense.

"Um, sure." I hang up and slowly walk out into the hallway.

"Who were you talking to?" Lily calls, spotting me from the living room.

I look at her in a daze.

"Trish?"

My three friends leap up and gather around me.

"What's going on?" Emma asks, gripping my arm.

"My brother is standing outside my front door," I whisper.

"Your *brother*?" Mags squeals.

"Which one?" Lily demands.

"Will," I mutter.

"Do you think we should let him in?" asks Mags.

I nod again. "Probably."

Lily steps towards the door, but I pull her back.

"I'll do it," I whisper. "You guys go sit down."

Reluctantly, they slink back into the living room and I take the five seemingly endless steps to the front door.

When I open it, my brother is facing away from me, looking across the street.

He spins around. "Hey, sis."

We stare at one another. Will's beefed up and his hair has grown out of the short military cut – the only hairstyle my brothers were allowed. It's hanging across his face, blond like mine. I can see my father in his mouth and jawline. His eyes are similarly dark blue, intense and watchful. But he has wrinkles around those eyes. Smile wrinkles. This throws me more than anything

Will steps forwards and gives me an awkward hug – something he's never done before in his life. I hug him back tentatively.

"Sorry to turn up unannounced. It was a spur-of-the-moment thing."

Lily's voice drifts towards us and Will lets me go.

"You're busy," he says. "I can come back—"

"It's m-my friends," I stammer. "Do you… would you like to come in?"

Will shrugs and I notice he isn't wearing proper shoes. He's in scuffed sandals. And there's dried mud on his left knee beneath his shorts. Who is this stranger?

He lifts his hand and bites the tip of his thumb. Deep worry lines crease his forehead.

"I'm not great with people," he mutters, his thumb still between his teeth.

I figure he's going to leave, but he continues to stand there looking at me.

"They're old friends from university days," I say. "You've met them once before. Briefly. At James' twenty-first."

The second to last time I saw anyone in my family.

Will nods slowly. I can't believe he hasn't drawn blood the way he's gnawing at his thumb. I want to pull his hand out of his mouth and tell him to leave it alone.

"It's up to you," I say, taking a step back. "No pressure."

Truth is, I don't really want him to leave. After the initial shock of seeing my brother, I'm nervous but excited. Someone in the family has actually decided to find me. Then I have another thought: he wants money. It makes much more sense. Why did I ever think a member of my screwed-up family would seek me out because they wanted to reconnect, to have a relationship with me? I feel like an idiot.

Will removes his thumb. "OK," he says. "I'd like to come in. Thanks, Trish."

I should send him packing now. Tell him I can see through his vulnerable "I'm not good with people" disguise.

I narrow my eyes and dip my head to indicate he can enter my house. I want him to know I'm on to him, though. And that I have the power in this situation, not him.

I follow my brother into the living room. My friends stand and introduce themselves, politely shaking his hand. No doubt remembering how important strict manners are to my family –I've told them often enough over the years.

Will does an impressive job at looking anxious and uncomfortable, even offering to sit on the floor when I move to find another chair.

"No, Trish," he says, resting a hand lightly on my arm. "I prefer the floor, really."

It's almost as if he's taunting me. Growing up, being caught sitting on the floor was akin to smoking weed in your bedroom.

He drops to the carpet, crosses his legs and leans back against the couch next to Lily's legs.

"So, Will," Lily says into the awkward silence. "What brings you to Trish's door?"

Attagirl, Lil, I think, giving her a half-smile. Straight to the point.

Will angles his neck to look up at her.

"I heard Trish was living in these parts and I was down here for an appointment so thought I'd look her up." He smiles nervously at me. "It's been a while."

"What do you do for a living?" asks Emma, getting in on the not-so-subtle interrogation.

God, I love my friends.

"I work for a landscaping company. I'm in the clean-and-clear team."

"The what?" Mags asks.

He shrugs. "We go into properties that haven't been looked after and clear away all the overgrowth. Take out anything that's in poor condition, trim branches and salvage what we can."

My brother spends his days outside bringing gardens back to life. It seems ridiculous to be jealous, but I am.

"I'm hoping to move into the design team soon," Will continues. "It would be a nice change actually to put plants in, rather than rip them out."

My friends nod encouragingly.

"It doesn't pay well, though," Will says. "I've been saving for ten years to buy my first house but I still don't have a big enough deposit."

And there it is. The true reason my brother has turned up on my doorstep. The bloody arsehole wants money. Well, he can take a flying leap.

Mags is sympathizing with him, of course – she can't see what he's angling for. She's telling him how she's still renting herself but hoping to buy an apartment soon.

Emma sneaks a hand onto my knee and squeezes.

"Should I give you a hand with those hot drinks, Trish?"

I look at her, startled.

"Oh, sorry, I forgot about them."

"Would you like a tea or coffee, Will?" Emma asks sweetly.

Will looks up from his cozy spot on the floor. Where are the nerves now? He looks like he's been lazing about in my house for years.

"A regular cup of joe would be great, thanks, Emma. Just a little milk, no sugar."

Emma and I enter the kitchen and then I round on her.

"Don't be nice to him, Em," I hiss. "He's only turned up because he needs money."

Emma's eyes widen. "What makes you think that?"

"You heard him. He's been saving for years. Still can't buy a house. I bet you he asks me for money. I bet you a million dollars."

"Trish, calm down. This is crazy talk."

"You don't know my family," I mutter.

"No, I don't. You never talk about them. We've met your brothers once at that bizarre twenty-first that could have been mistaken for a funeral. And I've barely laid eyes on your mum. The few times I've met your dad, he's asked a few polite questions and left."

I cross my arms and lean my bottom against the kitchen bench.

"I don't have a loving family like you, Em. I prefer to have as little to do with mine as possible."

"It does seem odd that he'd just turn up like this." Emma gets out another mug. "Have you spoken to him at all recently?"

"No."

The last time I saw Will was at our brother's wedding. When the invitation had arrived in the mail, I'd stared at it for ten minutes, then shoved it in the kitchen junk drawer and done my best to pretend it wasn't there. Pete found the invite three weeks later and insisted we go. He wanted to meet my elusive family, he said. He was so excited he sent an RSVP right there and then. We'd been together for twelve months at that stage and I was still in the "do anything for this gorgeous man who loves me" phase.

I'd never met James' fiancée, whose name, according to the invite, was Clare. I wasn't even aware he was engaged. The sole contact I'd had with anyone in my family was the occasional businesslike email from my father enquiring how I was getting on. What was the point of those emails? When I didn't reply, it wasn't like he became a worried father and tried to track me down. He didn't follow up my unanswered email with "Are you all right? I haven't heard from you in a while". He certainly didn't call. He just sent another brief email six months later. A replica of the one he'd sent before.

Pete thought the wedding was hilarious, in a "is this for real?" kind of way. He said later it was like he'd walked onto the set of a British period drama. Everyone impeccably dressed, speaking politely, the men all standing to attention or, as Pete said, "with a carrot up their arse". The women were well mannered, eager to please. It was everything I knew it would be, only worse.

My father greeted us when we arrived. He gave me a weak "we're in public" hug then shook Pete's hand, while giving him the quick once-over. Somehow Pete's suit passed muster, or maybe it was Pete's natural charm. Either way, Dad nodded once in approval before moving on to greet others, the medals on his military uniform glinting in the sunlight.

I didn't see my mother until we stepped inside the church. She was sitting in the front row facing the altar, her shoulders hunched. My brother Will sat beside her and neither of them turned to watch people file inside. They just stared straight ahead, as if they were alone on their own separate desert islands.

I knew better than to sit near the back. My father would demand we move up the front with the family members. So I sat directly behind Mum. I inhaled the scent unique only to her, which reminded me of all the hundreds of times I'd sat beside her bed, willing her to look at me, to smile, to let me know I existed. It hurt to swallow. It hurt even to breathe. And then, as I felt myself falling into an increasingly familiar dark place, Pete took my hand, squeezed it and whispered, "You're beautiful", in my ear. That was the moment I decided I'd love Pete no matter the risk.

With Emma's help, we finish making the tea and she retrieves a container of home-made shortbread from her bag. I place some on a plate, along with my store-bought chocolate biscuits.

"Juggling work with her appointments is the challenge," Will is saying as we re-enter the lounge.

Tears pool in Mags' eyes and even Lily looks close to crying.

"What did I miss?" I ask, looking accusingly at Will.

I bet he's decided to ramp up the sympathy levels with a sob story.

"Will's daughter was in a terrible car accident with her mother," Mags says with a choke.

"Her mum died at the scene," whispers Lily.

I sit with a thump in the corner armchair.

"That's awful."

Will has his head bowed and he's chewing the tip of his thumb again.

"It's not something I tend to talk about," he mutters.

"Was your daughter OK?" Emma asks.

When Will doesn't reply, Lily speaks for him.

"She crushed her foot, broke like a gazillion bones and has only just started to walk again. That's why Will's here – Matilda had an appointment with a specialist in Millwater Hospital down the road."

Emma gasps. "How old is she?"

Will lifts his head. "Tilly will be seven in a month."

Seven. He's had a daughter for seven years and I never knew about her. Why wasn't she with Will at James' wedding?

"I didn't even know Tilly was my daughter until she was four years old," Will says as if reading my thoughts.

"What do you mean?" asks Lily.

"Her mother, Rachel, and I were only together for a few months and then she moved away. I found out about Tilly when a friend of mine let something slip. Apparently, everyone in the world knew I was the father of the baby except me," he adds bitterly.

I feel as if my life has become a whirlpool and I'm going round and round faster and faster as I head towards the plughole.

"That must have been a-a shock," I stammer.

He fixes me with a stare. "Can you blame her, Trish?

She'd met Dad and heard about Mum. I imagine she wanted to raise her child as far away from them as possible."

"Don't you think she should have told you anyway?" says Lily. "Besides, we aren't living in the Dark Ages. You don't have to get your parents' approval."

I still have my eyes locked with Will's.

"It wasn't about getting Mum and Dad to approve, Lils," I say quietly. "That would never have happened."

"What was it, then?"

I was wrong – Will's eyes are different to Dad's. They're softer, and wary of what I might say next.

"Dad would have lost it," I say firmly. "Then Mum would have shut herself in her room for a month until we either managed to coax her out or she found another way to try to kill herself. And we'd have carried on acting like everything was just fine – or face the consequences. The way we were taught from the day we were born."

Will blinks several times, then gives me a ghost of a smile.

"That about covers it," he says.

"Well," Lily breathes. "Talk about intense. How come you never said anything?"

My friends are looking at me like I'm someone they don't fully recognize. Mags even looks a little scared.

I flick my thumb against my finger, desperate to steer the conversation away from my parents.

"Where's Tilly?" I ask Will.

"She's staying in hospital overnight. Usually I sleep – well, try to sleep – on the chair in her room, but she insisted I stay in the hotel down the road. I swear Tilly's seven going on twenty-one." Will smiles weakly and has a long, slow sip of his tea.

Lily let's out a noisy sigh. "I'm surprised you turned out as well as you did, Trish." She winks to let me know she's joking.

"You might want to re-assess that when you hear how I burst into tears and cried all over some stranger on the plane because he happened to mention my mother."

"But you never cry," Lily says, horrified.

"Exactly."

"Was this stranger the mystery guy who later took you to a wedding and confessed he was deeply attracted to you?" Emma asks.

Mags and Lily both leap out of their seats.

"What?" they shout in unison.

Will gives a small chuckle and shakes his head.

I grimace and punch Emma lightly on the leg.

"Thanks, Em."

She widens her eyes innocently. "I thought they knew about the lovely Scott."

"Jesus, he even has a name," Lily yells. "Boring middle-class name, but still. Who is this Scott character and why does he have the unflappable Trish blushing?"

By now Will is laughing so hard he's spilling tea on his shorts.

"I can see why you've stayed friends with this lot, Trish," he says.

"You should see them when they've had a few," I mutter.

"Yep, this is nothing," Lily says. "Now, Trish, tell us everything about this Scott, and start with the important details, like how much you'd like to strip him naked."

"Lily," Mags says. "That's revolting."

"Oh! don't be such a prude." Lily throws a cracker at

Mags. "If Scott was a hot girl, you'd want to know all the details."

Lily's voice is loud and her eyes glazed – a sure sign she's had more wine than I realized. Glancing at the bottle, I notice there's barely a drop left at the bottom.

"I'm sure Will doesn't want to hear about Scott," I say, reaching forwards for a piece of shortbread and hoping my cheeks aren't as red as they feel.

"Actually, I'm intrigued. Besides, the alternative is watching some awful movie alone in my hotel room."

Lily slaps Will on the back, sending another splash of tea over the rim.

"I like this brother of yours, Trish. Why on earth have you been hiding him from us all this time?"

I keep my eyes down and brush crumbs from my lap onto the carpet.

"Because I was a shit brother," Will says softly.

I glance up at him. "That's true," I say quietly. "But I wasn't a great sister, either."

"I guess we were too busy managing Mum and Dad to consider each other."

"I just figured you were like James, intent to ignore me at all costs."

"He's an arsehole, Trish. I try not to have anything to do with him these days."

A knot inside me starts to unravel. Will turned up out of the blue because he wanted to see me. But why? I won't let myself trust him. I can't let my defences down. No matter how genuine he seems.

16

My unborn baby wakes me early. For nearly half an hour, I lie with my hands on my stomach trying to process the fact that a tiny human being is rolling about in there. I'm the mother of this soon-to-be child. It defies comprehension.

The second I get out of bed and wrap my thin dressing gown around me, I'm ravenous. I wander into the kitchen and ignore the bench littered with the detritus of last night's gathering. Everyone left close to midnight and would have stayed longer, only Emma was worried her parents, who were babysitting Freddie, would be impatient. Finn is away for two months, working as a park ranger in the South Island. I know Emma misses him, but at least he's managed to get two months' leave approved for when their baby arrives.

Will offered to give a drunken Lily a lift home as it was close to his hotel. Which was very kind of him, I suppose, but also a small cause for concern. What did they talk about?

I make myself a tea and two pieces of toast and sit on the porch step in the sun. The second I've finished my toast, I phone Lily.

"Just checking you got home OK."

Lily groans. "Darryl was waiting for me, pacing like a bloody jealous husband."

"Is he there?" I ask.

"In the shower."

I can hear Lily taking several gulps of what I assume is water. I suspect she might have a slight hangover.

"He wasn't very pleased to see me dropped home by a handsome stranger, either." She laughs. "Serves him right."

"Lily, that's awful. I hope you explained."

"Of course I did. Last night and again this morning. He's still got the pip with me."

"I hope it's going to be all right," I say, fairly confident it will be.

"Yeah, it's fine. I promised I'd go to some war movie tonight with him as penance. Not that I did anything wrong. Anyway, enough about me – we should talk about last night. There's a lot to dissect, Trish, not least of which is this mysterious Scott. I think we should try to—"

"Not a chance, Lils." I use my no-nonsense work voice.

"All right then, Miss Enigma, how about Will? He asked me if you were pregnant, by the way. He said he didn't want to mention it in case you were just fat."

"Thanks."

"Well, he used nicer words, but you get the gist."

"What did you tell him?"

"The truth. That you were pregnant and the baby's dad had been narrowed down to one of two possibilities."

"Oh, God," I groan. "What did he say then?"

"Truthfully? He laughed, Trish. Honest – he thought it

was a crack-up. Said he was looking forward to getting to know you better."

I'm silent, processing this information.

"He seems like an all-right brother, Trish. It must be nice to have contact with someone in your family."

I know where this is heading. I'm not ready to talk to Lily about Mum and Dad. I'm not ready to talk to anyone.

"Well, I'd better dash. Just wanted to check you were OK," I say quickly. "Bye, Lils."

Once I hang up, I finish my tea and examine the garden. The border of pansies is looking straggly. It's time they came out. I'll have a quick shower then head to the garden centre to see what looks good.

My phone pings. It's a text message from a private number:

I had a great night, Trish. Thanks. It was so good to see you. Any chance I can stop by after lunch? Tilly would really love to meet you. Will

While I try to figure out what my answering text will be, another comes through. It's from a number I know well:

Sorry I reacted so badly to your news. It came as a shock. Please can we meet this afternoon to discuss? I want to make it work x Pete

Oh, God, what do I do now? My head is spinning with yes, no, maybe replies and since I can't make up my mind, I decide to have a shower.

Unfortunately, when I get out of the shower and check my phone, I have a message from Emma:

Been thinking about last night. Please can we have a chat? Come for cake this avo x Em

And a message from Mags:

I meant it about moving in when baby is born. Can find someone to take care of cats. Maybe you could talk to a psychologist about your parents. Just want to help x M

There's also one missed call and a message from another number I don't recognize.

"What the hell!" I say out loud as I hit the button and listen.

"Trish, it's Scott. From Tokyo. You very kindly came to my friend's wedding with me. Anyway, please don't think I'm stalking you, but I remembered the name of the company you work for and got your number from your boss – she's a dragon, by the way. I told her we'd met in Tokyo and I was interested in you doing some work for me. Small white lie.

"So, I was hoping... this is going to sound strange," says Scott, "But I wondered if there was any chance I could take you out for dumplings some time. Proper Japanese ones. There's this great place I know of and I really want to thank you properly for what you did and... well, also apologize in person for getting drunk and coming on to you – it was poor form. So, this catch-up would be as friends, obviously, but... well, I'd love to see you again." There's a long pause and I listen to Scott breathing. "Think about it, Trish. I'll... I'll leave it with you to decide. This is my number. You can work that out, of course. Anyway, I'll stop blabbering. Bye."

I place my phone carefully on my bedside table and sit on the edge of my bed in my wet towel. The carpet under my feet is damp from my dripping hair. It's too much. All of these people wanting to be in my life. I need to keep a distance between them and me. They're getting too close and I can't allow it to happen.

I snatch up my phone and send a quick message to Will:

Busy today sorry. Maybe another time.

Then Emma:

Can't today. Catch up soon x T

And finally one to Pete:

I need some time. Can I call you next week?

I think about responding to Mags and Scott but decide to stay silent. Instead, I get dressed and head to the garden centre. I wish I lived somewhere completely cut off from the rest of the world: a tropical paradise with a small house, a big garden and a person who delivers supplies once a week. Apart from that brief weekly contact with the delivery person where we might exchange a few innocuous remarks about the weather, I'd see no one and have no contact with the outside world. I could live happily in my bubble. Lead a simple, uncomplicated, unthreatening, pain-free life.

17

I spend all afternoon pottering around the garden. My phone has stayed beside my bed since this morning and I haven't checked it once. I'm torn between being blissfully unaware if anyone is trying to contact me and the nagging urge to check if anyone has tried to get in touch. What if I look at my phone later tonight and there are zero messages? I'd like to think I'd be relieved, but I suspect it'll have the opposite effect.

After an early dinner of poached eggs on toast with avocado and tomato slices on the side, I scroll through Netflix trying to find a movie. There are a thousand movies on there and not one I have the remotest interest in watching.

I turn off the TV and wander out into the hallway. The wall clock tells me it's not even 7 p.m. yet. For a while I stare at the front door as if I'm waiting for someone to knock. Which I'm not. Then I find myself in the spare room, looking at the immaculately made bed. One of my earliest memories is of Dad demonstrating the correct way to make a bed. The special three-tuck technique for the corners, the smoothing of the blanket from bottom to top. The exact placement of the plumped-up pillows. It was important to go around the bed twice to ensure everything was tucked in perfectly. Some lessons are hard to forget.

The walls of the spare room are the same pale grey they were when I moved in. I bought the grey linen bedcover to match. Plus the black-and-white striped sheets to complement the sophisticated look I was going for. Along with the dark grey curtains and the black wooden side tables, the room has a classic spare-room look similar to an upmarket hotel.

It's no nursery.

Crossing my arms, I narrow my eyes. Emma has informed me that for the first couple of months at least, the baby will probably be in my room, in a yet-to-be-purchased bassinet beside the bed. But eventually, I'll want to put the baby down to sleep in its own room. Plus, I'll want to feed and change the baby in his or her bedroom. The one I'm scrutinizing. Which means, said Emma, presenting me with a list, I'll need a cot, and a change table, and a comfortable chair for breastfeeding. Plus a gazillion nappies and wipes, and muslin cloths (you can never have too many), and clothes for the wee one, of course. And a buggy, and blankets and, most importantly, black-out curtains. If you invest in one thing, said Emma, make sure the baby's room is as dark as you can make it. If they see so much as a crack of light, they'll resist sleep.

I shut the curtains and the door and wait for my eyes to adjust. It's dark, but I can still make out the various shapes in the room. If I wave my hand around, I can see it clearly. Not only is there a strip of light visible either side of the curtains, but there's also a glow coming through the curtains, which gets brighter the longer I look.

I open the curtains and check my watch. Too late to go shopping now. Even the shopping centre will be closed. My heart begins to race. I spent all afternoon mucking about in the garden when I should have been getting ready for this baby. I've got nothing so far, not even a baby seat for the car. What if the baby comes early? I can't even bring it home from the hospital. That's assuming I can drive. What if I can't drive because I had to have a caesarean? I should have bought a bassinet months ago, or at least started researching. I can't just buy any old one It needs to be a top-quality one made of natural, non-toxic materials. The sheets should be organic cotton and the blankets 100 per cent wool. How can I be six months pregnant and so disorganized? I can't have a baby. I'm not ready.

I race to my room and pick up my phone, my breathing fast and shallow. Someone needs to help me calm down. Talk me out of this panic. But who?

There are no text messages. No missed calls. No one has tried to contact me again. Not that I can blame them when I blew them off.

With shaking legs, I crawl into bed and curl up on my side. My phone digs into my hip and I ignore it. I want my mum. Which is so ridiculous I laugh out loud. A short, barking, bitter laugh. It took me a while to accept the truth but eventually, I learnt never to rely on her for anything. One day I'd arrive home from school and she'd be bustling about the kitchen preparing afternoon tea and asking me about school like a normal person, and the next she'd be sitting on the porch staring into space. She wouldn't even acknowledge me if I said hi. Let's not forget the times she wouldn't even snap out of whatever mood she was in to wish her own daughter a happy birthday.

My chest hurts from trying to breathe.

"I can't do this," I whisper.

Closing my eyes, I will myself to calm down. I can't think about Mum. Instead, I focus on work. If I'm going to hand over the Omnus project, I'm going to make sure it's in the best shape possible. Which means I have to be in top form when I go back to Tokyo this Thursday. Which means I have to stop being a pathetic sap.

I drag myself off the bed and change into running gear. It's the last thing I feel like doing, but exercise always helps when I feel low. Well, nearly always.

Once I've laced my shoes, I tuck a front door key into my sports bra and head out. At first, my pace is slow and my legs seem made of cement, but after ten minutes, I begin to feel lighter. There's a faint pain in my lower abdomen, but I assume it's a stitch and keep going. The pain builds and I welcome it as a distraction. But what if…

I slow to a walk. What if this isn't a stitch? What if the deep ache emanating down my legs is to do with the baby?

I turn on my heel and walk with purpose towards home, the pain easing the closer I get. It's nothing, I tell myself. Everything's fine.

As I turn the corner into my street, I notice my underwear is damp. It could be sweat, but I don't think it is. My hands cup my belly and I press my legs together as I walk in short, careful steps. Finally, I reach my front door, fumble for my key, open the door and shuffle to the bathroom. I pull down my running shorts and stare at the blood staining my underwear.

I'm losing the baby. It's my fault. I should have got the baby's room ready and acted like I wanted to be a mum. For weeks, Emma has been telling me to ring her midwife, but I kept coming up with excuses. I should have faced up to the pregnancy like a sensible adult instead of ignoring it like some immature teenager.

I pull up my shorts and numbly retrieve my phone from the bedroom. I stand in the hallway and call Lily. The phone rings and rings until it switches to answerphone.

"Lily," I whisper, my voice trembling. "Could you come over, please? Something's happened and I—" My voice seizes. I shouldn't have left a message. "Forget it, Lils, I'm fine." I hang up.

If I call Emma, she'll have to find a babysitter for Freddie and she'll be all pregnant and glowing, which I can't face right now. And Mags will go into a panic and cry. I could ring Elliot or Pete, but they want nothing to do with me, or this baby. Maybe I don't ring anyone… That's it. I'll deal with this on my own.

I consider calling an ambulance but quickly dismiss the idea. Instead, I have a shower and get dressed. Then I rummage through my handbag until I find the piece of paper Emma gave me. With shaking hands, I make the call.

The midwife answers on the second ring.

"Leanne speaking."

"Hello, Leanne. I'm sorry to ring, but Emma gave me your number. She's a friend and I'm pregnant. I should have phoned you months ago, but I've been ignoring the pregnancy and now I'm bleeding and I didn't know who else to call."

"Is that Trish?" asks Leanne, her voice soft and composed.

"Yes."

"Emma told me you might get in touch. She also said she was worried you were leaving things a little late."

There's no hint of accusation in her voice. She's simply

stating facts plainly, much the way I do at work. It calms me immediately.

"Yes," I say.

"How many weeks along are you?" Leanne asks.

I'm embarrassed to answer. She's going to think I'm an idiot.

"Six months," I murmur.

"And have you had any complications so far? Any unusual bleeding?"

"No."

"Did you have your twenty-week scan?"

"Yes. It was fine, apparently."

"Good. Now, how much blood has there been, Trish? A few spots, or more of a gush?"

"Not a gush," I say quickly. "But more than a few spots. Somewhere in between."

"OK, and are you experiencing cramps?"

"No. There was this ache while I was out running. It got worse so I came home. But it's stopped hurting now."

"So there's no pain?"

"No."

"OK. What's your address, Trish, and I'll pop over?"

"Really? You'd do that?"

"Of course. That's what I'm here for."

This woman is too good to be true. Matter-of-fact, calm and in control. Everything I've tried to be.

I give her my address and Leanne says she'll be at my place in twenty minutes. She recommends I make myself a cup of tea and have something small to eat. Then I'm to lie on the bed until she arrives.

I do exactly as she says.

There's a knock at the door fifteen minutes later and I let Leanne in. She gives me a brief, no-nonsense hug.

"Right now, Trish. Back to your bed and we'll have a chat."

Once again, I follow her instructions.

Leanne perches on the bed next to my hip.

"I'm assuming you saw a doctor at some point to confirm your pregnancy?" she states.

"Yes."

"And they did blood tests?"

"Yes. I never heard back, so I assumed it was fine."

"I'm sure if there was anything out of the ordinary, they'd have contacted you. Did you have any morning sickness?"

I nod. "More like all-day sickness."

"Nausea or throwing up?"

"Both."

"How often did you vomit?"

"Probably four, five times a day."

Leanne gives me a silent stare. "That must have been hard for you, Trish. Did you see a doctor about it?"

I look down. "No."

"So, you haven't had a blood test since your first doctor's appointment to confirm your pregnancy?"

"No." I'm the worst mother in the world and I'm not even a mother yet.

"Right, well, let's have a little listen to the baby's heartbeat and we'll go from there – assuming you're happy to have me as your midwife?"

"Very happy," I say firmly.

Leanne smiles. "Excellent." She opens her bag and brings out a little white box with a cord attached. "If you can lift up your shirt, Trish, I'll introduce myself to your baby."

18

Leanne leaves half an hour later. I have strict instructions to stay home from work tomorrow and rest in bed until she can arrange an ultrasound appointment. Leanne is confident my baby is fine, but she wants confirmation all the same. I see now why Emma thought I'd like her.

My phone rings as I'm brushing my teeth. I leave it because I'm tired and fragile, and I also know I won't make it back to my bedroom in time to answer. I'm not allowed to rush. I have to take it easy. The best thing I can do for my baby right now is take care of myself. All things Leanne has told me tonight in her forthright tone.

"This is the time to put your health and well-being before anything else, Trish."

So, that's what I'm going to try to do. Starting with an early night.

The bleeding has stopped now and I'm feeling sleepy. Dopey, even. Like I've been given a pill to help me relax. Only, Leanne gave me nothing. Actually, she gave me exactly what I needed. She took care of me and I let her. The only other time that ever happened was when I stayed with Grammy Rose. Even then, I never fully let myself accept her affection because I knew it wasn't going to last. I'd have to go back home to Mum and Dad: to a house of empty looks and closed doors.

I'm almost asleep when there's a bang on my front door.

"Trish, open up," yells Lily. "For fuck's sake, open your door before I bash it down."

I drag myself into an upright position, my head foggy. I hear Lily mutter and other voices responding. Is that Mags? And Emma? Oh, God, they're all here. What's going on?

I reach for my dressing gown on the end of my bed.

"Coming," I croak.

When I turn the door handle, they burst in and surround me like a herd of bulls.

"What's happened?" Emma asks. "We've been calling and calling."

"Why didn't you answer your phone?" Lily demands. "After I listened to your message, I knew something was wrong and when you didn't reply—"

"We've been so worried," says Mags. "Is it the baby?"

"Calm down, I'm fine," I say, shaking my head.

I'm half loving the fact my friends have dropped everything to come running and half annoyed they've turned up unannounced when I was so close to sleep – something I've been in short supply of recently.

"You sounded terrible," says Lily. "Don't go acting all cool, calm and collected on us."

I sigh. "Look, I'm sorry I freaked you out. I was in a panic because I'd started bleeding and I was getting pains—"

"Oh, Trish." Mags is so distraught she has to lean on the wall for support.

Emma places a hand on my arm. "Did you go to the doctor?"

"Fuck," Lily says loudly. "Why the hell did I choose the one and only time my friend rings me in genuine need to be bonking Darryl's brains out on top the washing machine?" She covers her face. "Bloody Darryl," she mutters.

I giggle quietly. "Was the machine going at the time, Lils?" I ask.

"Trish." Emma squeezes my arm, her face serious. "Don't change the subject."

I remember Leanne's words and the vow I made to put myself first.

"I'm going to lie back down."

Nudging past Mags, I head to my room and climb into bed. The others follow. Lily flops onto the end of the bed and the other two sit either side like nurses tending to the infirm.

"OK, so after I left a garbled message on Lily's phone, I rang Leanne, the midwife Emma recommended," I say softly. "She checked me out and gave me a lecture on taking better care of myself. She thinks the baby is fine but that I'm probably low in iron, especially after not being able to keep much food down in the first trimester."

"I thought you'd been seeing your doctor about that?" Emma says.

"No, I haven't. Anyway, I've got an ultrasound and blood tests tomorrow and I'm under strict instructions to rest. Which I was doing until you all turned up."

"So, why did you start bleeding?" Mags asks.

I shrug. "The low iron might be a factor. Stress maybe. Pushing myself too hard. But the bleeding has stopped now. I'm honestly feeling fine." Which is surprisingly the truth.

"I knew we should have intervened earlier," says Emma. She stares accusingly at Lily. "I told you Trish was overdoing it."

"And I told you, Trish wouldn't listen."

"I am in the room, guys. And Lily's right, Em. I wouldn't have listened. I've been keeping myself busy because I didn't want to accept I was pregnant. But I do now. And I'm going to make a real effort to slow down. In fact…" I pause and take a deep breath.

"That was what set me off in a panic. I was looking around the spare room and realized that I hadn't done a thing to get ready for this baby. I haven't painted the room or bought a bassinet or joined an antenatal class. I don't even have a single item of clothing for the baby. Isn't that the first thing a parent-to-be goes and buys? A cute little outfit for their unborn child?"

Emma takes my hand. "You've got three months to go, Trish. Plenty of time to get that stuff sorted."

"And I've already bought two outfits for bubs," says Mags. "I was going to give them to you a couple of months ago, but I wasn't sure you'd be keen." She leaps off the bed. "I'll go and get them now."

"Mags," I say, smiling. "That isn't necessary."

Lily clambers off the bed and races out of the room. The next second she's back with the paper and pen I keep stuck to the fridge.

"Right. Let's make a list. I'm a dab hand with a paintbrush, so I'll come over this weekend and start on the painting. You just need to pick a colour, Trish, and I'm telling you now, I refuse to paint your spare room yellow."

"What's wrong with yellow?" Mags asks. "I like yellow."

Lily scowls. "It's the classic fallback colour when you don't know the baby's sex, but it's a try-hard colour, Trish. Trust me."

"I painted Freddie's first room yellow," says Emma.

"And you knew it was a mistake and changed it to green," Lily says.

"True. But only because it was the wrong shade of yellow. It was too bright. Like standing inside a tub of margarine."

I lean back against my pillow and rest my hands on my belly. The baby gives me a gentle wave.

"Could I get some sleep and maybe talk about the list tomorrow?" I ask.

My friends look at one another, considering my request.

"Seems reasonable," says Lily. She puts the pen and pad on my bedside table.

"Do you want me to stay the night?" asks Mags.

"No, really, I'm going to be fine."

Emma squeezes my hand. "I'll come with you to the scan tomorrow. Just let me know when it is and I'll pick you up."

Yawning, I curl up on my side. "Goodnight, guys. Pull the door closed on your way out."

They tiptoe exaggeratingly out of the room.

"Night," Mags says. "I'll call you in the morning."

"And I'll keep my phone beside me and tell Darryl to keep his filthy hands off me," Lily calls as she opens the front door.

I close my eyes and absorb the silence once they leave. It's a nice quiet. A calm quiet. My baby shifts about getting comfortable and we both drift off to sleep.

19

Leanne rings as Emma is driving me home from the doctor. I didn't think anyone in the medical profession made personal calls like this. I actually thought there might be a rule against it.

"How did it go?" she asks.

"Just as you predicted. My doctor said the scan shows nothing out of the ordinary and that I should start on some iron tablets, which I now have in my hands."

"Excellent. Are you going to rest for the remainder of the day?"

"Yes, boss. Emma's dropping me home now."

"Any more bleeding?"

"Just a couple of spots. Nothing, really."

I glance at Emma, who scowls at the road ahead. There may have been a slight withholding of information from my end. As in, I told Emma I hadn't bled at all.

"Well, take care, Trish. I'll pop round and see you in the morning."

"But, I... I mean, I'll be at work tomorrow."

There's a long pause and I know I've said the wrong thing.

"My advice would be to take another day off, Trish, and maybe look to reduce your hours."

"But I'm only six months."

"And your body is telling you to slow down."

I sigh. Tash sounded less than impressed when I rang her this morning to say I couldn't make it in. If I don't get back to the office soon, I suspect there won't be a job to go to. She'd better not renege on her promise to let me go to Tokyo. Speaking of which…

"Leanne, I need to go to Tokyo in a couple of days for work," I say firmly. "It's important." I steel myself, waiting for her disapproval.

"OK."

That's it? I was sure she was going to talk me out of it. Actually, I might have been secretly hoping she would.

"So I can fly still?"

"Sure. For the next two to three weeks. I'd suggest at seven months you avoid overseas travel."

"Oh. OK. Thanks."

"Of course, if the bleeding or pains start up again, you'll have to re-assess."

"Absolutely."

Emma turns her car into my street.

"Thanks again, Leanne."

"Bye."

The second I move my phone away from my ear, Emma opens her mouth.

"You told me you had no bleeding," she snaps.

I consider coming up with some story, but in the end I just say sorry.

"It's like in the past few weeks I've gone from thinking we're the closest of friends to wondering if I know you at all. Honestly, Trish, the four of us have been hanging out together forever and we've been each other's biggest support, but now... I feel like you've been presenting us with one Trish – the beautiful, confident, got everything under control Trish – when there's been this whole other Trish you've kept hidden."

"That about sums it up," I mutter.

Emma pulls up outside my house, turns off the ignition and faces me. "Why?"

"Why what?"

She narrows her eyes. "Why keep that part of yourself from us?"

I shrug. If only I could just get out of the car and leave.

"It's how I was raised, I guess. Get on with things, don't show your emotions, don't talk about stuff. It's the military way, Em."

"Bollocks. It was your father's way."

I nod. "True."

"I hope you'll talk sometime. About your dad and mum. Meeting your brother the other day made me realize the lack of family support you have. I feel bad for not recognizing how hard that must be."

"I'm pleased," I state, staring at my lap.

"Pleased?"

"I couldn't get away from my family fast enough. Anyway, you and Mags and Lily are my family."

"We are..." Emma trails off. "I just want—"

"Oh, shit," I exclaim, having spied Pete standing by my front door. "What the hell is he doing here?"

Emma glances at Pete and bites her lip. "Want me to send him packing?"

I shake my head. "No. He phoned asking if he could catch up and I fobbed him off. Might as well get it over with now he's here."

I open my door, hop out and thank Emma. She wishes me luck and drives away.

Pete watches me walk towards him. I can't tell from his expression which way this is going to go.

"I phoned you at work and they said you were off sick," he says, shoving his hands in his pockets and rocking back on his heels.

It's the way he often stands when he's talking to people. I used to find it sexy. I still do.

My palms ache as I stop a metre away from him, keeping space between us.

"I haven't been well, but I'm improving. Sorry I didn't get back to you."

He smiles faintly. "It's OK. I know you don't like these sorts of moments."

"What do you mean?"

He tips his head to one side and lowers his eyelashes – another of his mannerisms that used to melt my insides.

"Awkward emotional outpourings," he says softly.

I look away from him "Do you want to come in?"

Pete doesn't answer. Instead, he steps back so I can use my key in the door.

"How's the baby doing?" he asks.

I feel his breath on the back of my neck.

"Fine."

He follows me into the kitchen. "You've got a nice little bump happening."

Why is he sounding so friendly?

"Coffee?" I ask, flicking on the machine.

Pete pulls out a chair and sits at the table. "Thanks."

I sit opposite as we wait for the machine to warm up.

"So, what's with the surprise visit?" I ask.

Pete smiles and tips his head to the side again. I wish he'd stop doing that. Where's the angry guy who stormed out of the café gone?

"Sorry, I know you don't like surprises."

It's one of the things he used to tease me about. He'd ring me at work and say, "Just warning you – I'm going to arrive home with something different than planned for dinner." Or: "I have a birthday present for you and it's not one of the items on your list. Just wanted to let you know in advance so you don't freak out."

He knew me so well.

"I thought you weren't talking to me," I say quickly. "That you didn't want anything to do with this baby." I place a protective hand on my belly.

"I reacted badly. It was a shock, Trish. A big one." He clasps his hands on the table and leans forwards. "A few months ago, you didn't want me in your life. Then all of a sudden…" He waves his hand at my stomach. "This."

"I didn't plan for it to happen," I mutter.

"And that was the biggest shock of all," Pete exclaims. "It was so un-Trish-like."

"Thanks."

"What I mean is, you didn't plan to get pregnant but you did. So maybe it's a sign that, well, that things aren't supposed to be over between us. I still love you, Trish. The whole time I was in Sydney, I never stopped loving you."

My heart starts to beat fast. "You had a girlfriend, Pete."

He sits back in his chair and crosses his arms. "How did you know?"

I roll my eyes. "You do know what Facebook is, right?" When I saw the photo of Pete with a slim, dark-haired nymph less than four months after he took off to pursue the career of his dreams, I felt as if I'd been scraped hollow.

"She was a distraction, Trish. A way for me to try to forget you."

I finish making the coffee, slide it towards him and sit. "It's not important anymore."

"What about you?" he says. "You clearly haven't been a spinster."

I can't believe we're going down this path.

"What do you *want*, Pete?" I snap.

He suddenly reaches out and takes my hand.

"I want us to forgive each other for everything that's happened and to get back together. I'll have the DNA test and hopefully, the baby will be mine. If it isn't… well, we'll find a way to deal with it." His thumb strokes the top of my hand. "I want to be with you, Trish. So, so much."

I look into his wide hazel eyes. When Pete suddenly reappeared a few months ago after two years of nothing – no phone call, no email – I'd have done anything to hear him say those words. I thought he was still in Australia, but one evening he showed up at the bar where I always met my friends, came over to our table and chatted away as if he'd just been on a two-day work trip.

I reacted the only way I knew how: like it was no big deal. He sat down, had a few too many drinks with us, then threw his arm around me as we got up to leave. I ignored the looks from my friends who had been watching me all night with concern. Several times they'd suggested we head home, but I wanted to stay at the bar. I refused to show weakness. When Pete and I got back to my place, we couldn't get our clothes off fast enough.

It wasn't until the morning when I woke with him asleep beside me that I realized I couldn't do it again. Couldn't risk him hurting me. So I sent him packing and he made no attempt to change my mind. He never said he loved me, wanted to be with me. He just yelled that I was leading him along and left.

"I don't know, Pete."

He comes around the table and crouches next to me. Lifting my chin, he leans close.

"Please, Trish. Can't we try?"

I stare at his lips. Lips I've kissed over and over.

"Maybe," I whisper.

As if I've said yes, he smiles, tips forwards and brushes his lips lightly against mine. It's so achingly familiar. I don't want to be alone and pregnant. I'm exhausted from trying so hard. Pete is offering to be here for me and I should be feeling relieved, happy even. But I don't. I feel numb.

Pete is kissing my neck now. In the past, this would have been our secret code for "I want to take you to bed and ravage you", but I'm not interested in having sex. That's not what I need from him right now.

I push Pete away and stand up. "Emma took me to the doctors," I say as he rises, too.

He puts his hands on my waist and tries to kiss me again. I duck and move to the other side of the table.

"I've had some bleeding. I thought maybe I was losing the baby, but it seems to be all right."

Pete nods and I can see in his eyes he's still thinking about sex.

"I'm sorry," he says huskily.

"Pete, you'll have to go," I say loudly.

"But—"

"I need to rest. I haven't had much sleep."

The lustful look leaves his eyes.

"OK," he says. "Should I come back this evening? I could bring us some of Gino's."

My stomach growls. I haven't had Gino's for months. Pete used to bring it home every Friday night – when it was "his night to cook", he joked.

"It's a nice offer, but not tonight. Sorry, Pete. I... I can't."

Pete squints and his jaw clenches.

"Fine," he mutters, draining his coffee in one gulp. "I can see when I'm not wanted."

I'd forgotten how often he'd do this. Turn things around to make himself the victim. Rather than annoy me, it weakens my resolve. He's not as confident as he makes out. And he's not perfect, which means that I don't have to be, either.

"We're having a bit of a working bee here this weekend. Painting the spare room and getting it set up as a nursery. The girls are organizing it. You could... if you're free and you'd like to come—"

"I'd love to." Pete leaps around the table and throws his arms around me. "Of course I want to help," he says into my hair. Then he pulls back, grinning. "That was a weird feeling." He places a hand on my bump. "I could feel it when we hugged."

I smile and Pete smiles back. He places a palm on my cheek and gives me another soft kiss on the lips.

"I'll be here bright and early on Saturday," he breathes. "Have the coffee ready."

When we were together there was a running joke between us. Pete couldn't speak to anyone or do anything until he'd had at least two coffees to start the day. He drinks more coffee with more dedication and conviction than anyone I've known.

"I'll get another kilo of beans to be safe," I say.

Pete pecks me on the cheek. "Get some rest, Trish. I know how challenging that's going to be."

I follow him to the front door and close it behind him as he leaves.

20

Tash phones while I'm in the taxi.

"Well?" she demands.

"It went well," I say, trying not to sound as exhausted as I feel. "They were disappointed I'm handing the project over to Mark but were grateful I'd gone to Tokyo in person to explain the transition and talk through any concerns. They were very supportive in the end." *Unlike you*, I want to add.

"At least you didn't lose them," Tash mutters.

I close my eyes and rest my head back against the seat. How did I put up with this woman as my boss for so long? Scott's right – she is a dragon.

"I've arranged a meeting with Mark first thing Monday to go over everything."

"Good. So you're better now? You'll be working proper hours again?"

She speaks like my pregnancy was a bad case of the flu and it's been an inconvenience but thankfully is in the past.

"I intend to work full-time for as long as I can," I snap.

Tash sighs dramatically. "I've got to go." And she hangs up without so much as a goodbye.

The trip to Tokyo was harder than I thought it would be. Workwise, it was fine – I can still switch into being a focused fiend when I'm talking to clients – but the rest of the time was tough. The city was wet, crowded, noisy and lonely. My client offered to take me out for dinner, but I respectfully declined and ordered off the in-room menu instead – a miserable plate of rice mixed with cabbage and a weird-tasting dressing. The hotel room was airless, and a red light kept flashing on and off through the flimsy curtains all night.

The flights both ways were long and uncomfortable. Normally I'd have been pleased to have a row of seats to myself, but conversing with a stranger might have helped to take my mind off… well, my thoughts, mostly. The doubts and fears that kept swirling around in my head. Plus, every time there was so much as a niggle in my abdomen, I was convinced I was going to lose the baby.

Several times I wished Scott had been sitting next to me, talking about auras or some other bizarre notion. If I hadn't been hurtling along in a plane, I might have tried to call him. Not that I'd have known what to say.

I wonder how he is, what he's up to. I never asked him what he did for work, where he lived, what he liked to do. I'm so wrapped up in myself. I spend far too much time keeping my emotions in check, yet at the same time wallowing in self-absorption. I'm doing it now. I need to change. Start thinking more about others and less about myself.

Snatching my phone off my lap, I call Scott.

"Hey, Trish," he says, answering before I've had a second to reconsider. "Glad you rang."

"Hi, I… I've just got back from another quick trip to Tokyo."

"You have? Wow, I bet you're shattered."

"A bit." I hesitate. "Actually, more like a lot."

"How's the pregnancy going?"

"It's fine." I hesitate because I want to tell him the truth, not brush things off as I normally would. "It's been a little rough this week. I had a scare. Thought I was having a miscarriage."

I hear Scott take a sharp intake of breath.

"Trish that's awful. I'm so sorry."

"The baby's OK. At least that's what the midwife and doctor tell me."

"They generally have a pretty good understanding of these things."

In the next few seconds of silence, I remember why I rang. So far, this conversation has been all about me.

"How are you doing, Scott? Did you manage to check out of the hotel without running into your ex?"

"Yes, thankfully. I was kind of hoping I might bump into you so I could apologize for my disgraceful behaviour, but I slept in, woke with a hangover and took a while to drag myself to your door. By then you'd left."

I like knowing he came to find me the morning after the wedding: that I hadn't been forgotten. Also, he wasn't the only one to behave "disgracefully", as he put it. I was the one who kissed him in the lift, though he may not even remember that part.

"So, I'd still love to take you out for a meal, if you'd let me?" says Scott. "It's the least I can do, considering you not only came to a wedding with a virtual stranger in a foreign city where you knew no one, but you also put up with me making a highly inappropriate drunken advance on you. Which by the way I promise not to do again."

The taxi driver smiles at me in the rear-view mirror as I laugh.

"You make it sound far worse than it was."

"The drunken kiss was all right, then?"

So he *does* remember.

I know he's teasing by the tone of his voice, but I wonder could this be him ever so slightly flirting with me?

"I'm free now," I say.

What the hell brought that on? Five seconds ago, I wanted to get home, eat toast with lashings of peanut butter and have a long bath.

"Perfect," Scott says. "I was just finishing my last job here. Should I pick you up?"

While chatting at the wedding, we'd discovered that we live in neighbouring suburbs. I'll admit there's been a few times when I've been at the local supermarket or out walking that I've found myself looking around, hoping I might spot him.

The sensible thing to do would be to meet Scott at the restaurant. If he picks me up, he'll know where I live. Not that it's a bad thing. I completely trust he's not a psycho, but still, I need to stay in control of the situation.

"You don't have to."

"It's no problem. I work from home, so I'm close to your place right now anyway."

If he picks me up, it'll give me more time to recover, shower, get changed, question what on earth I'm doing. It's a perfectly logical, sensible idea. I don't know why I'm making a big deal out of it.

"OK, that would be great. Could you give me an hour? I'm actually still in the taxi from the airport."

"How about I pick you up at six, then? Give you a bit more time."

"That would be great." I reel off my address.

"See you soon. And it's casual. Nothing fancy."

"Good. I like nothing fancy."

Scott laughs. "Yeah, me too."

I picture his hair flopping over his face and his eyes so dark and penetrating, and my stomach lurches as if I'm still on the plane and it's dipped its nose forwards to begin a steep descent towards land.

21

"I'm stuffed." I lean back against the leatherette booth. "I should have stopped eating ten dumplings ago."

Scott grins and clasps another dumpling with his chopsticks. "It takes stamina, Trish. I've been training for years." He dips the dumpling in the dark soy sauce and puts the whole thing in his mouth in one go. "Not sure I can finish this last plate, though," he mumbles, his mouth full.

Giggling, I take a sip of water. Scott is on the water too, though he did drink a modest half-pint of beer when we first arrived.

"I love this place," I say, glancing around at the other small raised booths crammed with happy, chatting customers. "Can't believe we got a table."

Scott nods and swallows. "It gets booked up pretty quick. I rang them as soon as I got off the phone with you and was lucky they still had space."

"The funny thing is, I've driven past about a hundred times and never thought to eat here."

"Yeah, it's not particularly appealing from the outside."

A loud gong bangs quickly five or six times and there's a chant from the chefs in the open kitchen as a group of satisfied diners head out of the door.

"Do they really carry on like that every time anyone comes in or out?"

"Yep. You should see what they do when it's someone's birthday."

Red lanterns and flags hang everywhere. Waitresses dressed in colourful Japanese kimonos float about looking completely unruffled as the worst pop music I've ever heard blares in the background. I'd have thought it would make me wish I'd never left home, but being here energizes me, makes me feel more alive and excited than I have done in weeks. It could also be because I'm sitting opposite a guy I'm finding it extremely hard not to throw myself at. I need to snap out of this. Fast.

"So, how long have you been running your own business?" I ask, watching Scott swallow yet another dumpling.

"About three years."

"Did you always want to be an architect?"

"No. I thought I was going to be a famous wildlife photographer."

"What happened?"

"I tried to photograph my neighbour's cat and it attacked me. Viciously, I might add. I still have the scar." He shows me the inside of his wrist and points to a faint white line. "Talk about being scarred for life."

I want to run my finger over the scar. *What is happening to me?* I must act calm.

"How old were you when this savage attack took place?"

"Ten."

"Where did you study architecture?"

Scott lifts his eyebrows. "Do you always interrogate people like this?"

My cheeks grow hot. "I'm just interested."

"Trish, I'm hassling you. You looked so serious and earnest, like you were interviewing me for some report."

"Thanks a lot." I cross my arms and pretend to look cross, though I'm relieved he didn't read something else into my expression.

Scott eyes me as he takes a gulp of water.

"How about you start answering some of my questions? Conversations are supposed to go both ways, you know. It hasn't gone unnoticed that every time I ask you anything, you change the subject or turn it around into a question for me instead."

Damn him and his overly perceptive ways. "I don't really like to talk about myself."

"Why not?"

"Because my life has been very boring."

"Rubbish. What do you like to do when you're not beavering away at work?"

"If I tell you, you'll think I'm the most boring person on the planet."

"Again, rubbish. Spill."

"All right. I love gardening. I'm like an old nana."

"That's fantastic." He looks genuinely excited. "I mean... I wouldn't have picked it. You're always so... I don't know, well-dressed and perfect, yet you get stuck into mud and... wait..." Scott holds up a hand. "Please tell me you have wellingtons."

"Of course I do."

Scott slaps the table with his palm. "I knew it. You are anything but boring, Trish."

"I'm glad I amuse you."

Scott laughs again. It takes so little to make him look genuinely happy.

"Tell me more about your garden – assuming there's one hiding at the back of that pretty house of yours."

I narrow my eyes. "I can't tell if you're teasing me."

Scott's happy face drains away. "I was trying to make you relax, but I have this habit of taking things too far. I honestly am not teasing you, Trish. I want to know more about you and I admire the fact you garden. I can't tell a weed from a daisy, or maybe a daisy is a weed…"

"What do you do outside work?" I ask.

"Oh no." Scott waves his chopsticks. "We are *not* turning this conversation back to me just yet."

It's an inbuilt tactic of mine. Besides, most people are happy to talk about themselves. Pete always was. I'm beginning to think Scott isn't like most people.

"I was asking because for me, gardening is therapy," I say, instantly squirming in my seat.

This isn't something I've discussed with anyone before. My friends know I like to garden, but they don't understand why.

"Therapy for what?" Scott asks softly.

I look at my hands, clasped tightly on the table. Am I really going to talk about this? With a virtual stranger?

"When I was growing up, my mum spent a lot of time in bed and not a lot of time playing happy families. She also tried to kill herself a few times, which wasn't great. Sometimes it… I can get a little down." I'm too scared to look up.

Once – when I was having a down moment and couldn't drag myself out of bed – I told Pete about Mum. He brought me a coffee and said I'd snap out of it. I just needed to stop working so hard, he'd said, giving me a peck on the forehead. Maybe I'm testing Scott, seeing how he'll react.

Slowly, I raise my head. He's looking at me with such compassion and tenderness I want to collapse into his arms.

"I'm sorry, Trish. That might go some way towards explaining your tears on the plane."

"Yeah, well, you caught me off guard talking about Mum's aura." I smirk.

Scott grimaces. "Can't believe I said that stuff." He hesitates. "Have you seen a doctor about your depression?"

I sit back as if I've been slapped. How dare he.

"Excuse me?"

"Well, I know it often runs in families, and you said gardening was therapy. I assume this means you have depressed moments, too, like your mum. Gardening helps to lift your mood."

"I'm not depressed," I snap.

"OK. Sorry."

I stare out of the window wishing I could leave and never see this guy again. Who does he think he is, trying to diagnose me? I'm nothing like my mother. Nothing.

"I knit," Scott says.

I glare at him but don't speak.

"If anyone's a nana here, it's me," he continues. "And just so you know, I keep this information very much to myself."

"You knit?" I croak.

Scott nods. "It's my therapy too, I guess. My little sister taught me while she was… She spent a lot of time in hospital after she had to have surgery on her spine and she was a big knitter. I was always going to the wool shop with a list and bringing her in supplies. One day, I asked her to show me and that was it. I was hooked – excuse the pun."

I resist the urge to hassle him. Lily would have a field day on this one. All of my friends would. I hope for Scott's sake they never find out.

"What do you knit?"

Scott's cheeks are red with embarrassment.

"All sorts. I started out just knitting scarfs, but then I got better and now I knit jumpers and beanies. I knitted a blanket last year. It was a difficult pattern – took me forever."

"I can't believe you knit," I mutter.

"My ex-wife was horrified when she found me at it one day. I swear the way she looked at me when she walked into the bedroom – it was like she'd just caught me in bed with another woman."

I can't help but smile. "That's harsh."

"She was a harsh woman. Sometimes I wonder why on earth we married."

"I thought you were madly in love with her. You seemed pretty heartbroken in Tokyo."

"I was in love with her, but I was also in love with the whole ideal. The wife, the nice house, the trips back and forth to Japan – the whole 'till death do us part' thing. It was important for me that our marriage was a success. But it failed."

I nod. "I guess everyone wants their marriage to work out."

"My parents divorced when I was fourteen," Scott says, a slight catch in his throat. "It was brutal. They went from being nice people, to being savages. I swore when I married, it would never end that way."

"I'm sorry."

"Yeah, me too. After their divorce, Dad moved back to Fiji and I've barely seen him since."

That would explain Scott's lovely brown skin.

"So, your dad is Fijian?"

He nods. "Mum's a Kiwi. Dad wanted to move back to his home country and Mum refused. They used to fight about it constantly."

"I'm surprised you didn't go and visit him more often. I love Fiji – well, the couple of times I've been I've stayed in fancy resorts, so…" I trail off.

"It's a beautiful country, but Dad remarried and had four kids. I wasn't really made to feel all that welcome."

"That sucks."

Scott shrugs. "I got over it."

It's his turn to stare out of the window and we both sit in silence. The baby tries to get my attention and I put my hand down to feel the kicks.

"The baby's gone mental," I mutter.

Scott looks at my stomach. "Can you feel it move?" he asks.

Nodding, I take his hand and place it underneath mine. He frowns and goes extremely still. The baby gives an almighty nudge as if to show off and Scott widens his eyes.

"Oh my God, Trish. That's amazing."

I think Scott's going to lift his hand, but it stays there, warm beneath mine.

"I hope I get to be a dad one day," he murmurs, then grins as the baby moves again.

We lock eyes for a second and I hold my breath, captivated by his deep brown eyes and long dark eyelashes.

Scott lifts his hand away and sits back.

"We should make a pact," he says, his voice light.

I wish I didn't feel suddenly so on my own again.

"What sort of pact?"

"I'll show you mine, if you show me yours."

I choke. "Excuse me?"

"I'll show you my knitting, if you show me your garden."
He holds out his hand and winks. "Deal?"

I'm beginning to think I'm not the only one who avoids
uncomfortable situations. But I'm glad the bantering, chilled
Scott is back. He's much easier for me to handle. I shake his
hand briefly.

"Deal."

My phone rings as we walk towards Scott's car.

"I feel as if eating all those dumplings has actually started
turning me into one," I say to Scott as I fish in my bag for
my phone.

Scott laughs and unlocks the car as I retrieve my phone
and answer.

"Hello?"

"Hey, Trish, how are you?"

"Pete," I murmur.

Scott opens my door like a gentleman before walking
around to his side.

"Good," I say.

"Listen, I'm still at work and I know I said I'd help out
with your little working bee tomorrow, but I have to get
this project out the door by Monday. I'll be spending all
weekend slaving here."

I stand beside the car and stare at Scott, who is now sitting in the driver's seat, checking his phone.

"No problem."

"I'm really sorry, Trish, but you know how it is."

I do know how it is. This was something I faced regularly when we were together. Work first. Trish second. I shouldn't be so disappointed.

"I'll phone you early next week."

Pete has his distracted voice on. He's probably reading a work email or jotting down some notes.

"OK," I say, getting in the car and trying to sound chilled. "Bye." I hang up and shove my phone in my bag. "Sorry about that," I say brightly.

"Bad news?" Scott asks.

He's seen right through me.

"Nothing I haven't heard before," I say in a clipped voice.

Scott starts the car, reverses out of the space and pulls out onto the road.

"Anything you want to get off your chest?"

Oh, what the hell.

"It was Pete. Ex-boyfriend and possible father of my child."

"Ah." Scott pauses. "I thought it was best I avoided that topic tonight."

"Very wise."

"Does he know?" Scott asks, his eyes on the road.

"Yeah. He freaked out initially. Wanted nothing to do with it. Then he turns up at my door earlier this week and says he wants to work things out."

"And what did you say?"

I shake my head and take a moment to reply.

"I thought he was the one. We were together for so long – lived together, talked about travelling the world together, starting a family together, all that stuff." I pause. Am I really going to offload this shit on Scott? Oh, why not? Since we seem to be so freaking honest with each other. "He left about two years ago because he was offered some big fancy CEO role in Sydney. Dream job. Dream location. He said it had been the most difficult decision of his life, but an opportunity like this only comes along once in a lifetime." I decide to leave out the sex with someone else part.

"Did he ask you to go with him?"

"Nope. He said he couldn't expect me to drop everything and join him. It wasn't fair on me because he knew his focus would be on his job. He couldn't be worrying about me, too."

"The fucker," Scott mutters.

I grin. "That's what my friends called him, too."

"But he came home from Sydney and you got back together?" Scott lifts his eyebrows and looks pointedly at my belly.

I grimace. "He turned up at the bar where I often go with my friends. Just walked in and sat next to me. I tried to act casual. We had too many drinks and ended up back at my place."

"And had sex," Scott states.

He sounds unimpressed with my story so far. Not that I blame him.

"I sent him packing the next morning. Didn't speak to him again till a couple of weeks ago when I told him I was pregnant." We're almost at my house and I'm looking forward to collapsing on the couch. I'm so tired, it's hard to keep my heavy head upright. "Pete was supposed to be helping out tomorrow. My friends have arranged to come over and paint the spare room and set things up for the new arrival because I've been living in denial for so long, I haven't done anything to get ready. But now he's pulling out owing to work commitments. Something he used to do on a regular basis."

Scott stops outside my house and turns off the ignition. He swivels to face me.

"No offence, Trish, but he sounds like a complete twat."

I smile and shake my head. "You're not the only one to have called him that, either."

"I've got a free weekend. Can I help?"

"No, that's fine, it's—"

"Please, I'd like to. Plus, I'd get to meet these friends of yours, who sound like excellent types."

"Scott, I'm not sure—"

"I could see your garden, too."

"It's a really nice offer..."

I pause and decide not to follow up with a "but". If he wants to come over tomorrow, why stop him? He'd be good company and the girls could interrogate him, which would be fun. Plus, I could show off my garden. And I'll admit, the thought of spending more time with him is tempting.

"Thanks," I say, opening my door.

"Is 9 a.m. OK?"

"Perfect." I climb out of the car then lean back in. "Thanks for the dumplings. They were excellent."

"You're very welcome. Thanks again for coming to the wedding with me."

He doesn't mention the drunken kiss, but I know we're both thinking about it.

Scott starts the car. "See you tomorrow, Trish, and get some rest."

I wave as he pulls away. Then I stagger into the house, kick off my shoes and collapse.

22

"I'll get it!" Lily yells, even though she's standing right next to me.

They arrived en masse at eight thirty this morning, painting gear on, Mags and Lily complaining about how early it was, and Emma announcing she'd already walked the dog, eaten breakfast with Freddie, made a tray of biscuits and played four rounds of snap. All that on top of the fact she's about to pop out baby number two. Emma's been watching us with disapproval as we devoured the box of doughnuts Mags picked up on the way here.

Lily shoves her mug and me, winks and charges to the door. The second I told them Scott was coming to help, she's been hyped up and asking questions. The poor guy doesn't know what he's got himself in for. I'm looking forward to them meeting each other though. Should make for an entertaining day.

Lily's voice sails back to us.

"So, this is the Scott who scandalously told our Trish her aura was fucked and then forced her to go to some lame wedding."

Emma raises her eyebrows at me. "You'd better get out there."

I race down the hallway, waving to Scott. "Leave him alone, Lily."

Rather than looking like he wants to run, Scott appears to be enjoying himself.

"Looks like your aura contains flashing lights," he says, holding out his hand to Lily.

She shakes his hand and grins at me. "I like this one, Trish." Then she throws an arm around his shoulder and guides him into the kitchen to meet the others.

Mags does her usual stare at him without speaking, and Emma gets all serious and mother-like, but otherwise it's a fairly tame welcome. Until Darryl walks in. I'd forgotten he'd come over with the others. He's been in the bedroom placing masking tape around the window frame – Lily set him to work the moment they arrived.

"Darryl," Lily exclaims, grabbing his hand and giving him a passionate kiss better suited to the bedroom. "This is Scott, Trish's new *friend*."

I cringe as she emphasizes the word "friend".

"Hey, man," says Darryl, shaking Scott's hand. "It's not too late to do a runner. I can guard your back, if you like. Until Mags here tackles me to the ground."

Mags punches Darryl on the arm and he staggers back. I know from regular first-hand experience this isn't for effect. When Mags whacks someone, they know about it. For someone with such a gentle soul, she's surprisingly violent.

While Darryl rubs his arm, Scott laughs.

"I'll take my chances, but thanks for the offer."

I can see him eyeing the two remaining doughnuts on the table.

"Looks like you've already had breakfast." He shrugs off

his backpack. "But I bought along some banana bread, if anyone wants a slice?" He pulls out a container and places it on the table.

Emma immediately pulls off the lid.

"Did you make this?" she asks, eyeing the loaf with suspicion.

"I was up early, so…" He trails off, looking embarrassed.

Lily's eyes widen. "Hear that, Darryl? Scott here can whip something up. In the kitchen."

Darryl slips his arm around Lily's waist. "I bet he doesn't have Zico's on speed dial."

"Actually, I do. They make a great pizza."

Emma has surreptitiously pulled off a corner of the loaf and is chewing slowly. Scott has no idea how much his life depends on this moment.

"It's pretty good," she finally mutters.

"Wow, Scott," Lily grins. "That is high praise coming from Em."

"Thanks. It's my mum's recipe." Scott suddenly rummages in his bag again. "Trish told me you've recently opened a café, Emma. I was given two of these last Christmas and I was going to donate one, but I wondered if you might have any use for it."

"Oh my God!" Emma takes the weird-looking metal thing and clasps it to her chest. "I've been wanting a microplane ever since mine broke last year."

I've no idea what a microplane is, but I know Scott has gained some serious brownie points. Even Mags is nodding in approval, though I bet she doesn't have a clue what the bloody thing is, either.

"Coffee, Scott?" I ask, pulling a mug from the cupboard.

"Thanks. I'd love one." He comes to stand beside me. "Any chance you can show me your garden? I'm dying to see it."

"Sure."

I feel myself blush and my heart starts racing. He only wants to see my garden. What's the big deal? It's not like he just asked if he could see me naked. Oh, God, where did that thought come from?

"So, what's the plan for today?" Scott says loudly, shifting his weight and looking about the room.

"First, we need to move all the furniture out," says Emma. "And I'm going to take Trish shopping for a few essentials: a bassinet, for starters."

"Is that so you don't have to do the heavy lifting, Em?" teases Lily.

"You're welcome to take Trish to baby shops if you'd like, Lily?" Emma hassles back.

I don't have to turn around and look at Lily's face to know how much the thought of going into shops full of baby stuff is making her panic. She's great with Emma's boy, Freddie; he completely adores her. But she's in no way ready to surround herself with little people paraphernalia. She admitted only recently she often crosses the street when she sees a mother and pram coming towards her. She's worried they might infect her with a sudden urge to procreate.

"Nah, it's cool. I'll stay and make sure Darryl here doesn't slack off."

I hand Scott his coffee and he murmurs thanks before taking a sip. If I wanted to – which I don't – I could lean against him, he's so close.

"Don't know about you, but I'm going to have a slice of

Scott's loaf," Mags says, pulling a knife out of my cutlery drawer. "Anyone else?"

"Love a piece," says Darryl, "especially as the doughnuts are gone." He makes a quick lunge for the last two and shoves them in his mouth at once.

"Gross," says Lily. "Remind me why we live together?"

Darryl shakes his head as he chews. "The mind boggles," he mumbles, sugar flying from his mouth.

We all end up eating a slice of the banana loaf before I take Scott out onto my back porch to view the garden. He seems impressed. Definitely makes the right noises.

"I bet you spend a lot of time sitting here in the sun," he says. "I know I would."

"Yeah, I do."

He's standing so close I can see his chest rising and falling.

"It sounds like they're moving things," I mutter.

"We should go and help."

Scott's voice is low and hoarse. Is it my imagination, or is he leaning towards me?

I step back, turn and hurry towards the spare room.

"Hang on, guys," I call. "I haven't worked out where to put things yet."

"Well, I think it looks amazing," says Lily.

She's holding the ladder while Darryl attaches the last of the curtain hooks to the rail.

"More than amazing," I say, a lump in my throat. "It's better than I ever thought it would be, thanks to all of you."

Mags is holding a wheel onto the bottom leg of the changing table while Emma screws it into place. Job done, they turn it upright and roll it into position next to the window.

"You'll be able to distract yourself by looking at your garden while cleaning up baby poo," says Mags enthusiastically.

Emma flops into the new chair in the corner. It was an impulse purchase from the designer furniture place on Stone Street. Emma insisted my number-one investment should be a comfortable chair in which to feed the baby. She looks tired as she rests her hands on her stomach. I shouldn't have let her help out all day. She's more pregnant than I am and I feel completely shattered. But the room is transformed and I love it.

Scott walks back in. He's been breaking down the cardboard boxes the new baby gear came in and putting them in his boot, having offered to take them to the recycling centre.

"There's some guy outside wanting to see you," he says to me flatly.

"Who?" Lily asks.

Scott shrugs. "He didn't offer up a name."

I brush past him and out of the front door.

"Will!" I exclaim.

My brother's standing by the letter box, looking uncomfortable.

"Hey," he says, taking a couple of steps towards me. "I'm sorry just to turn up like this. I finished that job down the road and was heading home and thought I'd see if you were here."

I wave him towards me. "Come in," I say, strangely pleased to see him. "Sorry about not being able to see you and Tilly last time."

Will hesitates, his eyes on something behind me.

"I don't want to intrude…"

I glance back to see Scott leaning against the door frame scowling.

"Scott," I say firmly. "This is my brother, Will."

The scowl disappears and Scott gives a welcoming nod.

"Hey, Will."

My brother approaches and I hook my arm through his.

"Come and see what my friends have done," I say, marching him inside.

Scott steps aside to let us through and I avoid his eye.

"Will!" calls Lily from the doorway to the baby's room. "You're just in time for bubbles."

"Hi, Lily," Will says quietly.

He admires the new nursery, says hello to Mags and Emma, and is introduced to Darryl, all the while gripping his hands like he has to hold himself together.

"You OK?" I murmur as we head to the kitchen for champagne glasses.

"Not really." Will slumps into a chair and sighs. "Tilly's back in hospital for more tests. I need to go and pick her up shortly." He waves a hand at the bottle of bubbles. "I'll have to take a rain check on the drink."

"Is she OK?"

"I guess."

He looks so dejected and still. It's like he's shrunk inside himself.

"Will, is there something I can do to help?"

He sighs again. "I work under contract and I thought I had another job lined up, but it fell through. I hate not having a secure income coming in."

A small voice in my head starts to wonder if Will is putting on an act. He looks genuine, but maybe I was right the first time.

"Do you need money?" I ask harshly.

Will looks at me quickly.

"No, Trish. I don't need money. Do you think that's why I'm here?"

I don't answer.

"Not that it's any of your business, but I'm careful with finances. Always have been. I have a reasonable stash in my savings account for situations like this. I'm not here to fleece you. I'm here to try to give Tilly a family. She hasn't got any relatives, you know. Well, our side doesn't count and Tilly's mum – her parents died ten years ago and her only sister lives in Iceland, of all places. I'm it. There's only—" Will breaks off and drops his head in his hands.

"Will, I'm sorry."

"Forget it," comes his muffled voice. "I should go."

"Look…" I put a hand on his shoulder. "Until recently, I thought you were like the rest of our family. You didn't want to have anything to do with me and that was fine, because the fewer reminders I had of my childhood, the better. But it was great to see you – to know there's someone in my family who isn't, well, you know…" I take a deep breath. "I'd really like to meet Tilly. Why don't you pick her up and bring her back here? We're going to order takeaways. It might be a little chaotic for her, but you don't have to stay long… unless you want to?"

He lifts his head. "She's usually tired after being in hospital."

"Well, see how she is when you pick her up. Let her choose."

Will nods slowly. "Are you sure?"

"Of course I'm sure. She's my niece. I'd like to get to know her."

Suddenly, Will is on his feet. He pulls me into a tight hug and I try to relax my tense body. A member of my family is voluntarily hugging me. It's beyond comprehension. I carefully put my arms around him and squeeze in return.

Will's body begins to shake and I think he's crying – again something unheard of – until he pulls back and I discover he's laughing.

"If only our parents could see us now," he says.

I laugh softly. "They'd be horrified."

Mags comes into the kitchen.

"Lily has sent me to enquire as to the whereabouts of the glasses," she says, eyeing us carefully.

Will takes a step towards the door. "I'd better go and check on Tilly." He gives me a fragile smile. "We may or may not be back soon."

"Fantastic!" Mags says with her usual enthusiasm. "I'd love to meet Tilly."

"Me too," I say with a lot less volume but with just as much conviction.

"Bye."

Will leaves quickly without another word to anyone.

"Everything all right?" Mags asks, handing me some glasses to carry.

"Yeah."

She lifts her eyebrows, but I ignore the questioning look.

We gather in the nursery and fill our glasses with bubbly liquid – sparkling water for Emma and me, and sparkling wine for the others.

"Here's to all of you," I say, raising a glass. "The best friends a person could wish for." I cough as my throat tightens. "Thank you so much. For everything."

"To Trish's baby," says Emma, raising her glass and giving me a wink. "He or she is going to have the best mum in the world."

"Hear hear," everyone says, chinking their glasses and grinning.

"Thanks for letting me be a part of today," says Scott.

Lily gives him a nudge. "You did all right. We might allow you to hang out with us again. For a price."

"And what price would that be?" he asks.

Lily considers his question for a few seconds.

"I'm not liking the look of this, Scottie," says Darryl. "She's scheming something."

We wait, knowing Scott's initiation is far from over.

Lily snaps her fingers. "Got it! You can take Trish to those antenatal classes she's been avoiding."

Silence swamps the room.

"Sorry?" Scott squeaks.

I try to speak, but my throat is blocked.

"That might be taking things a little far," Emma murmurs.

Lily stamps her foot. "It's not. Trish needs a partner to go with her. Both possible dads are MIA, so Scott here can help out." She glares at Scott, daring him to speak. "You don't have to do much. Pretend you're some clueless husband who's been dragged to a meeting with loved-up annoying couples called Claudia and Dwayne or something. Act like you actually want to know all about labour and childbirth, then leave."

Scott's eyes are wide and his face has drained of colour.

OLIVIA SPOONER

"I'm not sure it's…"

I'd better save him before he starts to hyperventilate or pass out.

"Lily, I'm quite capable of attending antenatal classes without resorting to a fake husband."

"Yeah," Mags says loudly. "We're not living in the fifties, Lil. A woman doesn't need a man in order to fit in with some bullshit stereotypical norm."

"Exactly," I state firmly.

For a moment we all stare at our glasses in awkward silence. Then Scott clears his throat.

"Well, since it appears I'm not required to be a pretend husband, I hope I'm still allowed to hang out with you again anyway."

Lily wrinkles her nose, then sighs dramatically. "I suppose," she murmurs.

"Hear hear," Darryl shouts, raising his glass and blowing Lily a loud kiss. "To the craziest bunch of girls I've ever met."

Mags gives Darryl another fairly forceful punch in the arm and he yelps.

"Serves you right," snaps Lily, and we all begin to laugh.

I can't speak for the others, but my own laughter is certainly one of relief. What on earth was Lily thinking suggesting Scott attend antenatal classes with me? Talk about mortifying.

When there's a knock on the front door half an hour later, I assume it's the pizzas being delivered, but when I open the door, Will is standing holding the hand of a thin, beautiful young girl with a shy smile.

154

"You came," I exclaim, grinning. "Hello, Tilly. I'm Trish – Will's sister."

Tilly holds out her hand, but instead of shaking it, I pull her into a hug.

"I'm so excited I have a niece," I whisper into her hair.

She feels so fragile in my arms. Releasing her gently, I smile shakily at Will and take a deep breath to get myself under control. I'm nearly as emotional as Mags, for God's sake.

"Thanks for coming back."

"Thanks for inviting us," he says. "The second I mentioned a long-lost aunt, Tilly went from being tired and wiped out to bursting with excitement."

"Come in." I usher them inside. "Tilly, I hope you're up to meeting a few of my friends."

I lead them to the living room and quickly introduce everyone. Tilly grips her dad's hand and presses against his side, her face half hidden behind his baggy T-shirt. I imagine having a roomful of adults all staring (admittedly, everyone is smiling encouragingly) would be a tad overwhelming for a child.

Emma, bless her, senses my rising panic. She crouches in front of Tilly.

"I've got a little boy called Freddie who's only a couple of years younger than you and his favourite drink in the world is apple juice mixed with lemonade. Would you like to try it out?"

Tilly's wide eyes look from Emma, up to her dad, then back at Emma.

"OK," she says.

"Please," Will says gently.

"OK, please."

I watch Tilly and Will follow Emma out of the room and notice Tilly's stilted walk. The poor girl has been through so much. I feel a sharp pain in my chest and my stomach contracts so painfully, I put a hand on it and suck in my breath. Needing a second to myself, I slip into the hallway, still clutching my belly.

Scott appears beside me and puts a hand on my lower back. He rubs gently.

"You OK?" he whispers.

The pain begins to ease and I let out a shuddering breath.

"It must be so hard for Will... and Tilly. They're so... they're so..."

"So what?" he asks, his hand still resting on my lower back.

I want to lean against him, for him to put his arms around me, make me feel less...

"So alone," I whisper.

Scott brushes the hair back from my face, too intimate a move, surely, for a guy who isn't my boyfriend and can't be my boyfriend because I'm pregnant with someone else's child.

"They're not alone, Trish. They have you."

I take a step back to create more space between us.

"But I barely know them. This is the first time I've even met Tilly."

"Really?" Scott asks, confusion – or is it disappointment? – on his face.

"A couple of weeks ago, Will turned up here out of the blue. I hadn't seen anyone in my family for years. I didn't even know Will had a daughter. I swore I'd never have anything to do with any of my family... They all... they all made me..."

It's too much. The look of sympathy on Scott's face, the fact he's fucking gorgeous and I like him, as in *really* like him... But what's the point? It's not as if...

I jerk away and take a step towards the kitchen.

"Trish—"

"Forget it, Scott," I say over my shoulder. "It's this bloody pregnancy making me all emotional."

As I pass the front door, someone knocks and I jump.

"That'll be the pizza," I say too brightly.

Ignoring Scott, who I know is staring at me, I open the door and give the young, pimply guy a massive grin. He looks shocked, which makes me suspect I might look as demented as I feel.

"Fantastic," I say, grabbing the stack of pizza boxes. "I'm starving. Thank you."

Slamming the door far too hard, I charge into the living room.

"Who's hungry?"

Lily frowns. "You all right there, Trish?"

"Of course."

I place the boxes on the coffee table as Tilly, Will and Emma return from the kitchen.

Scott slips into the room. He waits for the others to help themselves, then reaches for a piece of pizza and takes a bite. When his eyes turn towards me, I quickly look away.

It's time to stop blurting out my life story to a practical stranger. Scott is not my knight in shining armour and I'm not some damsel in distress who needs saving. I'm ball-busting, take-no-prisoners, I-don't-need-anyone Trish. That's the way it needs to stay.

23

My phone starts to ring and I refuse to drag myself out of my chair to answer. Instead, I glare at the glowing screen resting beside the toaster and will my phone to shut up. I've had the day from hell and I'm in no mood to talk to anyone.

In a pathetic act of defiance, I swallow my piece of toast and take a sip of my lukewarm peppermint tea, determined to ignore my phone as if I might somehow hurt its feelings. I realize with a jolt the kitchen has become dark all of a sudden. I glance at the window and am shocked to see it's no longer light. How did the evening suddenly speed up? I feel like I've only been home from work for a few minutes.

I'm too tired to get up from the kitchen table. Too tired, too grumpy and too fed up. Surely the phone will stop ringing soon. I mean, who hangs on that long? Unless... What if it's Emma? She could be in labour. I leap to my feet and grab the phone.

"Hello?"

"Oh, Trish. I was about to hang up."

It's Will. I can't decide if I'm relieved or annoyed.

"Hi."

"Is this a bad time?"

I take a deep breath and let it out. Just because I've had a bad day doesn't mean I should take it out on my brother. If only I didn't have to be an adult all the time and act accordingly.

"It's fine, Will," I say as enthusiastically as I can. "How are you? How's Tilly?"

"She's great. Actually, that's why I'm ringing. We were wondering if you wanted to go to the zoo with us this Saturday. It's become a bit of tradition over the past couple of years to go to the zoo on Christmas Eve. Tilly has been at me all day to ring and ask if you'd join us."

I'd forgotten all about Christmas. Or tried to, at least. When you don't have family to spend time with during the festive season, it ceases to be a magical time of year.

Will is talking again.

"Tilly hasn't stopped going on about you since our visit. She thinks you're gorgeous, by the way... And that you have the nicest house in the world... and the coolest friends. I feel pretty inferior by comparison."

I almost feel like smiling. Almost.

"I haven't been to the zoo in forever."

"It's much the same. Though there is a new baby elephant, and an awesome chimpanzee enclosure."

I hesitate. A part of me wants to go and hang out with my brother and niece, but another part would rather stay home and avoid all human contact.

"No pressure, Trish. I understand if you'd rather not." Will's voice is flat and distant.

"I'd love to come," I say firmly in an effort to convince myself.

"That's great!"

I hear Tilly squeal excitedly in the background. The growing baby inside me must hear her, too, and does a giant somersault. I place a hand on my swollen stomach and close my eyes. I'm so overcome with guilt I feel light-headed. I don't deserve to be a mother after the thoughts I had earlier today. If I'm honest, not thoughts plural – there was only one thought reoccurring in my head as I handed over my work to Mark.

"Trish?" Will interrupts my guilt. "Are you OK?"

I'm already regretting my decision. I should have said no to the zoo trip.

"I'm fine."

"You don't sound fine. Is there anything you want to talk about?"

"No." My voice cracks and I know if I have to say another word, I'll cry.

"Did something happen today?"

Clearing my throat, I do my best to make my voice sound normal.

"Nothing happened. I'm just tired."

"Can I do anything to help? Tilly and I could come over and keep you company. Only if you want some – you've just said you're tired. You might prefer—"

"Will, I'd better go. I… I'm running a bath."

"OK. We were thinking of going to the zoo first thing on Saturday. Beat the crowds. Does 9 a.m. sound all right?"

I want to tell him I've changed my mind, but I keep picturing Tilly limping slowly around the zoo.

"Perfect," I mutter. "I'll see you there."

"No, no – we'll come and pick you up. Will be at your place at eight thirty."

If I go with them, I can't make a rapid escape.

"It's better I meet you there. Sorry, Will, but I really have to dash."

Without waiting for a reply, I hang up, place my phone back on the kitchen bench and sit down. Slowly, I lean forwards and place my forehead on the table.

All those years of working my butt off feeling like I was someone important. Then, today I hand over my accounts to a smirking Mark and instantly become worthless. The pregnant woman who can no longer do her job.

Every part of me resisted. My head, my body, my heart. I never realized how much importance I'd placed on my work until it was taken from me. Of course, it happens to women all the time. I'm not going through something unique or unusual. And that only makes me feel worse. That I just have to accept it, the way scores of other women have.

The baby gives me a gentle kick in the ribs – no doubt feeling too cramped in my hunched-forward position – and I straighten up. Retrieving my phone, I text Emma:

Did you ever feel like being pregnant was a bad idea?

Within seconds, my phone rings.

"All the time," Emma says the moment I answer. "It's OK to wish you weren't a human incubator sometimes, Trish. Normal, even. You should see the stretch marks this little foetus is giving me, plus I barely slept last night because my hip is so sore."

I don't reply. Instead, I let a tear roll slowly down my cheek.

"Trish, what's up?" Emma murmurs.

"I had to hand over all of my big projects to some smarmy little brat and he'll get to reap the rewards of all my hard work and probably get a promotion. I'll go back and probably have to work for him and start from the bottom all over again."

"Oh, honey, I'm sorry. It sucks."

"Yeah."

"This doesn't have to mean your career is over. You're just on a different path for a while."

I stay silent.

"Trish, it's OK to be pissed off that you're pregnant."

Emma is getting far too close to the truth.

"Trish? Talk to me. I swear whatever it is, it's not as bad as you think."

"I kept thinking all day…" I trail off.

"Thinking what?"

"I kept thinking, if I, if only…"

"If only you weren't pregnant?"

I nod. She can't see me, but somehow she knows my answer anyway.

"Trish, I think that nearly every day. I mean, I'm happy I'm pregnant, but I also curse the day and wish it had never happened. It was the same when I was pregnant with Freddie."

"Really?"

"Yes. Really. Bloody hell, Trish. This whole having a baby thing is terrifying, not to mention it pretty much destroys your identity. And your body."

"That's not exactly making me feel better."

Which isn't true – I already feel lighter, less alone than I did a few moments ago.

Emma laughs. "Trish, I hate to break it to you, but this is some big shit you're going through. Cut yourself some slack, girl. Get grumpy if you want to, throw stuff if it makes you feel better, wish guys would keep their sperm to themselves, dream about how life would be if you hadn't got pregnant, but don't think that it makes you a bad person. And don't ever think it'll make you a bad mother."

As Emma talks, I walk down the hallway and into the nursery. I lower myself into the fancy nursing chair and rock gently.

"I don't always feel this way," I whisper. "There are times when I love it... love the baby. Lots of times. But, Em, there are times when..." I can't say it.

"Trish, it's OK," says Emma.

"Is it?"

"Absolutely."

We're both quiet for a moment. I enjoy knowing my friend is there at the other end of the phone, sitting with me in silence.

"OK, well, I feel a little better now," I say finally.

I hear Emma take a breath as if she's about to speak, then stop.

"What?" I ask.

"Trish, you know I love you. We all do. But sometimes I think... well, I worry really that maybe you're a bit lonely. You know, with no family – except Will now, which is great – but it must be hard for you. You deserve someone special."

"A guy, you mean?"

"Yeah, I suppose. I'm sure I should be saying you can do this and you don't need a man, but I've kind of been there and it's tough, and... and lonely."

"Yeah," I whisper. "It is."

"If things were different, if you weren't pregnant and you'd met Scott on the plane and hit it off—"

"Em, why are you bringing him up?"

"You know why," Emma says softly.

I sigh and stare at the bassinet – all made up, ready for a newborn baby.

"I guess we'll never know," I murmur.

"He might still be interested, even with—"

"Emma, no guy is going to want to hang around with some woman who's pregnant with another man's child."

"Maybe, but look at Finn. He loves Freddie and he's not the biological dad."

"That's different."

"How?"

"Because Freddie and you were a package deal from the start."

"So are you and that little baby growing inside."

"It's still different. Anyway, I barely know Scott."

"If you say so."

"I do."

My phone pings and I look at the calendar notification on my screen. "Shit."

"What?" Emma asks.

"I've got my first antenatal class tonight."

"Oh."

"I'm not sure I'm up for it."

"I could come. I can get Mum and Dad to babysit."

"Thanks, Em, but I'll be fine."

Freddie starts to scream in the background.

"Crap," Emma mutters. "I think Freddie just got a bee sting."

"You'd better go."

"Yeah. I'll call you after the meeting and see how it went, OK?"

In other words, she'll phone to check I actually went.

"'K," I say, listening to her hang up.

I've barely taken a breath before there's a knock on my door. My heart leaps as I picture Scott standing outside.

Why would I think of him? He's hardly going to turn up unexpectedly. Maybe I shouldn't answer. I could sit here silently until whoever it is leaves.

There's another knock and I hear my name.

It's Pete. Damn him.

When I open the door, he's holding a bunch of blue hydrangeas in one hand and a giant present with a thick yellow ribbon in the other.

"I'm so sorry, Trish. It was shit of me to cancel on you like that. For work of all things."

He looks apologetic. Plus, he's in the pale blue shirt I bought him several years ago. It looks just as good on him now as it did then.

"You do remember how much I dislike people just turning up at my house, don't you?"

Pete nods, his expression trite.

"Yes, but I also wanted to apologize in person."

I glance at the flowers. "Are they for me?"

He holds them out, a hesitant smile on his face.

"I wasn't sure if they're still your favourite…"

I accept the hydrangeas without smiling. "One of them."

His smile widens. "Phew, at least I didn't mess that one up."

"And the present?" I glance at the large box tucked under his arm.

He holds it in two hands in front of him but keeps it close to his chest.

"Actually, this is for you and the baby. I know it in no way makes up for the fact I should have helped out the other day, but I wanted to get something special and I spent the whole day trying to find the right thing."

I stare him directly in the eye and wait. He deserves to squirm for a little longer.

"Anyway…" Pete shuffles from one foot to the other. "Can I come in? At least while you open the present"

This isn't a side of Pete I've seen for a long time. It reminds me of the first few weeks after we got together when he was slightly nervous around me, afraid to put a foot wrong in case I sent him packing. Once he was sure I was well and truly in love with him, he gained more confidence. Stopped trying.

I turn around and step inside, indicating with a small dip of my head for him to follow. When we reach the living room, I place the flowers on the coffee table and sink onto the couch. Pete sits beside me, so close his leg touches mine.

Pete places the present on my lap with a flourish.

"Sorry again for bailing on you, Trish. It was poor form."

"I had enough help in the end."

For a split second I think of Scott, then I quickly turn my attention to opening the present.

"Wow," I say, genuinely stunned when I remove the wrapping paper.

"It's not something useful or anything, but when I saw it, I thought of you. It lights up with this soft glow – they showed me in the shop – and I thought you could have it in the baby's room and look at it together. You could point out all the places you've been and tell the little one about what an amazing, talented mummy you are. And I figured it must be hard for you – you're probably going to miss it, the whole work thing – but this will be a nice reminder. You can look at all the places you've been and imagine all the places I'm sure you'll get to one day."

As Pete talks, I open the box and carefully pull out the most beautiful globe I've ever seen. I spin it around on its brass stand and run my finger over the bumps and contours on the surface. In all the years Pete and I were together, he never came close to buying me such a beautiful, thoughtful gift.

"I love it," I whisper. "Thank you."

Pete clears his throat. "Can we maybe plug it in? See how it looks? I'd love to see the baby's room."

Who is this guy sitting next to me? He's almost a stranger.

"S-Sure," I stammer.

In a fluster, I fling the ripped paper and box to the floor and stand.

"You won't recognize it," I say, trying not to sound excited.

He stops at the threshold to the nursery and stares.

"Wow," he whispers. "Trish, this is amazing."

I watch him as he walks slowly around the room, gently fingering the woollen blanket on the basinet, running his hand over the back of the nursing chair, standing at the changing table and looking with a goofy smile at the waterproof mattress as if he's imagining a baby lying there kicking its pudgy little legs.

My hands rest on my stomach. "Not bad, eh?"

Pete looks at me with such tenderness I catch my breath. He steps towards me, places his hands on my cheeks and kisses my forehead.

"It's perfect, Trish," he murmurs, his lips dusting my skin as he speaks.

My heart beats hard and fast. "Thanks."

He lets go of me and steps over to the window.

"Garden is looking great as always. Once the baby arrives, you can spend time out there together. Aren't babies supposed to thrive on fresh air?"

My enjoyment of gardening was never something Pete could understand. He'd often get annoyed with me when I spent so much time out there. Once, he even offered to hire a gardener, thinking it would free me up to spend more time doing other "more meaningful things", as he put it. Pete couldn't see it was my therapy, even when I tried to explain how much it meant to me. And now he suddenly seems to get it.

Pete turns to face me and clears his throat.

"Any news?" he asks.

"About what?"

"The tests. You know, to find out who the dad is."

"Not yet. Sometime in the next day or two, apparently."

He nods and shuffles from one foot to the other.

"I've been thinking about it, Trish. A lot. And I wanted to let you know… well, I really hope it's mine. I'm ready to be a dad, to have a baby with you. Work has always taken up so much of my life and this could be just what I need, you know? A chance to re-assess my priorities. A chance, maybe, to have a second chance with you, too. If you'll let me." He wrings his hands nervously as he speaks.

"Hell, I don't know what to say to that, Pete. Are you OK? Is there something you're not telling me? Like, you've only got a few months to live or something."

It's harsh, but then, I'm more than a little freaked out.

Pete steps quickly across the room.

"I'm serious about everything I've said." He grasps my arms. "And I'm not putting pressure on you or suddenly expecting you to welcome me back into your life. But I want to be honest with you about my feelings. I never stopped loving you, Trish."

"You had a funny way of showing it," I mutter.

"Please, Trish. Give me another shot. I swear I'll be a better person." He places a palm gently on my hand resting on my stomach. "And a good father," he whispers.

I've lost all feeling in my body. Shut down. Even my heart seems to have stopped beating. Pete has given the perfect speech and yet, I can't seem to register it.

"Say something, Trish."

Pete runs a finger down my cheek, along my collarbone and over to the back of my neck. He knows what effect it has on me; how I melt when he touches me that way.

I take a quick step back. "I have to go out," I say rapidly. "I'm late."

Pete frowns. "Where?"

"I've got my first antenatal class. Probably going to be me and a roomful of loved-up happy couples, but…" I shrug.

"Let me come," Pete says.

I widen my eyes. Never in a million years did I think Pete would offer to join me.

"Did you hear what I said?" My voice is high-pitched and breathless. "It's an antenatal class. Where they talk about labour and birth and you do those stupid breathing exercises." Blood is pumping around my body now so fast I feel sick.

"Trish, calm down." Pete takes my hand and squeezes it. "You don't always have to act like it's you battling the world."

"I don't."

"I want to come, support you, learn about this stuff. You're possibly carrying my baby; surely I'm allowed to be involved. Please."

I shake my head. "You don't have to do this."

"Please, Trish. I genuinely want to be there." He takes my other hand and holds them both against his chest. "With you."

I let him lean in and kiss me, softly at first, then harder. After a long time, he pulls away.

"Is that a yes?" he says, his voice gruff.

Oh, how I've missed him! When we were together, I felt a part of something. I belonged to him and he belonged to me. Since he left me, I've felt untethered, adrift. Chances are he is the father of my baby. Maybe I can risk letting him back in. Maybe my heart can take it. Maybe this is the sensible, logical thing to do.

"OK," I state firmly, as if to convince myself.

24

The antenatal class is being held in a small community hall next to the local library. It's an unattractive square brick building set back from the road behind a patch of weed-filled grass. I never knew it existed until Google Maps led us here. I stare at the row of dirty windows and sagging front porch lit by a harsh white light that illuminates the scuffed and worn double doors. One of the doors is closed, the other propped open with a squat brown stool.

"Interesting," Pete says, turning off the engine.

A car pulls up across the road and a couple step out. The woman is petite, blonde and pregnant. Begrudgingly, I have to admit her rounded stomach looks perfect as it juts out beneath her tight crop top. The man is short, squat and at least ten years older judging by his balding hair and sagging pot belly. The man takes her arm and they hurry towards the hall. I watch him pull the door wider and give a slight bow, then as she moves past, he places a hand on her lower back and ushers her inside. He glances at us sitting in the car, smiles briefly – probably hoping Pete is admiring his attractive younger partner – and disappears, letting the door swing back and rest on the stool once more.

"Better get it over with," I murmur, reaching for the door handle.

Pete grins. "That's the spirit, Trish." He leans in to kiss me again on the lips and we make our way inside.

It's worse than I'd imagined – and that's saying something. There's a small raised platform at the far end of the room with a lectern and a couple of old wooden benches. A thin black curtain hangs pathetically to one side. Scattered about the hall are a few trestle tables and faded blue plastic chairs stacked against one wall. Some of the blue chairs have been placed in a circle and sitting in those chairs, staring at us with matching polite smiles, are the antenatal group.

There are four couples and a middle-aged woman in a loose linen dress with a clipboard in her arms. She stands and quickly moves towards us.

"Welcome," she says loudly. "Are you here for the antenatal classes?"

I'd have thought that was fairly obvious.

"Yes," I mutter. "I'm Patricia. Trish."

The woman surveys her clipboard. "Ah, yes. Patricia Kirkpatrick. Excellent. My name is Margot." She squeezes my hand hard as we shake. Then she turns to Pete. "And I take it you're Trish's partner in crime?" she says, laughing at her own joke.

"Absolutely. I'm Pete."

Easier for me to let that one slide for now, rather than try to explain the whole sordid story.

They shake hands, then Margot shoves the clipboard under one arm, grabs one of my hands in her left hand and one of Pete's in her right. She pulls us towards the centre of the circle.

"Everyone, this is Trish and Pete."

There are murmured greetings and I'm pleased to see everyone is as uncomfortable as I am right now. It feels like any minute Margot is going to start chanting and throwing our arms in the air. I want to snatch my hand away and make a dash for the door, but Margot's grip is ferocious.

"Trish and Pete missed the intro class last week, which is a shame, so let's go around the room and you can all say your names and tell us a little about yourselves. Why don't you go first, Becky and Ben?"

An extremely young, pimply, skinny girl with a flat stomach stands and pulls a gorgeous dark-skinned boy, who surely can't be out of school yet, onto his feet

"Hi, Trish," she says, her voice wavering with nerves. "I'm Becky and this is my husband, Ben. I'm six months pregnant and still don't have a thing to show for it." She pats her surfboard stomach. "But I am feeling movements and the doctor assures me there's definitely a baby girl in there."

"Course there is, babe," whispers Ben, leaning in to kiss her shoulder.

"A girl?" Pete blurts, and I stare at him, shocked by his outburst. "I didn't realize you could find out," he murmurs.

There's a collective intake of breath from the room.

"It's common to find out the sex of the baby," says Margot in a no-nonsense teacher voice. "From as early as four months." She looks at me. "Surely you've had your five-month scan, Trish?"

"Yes," I state, staring at the floor.

There's a long pause as everyone tries to work things out.

"Did you not go to the scan, Pete?" asks Ben finally.

"No, he didn't," I state.

Narrowing my eyes to thin slits, I look about the room. If anyone so much as opens their mouths to comment, I'll push them off their ugly blue chair.

Margot clears her throat. "Right, well, who's next?"

A couple of immaculate corporate types in suits and matching wire-rimmed glasses stand up and introduce themselves. Victoria's a lawyer and has been trying to conceive for five years, Ethan is also a lawyer who hopes to be made a partner at Simmons & McCloud – one of the top law firms in the country. Ethan has a slightly hysterical look in his eye, like a wild horse trying to act tough, when clearly the whole being a dad thing is terrifying.

Next comes the couple we saw enter the building earlier. Their names are Seb (short for Sebastian) and Aria. Aria barely speaks at all and seems very happy to leave Seb to do all the talking. They met at a yoga retreat in Bali two years ago and have been soulmates ever since, Seb says proudly. Aria was one of the yoga instructors and offered to give Seb some "private lessons", Seb says with a wink. I hate the guy already.

When Seb finally sits, I glance at the next two Margot encourages to take to the floor. I've been looking forward to hearing their story. Mags would be thrilled to see the two women who introduce themselves as Erin and Priya stand, hands together, and announce they can't wait to be Mum One and Mum Two (apparently, this has something to do with Thing One and Thing Two from a Dr Seuss book and I should find the analogy extremely funny as everyone else in the room clearly does, gripping their sides with laughter). When the room has recovered, Priya explains that her friend Dan provided the sperm – "Isn't he just the best," Erin gushes – but they've decided to call him Uncle Dan, so as not to confuse things. I refrain from pointing out that calling your father your uncle might be more confusing than the truth.

With introductions over, Pete and I are finally able to sit, and Margot claps her hands.

"Right, this class is going to be all about the stages of labour. Who can tell me some of the signs of labour?"

"Contractions," announces Ethan.

He strikes me as the type who's studied up hard on the subject.

"Yes," Margot says. "Now, let's get a better understanding of what contractions are, how they progress and some of the ways your partner can help you to manage them."

Smirking, I turn my head a fraction to look at Pete. I'm predicting he's broken out in a cold sweat, desperate to do a runner. But he's leaning forwards, elbows on his knees, eyes fixed on Margot, and he looks more than pleased to be here. He's enthralled.

A couple of hours later, I'm finally released and stride outside. Pete stays behind to ask Margot more questions and I wait by the car. My stomach is churning. I knew labour meant pain. Of course I did – who didn't? I also know it's good to be prepared for childbirth. But I wish I could go in blind, deal with it as it happens, instead of knowing what lies ahead. Margot hasn't even started talking about the actual delivery of the baby yet – that's being kept in store for next week.

As the other couples leave, I smile, wave, call out "see you next time" and hope they can't see how much effort it takes. Then I sit in the car and watch as Pete jog towards me.

"That was awesome," he says, climbing into the car. "I never knew about any of that stuff."

"Glad you enjoyed it," I snap.

"Hey, are you OK?" Pete puts a hand on my leg.

I nod, blinking back the sudden threat of tears. Why does Pete have to be so positive and nice all of a sudden?

"I'm fine," I mutter. "Just tired."

"Yeah, well, you know what Margot says – a lot of energy goes into growing a baby. You've got to take care of yourself."

"Thanks for that nugget of wisdom."

Pete gives my leg a squeeze.

"What are you up to tomorrow night?" he asks.

"Nothing."

"Good. I'm bringing you dinner and I'm going to give you a long shoulder massage while we watch a movie – your choice."

I shake my head. "Did you hit your head this morning?"

Pete laughs. "Get used to it, Trish. From now on, I'm the new and improved Peter. Peter 2.0, if you will."

"I'm not sure about this upgrade. It has a lot of advanced features." I'm trying to keep things light while I figure out what's going on between us.

Pete's hand slides further up my leg. "You haven't seen the half of them yet," he murmurs.

My heart flutters, my skin prickles and my pulse pounds

in my ears. I like his hand on my leg. I like the look he's giving me.

This isn't good. This is not good at all.

Pete claims he never stopped loving me, but why did he leave? Why was a job in Sydney so appealing he was able to take off without a backwards glance? And why, oh why am I allowing this man back into my life?

25

"Trish!" Emma walks out of her café kitchen and spies me hovering by the coffee machine.

She envelops me in a hug and I feel our stomachs press together.

"Come and sit down. I've just pulled a plum cake out of the oven and there's a piece with your name on it." She leads me over to the table by the window. "I've got a couple more things to sort and then I'll come join you. Do you want a drink?"

"I'm good," I say, surreptitiously slipping off my shoes under the table. "Take your time, Em. I've got a work email I need to deal with anyway."

Emma dashes back into the kitchen and I take a moment to survey the café. It's almost 3 p.m. on a Saturday, but there are still a couple of groups tucking into a late lunch. My mouth starts to salivate as I watch an elderly man take a big bite of his bacon and egg pie. I've only eaten an apple, cheese and crackers, and a packet of crisps since breakfast. Not that I'm going to tell Emma I'm starving – she'll be sure to give me a lecture about the importance of eating well. I hope she's not too long bringing out the cake.

Emma places a plate of deliciousness on the table ten minutes later, and flops down beside me.

"Man, it's been busy."

"Who's that?" I mumble, my mouth already full of cake.

I dip my head towards a tiny olive-skinned girl with short black hair, black jeans, a tight-fitting tie-dyed top and about twenty bits of jewellery piercing various parts of her face.

"Oh, that's Mia. What a godsend. She's here from Italy on a working holiday visa and saw the ad I put in the window."

"How is she at making coffee?"

Emma has been complaining about how hard it is to find a decent barista for weeks. Plus, I'm angling for a good decaf.

"Amazing." Emma waves Mia over. "Mia, this is my friend, Trish. I'm sure she wouldn't say no to a decaf flat white."

"You read my mind. Thank you, Mia."

"So the others have bailed on us," Emma says as Mia heads towards the coffee machine.

"Oh no."

"Mags forgot it was her and Phoebe's three-month anniversary and they're going to some swanky restaurant to celebrate, and Lily's going on a last-minute weekend away with Darryl. He booked them into a posh hotel with a private spa pool on the balcony."

"Lucky her. We could have cancelled."

"I still wanted to see you. Besides, you haven't told me how your antenatal class went."

I wrinkle my nose.

"That bad, eh?"

"I wonder if I'm better off not knowing all that stuff."

"Did you at least meet some nice people?"

I shrug. "Pete thought so."

"Pete!" Emma shouts. "What was he doing there?"

"He turned up at my place just after I spoke to you and somehow ended up coming with me."

"He voluntarily went with you to an antenatal class? Pete?"

Emma looks incredulous and I don't blame her. This is the same guy who balked whenever two-year-old Freddie went anywhere near him.

I nod. "He says he's ready to be a dad and a part of my life."

Emma leans back in her chair, crosses her arms and narrows her eyes. "He wants to get back together with you," she states. "What a nerve."

"I shouldn't have brought up his name."

I look at my hands resting on the table so Emma can't see my eyes filling with tears. My friends think the worst of Pete and yet all week, he's been coming over after work with a healthy meal for two selected carefully from a deli he tracked down as he looked for places that provided tasty meals to go. We've sat on the back porch eating and chatting about all sorts of things, and he's hardly ever brought up work – his or mine. Every time he puts a hand on my stomach to feel the baby kick, his eyes light up and he tells me I'm amazing, and he's never once pressed me by asking if he can stay the night.

"Trish, I'm sorry." Emma reaches across the table and puts her hand on mine. "He just hurt you so much and I find it hard to forgive him. Or trust him."

Mia appears at my side and places a steaming coffee next to my half-eaten cake.

"Enjoy, Trish," she says in her Italian accent. She glances at Emma, who's rubbing her eyes. "You OK?"

My friend smiles weakly. "I'm fine, Mia. As soon as that last group leave, you can close the doors."

"Sure thing."

I take a slow sip of my coffee and watch Emma. She's wrestling with whether or not to speak. When you've been close friends for as long as we have, it's easy to read one another.

"Trish," she starts. "People can change for the better and it's not like Pete is a demon. When you were together, you were both happy – at least most of the time. I could see you were crazy about each other."

"But…" I prompt, knowing there's going to be more.

Emma gives a small smile. "But he broke your heart, Trish. And though you always act as tough as nails, we saw what effect it had on you. You became harder, put up another wall—"

"That's ridiculous."

"No, Trish, it's the truth." She pauses. "You know what I've been thinking about for the past few weeks? Lily and Mags have mentioned it, too."

I have a feeling I don't want to know where this is heading and take a large bite of cake. It lodges in my throat and I have to swallow hard to force it down.

"Your brother, Will," Emma says. "It was so great to see you with him and Tilly. It made us realize that up till now, it's been you, on your own."

"What's your point?"

Emma sighs. "Oh, I don't know. I guess it's like there have been these chinks in your armour recently. Maybe it's time to talk to someone about your past. Any mention of your parents, you clam up."

"We weren't all blessed with a golden childhood."

Emma shakes her head. "Trish, I'm not attacking you. Why are you on the defensive?"

"I'm not. Anyway, what has my useless excuse for a family got to do with Pete?"

Emma purses her lips and doesn't say a word.

"I thought you and Pete got on well," I say.

"We did. Sort of." Emma sighs. "What if he isn't the dad?" she asks softly.

"He probably is."

"But if he isn't, will he still support you? Will he... will he stick around?"

I shrug.

"You deserve someone who wants to be with you no matter what."

"Are you saying he's only back because he wants some sort of ownership of this baby?" I place a protective hand on my belly.

"I hope he isn't."

"Wow, you really don't have much faith in the guy."

I want to tell her about the foot massage Pete gave me last night, his excitement at every kick the baby gives, the way he looks at me with such desire I know he'd like nothing more than to take me to bed. But before I can mention any of these things, Freddie bursts through the door, closely followed by Finn.

"Mum." Freddie throws himself at his mum.

She lifts him onto her lap, smiling. "Hey, little man. Look who's here."

Freddie gives me a toothy grin. "Hi, Trish."

"He wanted to say goodbye. We're off to the park with Kai," Finn says, ruffling Freddie's hair then bending to kiss Emma on the cheek.

He's a good-looking man that Finn, and he knows it.

"Hi, Trish." Finn gives me a peck on the cheek.

"Welcome home, how did your first experience as a park ranger go?"

Finn's eyes light up. "It was brilliant. Absolutely the best job I've ever had. It's simply stunning down there, Trish. The mountains remind me of Scotland. I hope you can all come and visit someday."

"I'd love to."

Apart from a short work trip to Christchurch and a weekend with Pete in Queenstown, I've spent hardly any time exploring the South Island. Funny, really, considering how many times I've been overseas.

"Glad to be back, though," says Finn, placing a hand on Emma's shoulder and looking at her tenderly. "I kept worrying Emma would go into early labour. Speaking of which, how's the pregnancy going, Trish?"

I've learnt that when people ask me this question – which they do endlessly – the correct answer is always, "Great, thanks."

Finn nods as I give the obligatory reply. "I suspect that's some semblance of the truth. I hear you have a long-lost niece, too?"

"I do. In fact, I'm going to the zoo with her tomorrow."

"Fantastic," Emma says.

She winces as Freddie squirms about on her lap. I imagine her baby is feeling a little cramped right now.

"OK, Freddie," Finn says, noticing Emma's face. "Let's get going."

Freddie leaps off his mum and eyes my leftover cake.

"I can finish it, if you want?" he says sweetly.

Laughing, I pull the plate closer to me. "Not a chance, dude." Emma laughs, too. "You can have a piece after dinner."

We watch them leave and I tuck into the rest of my coffee and cake.

"Did you eat much for lunch?" Emma asks.

Ignoring her, I scrape the plate clean.

"Trish, I'm sorry I gave you a hard time about Pete."

She shuffles forwards and I reluctantly meet her eye.

"It's fine."

I know Emma means well, but I feel a distance between us. Almost like I'm on one side of a thick pane of glass and she's on the other. Even her voice has become more muffled. Oh no, this better not mean what I think it does.

Pushing back my chair, I scramble to my feet.

"Trish?" Emma stands and puts a hand on my arm. "What's wrong?"

"Nothing. Honestly, it's just... I'm suddenly really tired. I think I need to go home, have a bath and lie down for a bit."

Emma frowns. "All right."

Gathering my things, I head for the door, waving a thank you at Mia and doing my best to look like I'm OK. Emma follows me outside.

"I'll call you later," she says, giving me a quick hug. "And if you feel like company at Christmas, the usual offer stands."

Every year, Emma asks me to join her for Christmas

Day at her parents' house. Mags and Lily have also insisted fairly regularly that I spend Christmas with them and their families, too. They can't seem to accept I prefer to be on my own rather than surrounded by someone else's happy family. Also, I have my own traditions for the day, and they're as worthwhile and important as sitting round a table laughing at dismal cracker jokes.

Christmas Day to me is walking to the beach for a swim, followed by coffee, a large bowl of summer berries, and a toasted croissant with ham and cheese. Then I throw on my elf hat and spend the rest of the day at the Auckland City Mission helping to prepare and serve a special Christmas lunch for the homeless. It's impossible to feel like a sad, lonely sack when I'm in a roomful of people less fortunate.

"Thanks, Em, but I'll be doing my usual thing." There's a dark mist hovering beneath my upper eyelids and a sense of dread so powerful I can taste its bitterness. "Bye."

I drive home fast, my vision blurring, my chest hurting with the effort of breathing. Mags is celebrating with her girlfriend, Lily is off on some romantic weekend with Darryl, Emma has the adoring Finn and I'm on my own with a baby on the way. Why did Emma have to be so negative about Pete? He's been nothing but thoughtful and loving. Yes, there's a chance he's not the baby's dad, but I deliberately haven't allowed myself to think what that would mean. I want Pete to be the dad. I need him to be the dad. I'm supposed to be tough and brave, but I don't feel it right now. I don't want to go through this on my own.

The moment I get home, I head to my bedroom, shut the curtains and climb into bed. I pull the covers up to my chin, curl into a ball and wait for the dark shadow to descend.

26

I wake the next morning, groggy and thirsty. Blinking in the early morning light, I assess my situation. My vision isn't blurry and I'm not straining to keep my eyelids open. I feel tired, but not as if my body is pinned to the bed by an invisible weight. I have numbness in my limbs, though it's not so severe that the thought of getting out of bed is impossible.

The baby gives me a gentle nudge as if to reassure me I'm OK. I'm not alone. Taking a deep breath, I prop myself up on my elbows and wait. A wave of trepidation causes my breath to catch, but then it fades and I manage to swing my legs out of bed and slowly stand.

The clothes I slept in stick to my body and I sit back on the bed to peel off my trousers. Walking carefully into the hallway, I extract my phone from my bag lying beside the front door and check the time. It's 7 a.m. I have two hours until I need to meet Will and Tilly at the zoo. I also have three missed calls from Emma, one missed call from Pete and a text message from Scott.

My heart gives a thump. Without wanting to admit it, I've been disappointed Scott hasn't made contact since he helped out with the baby's room. Not that he had any reason to. It's probably for the best anyway. With Pete back on the scene, it's easier if Scott isn't around to confuse matters.

His message reads:

Hi Trish. Sorry I haven't been in touch – had to go away for a few days. How are you? I have something for the baby. Any chance I can pop round later today? Scott

Wandering onto the back porch, I stare at the garden and wonder how I should respond. Before I can decide, my phone vibrates in my hand. Reluctantly, I take the call.

"Hi, Emma. Sorry I didn't hear you call last night. I crashed the second I got home."

"Are you OK?" Emma asks. "Be truthful."

I consider her question.

"Yes," I say honestly. "I'm OK."

Emma sighs so loudly I have to hold my phone away from my ear.

"I was worried."

There's a weird moment of silence before Emma speaks again.

"So, are you still going to the zoo today?" she says brightly.

"Yeah, I'm looking forward to it."

I'm mildly shocked to realize I am actually looking forward to spending the day with my brother and niece. Normally after being as low as I was last night, I don't want to see anyone for days. Even getting out of bed would have been impossible. Yet here I am, standing in the sun.

"Really, Em, you have to stop worrying about me so much."

OLIVIA SPOONER

"Can't help it. Comes with the friendship."

I smile and notice a scattering of pink buds have appeared on the climbing rose I've been training along the back fence. How can something so small and seemingly unimportant bring such a surge of joy? I need to remember to write it down as something I'm grateful for.

After I finish the call, I walk barefoot around the garden. It's turning into a scorcher – looks like summer has well and truly arrived. Feeling rejuvenated, I pull on my running gear and set out for the beach. The weight of my belly pulls me forwards, throwing me off balance until I find a position and rhythm that works. I imagine in another week or so I won't be able to run anymore. I'll have to be content with a fast-paced waddle.

In less than twenty minutes, I'm stepping onto the sand and inhaling lungfuls of sea air. There are a few people sunbathing, a few bobbing about neck deep in the water and several standing half in, half out, undecided if they should go all the way or back out. I could never do that. My approach is to dash in and dive under, or don't get in the water at all.

I expect the sea temperature is chilly, but I'm hot and the water looks so inviting I'm contemplating a swim. My first swim of the summer, I realize. Ever since I bought my house, my Sunday ritual from early December through to late April has been: run to the beach, swim and run back home to shower. But this month I've been so wrapped up with work, and pregnancy, and the appearance of family members, ex-boyfriends and guys who knit and smell of lavender, I haven't even thought about coming to the beach.

188

I pull off my shoes and socks, yank my singlet over my head, and charge across the sand in my shorts and sports bra. Plunging into the water, I do an ungainly flop onto my back, widen my arms and legs into a starfish shape, and float. It's deliciously cold and I feel weightless. Why haven't I done this sooner? Glancing down at my stomach sticking out of the water, I notice my belly button is now a fully-fledged outie.

After a short, lazy attempt at backstroke, I retrieve my gear, rinse my feet under the tap, then sit on a bench to wrestle my socks and shoes onto my wet feet. Surprisingly, I decide to walk home rather than run. I simply don't have the urge to push myself so hard anymore. I've even stopped going to the gym. It's a pleasant change from the constant pressure I always felt to be better and do more.

After a shower, I make myself toast with smashed avocado, mushrooms and poached eggs.

As I'm cleaning up the dishes, I think about Scott's message. I'm not sure how comfortable I am with him buying a present for the baby. If it's something expensive or – even worse – hideous, I'm going to find it excruciating. Also, I'm nervous about seeing him again, mainly because it'll remind me of that kiss in Tokyo and the strange moment the day he helped out, when he was standing so close and I wanted to...

My phone beeps and I snatch it off the table. It's a text message from Pete asking if he can take me out for lunch. I should probably ask him if he wants to come to the zoo, but I was looking forward to it being just the three of us. A chance for me to get to know Will and Tilly, and hopefully for us to relax in each other's company – maybe even feel like we're family.

I quickly text Pete back saying I'll be busy for the day and suggest we have dinner out instead. He responds immediately with one word – perfect – followed by three heart emojis. Since when did Pete start using them? He's always complained they were "stupid and juvenile". I stare at the pink hearts for a long time, trying to figure out how they make me feel, and fail to come up with an answer.

When it's time to go, I head to my car, sit for a few seconds, then message Scott to say I'll be home from 4 p.m. if he wants to stop by. The moment I hit "Send", I want to take it back.

27

"Sorry," I call as I spy Will and Tilly waiting by the entrance.

The traffic was worse than expected and I'm over ten minutes late. I hate being late to anything and have secretly taken pride in always being early. Until now.

"No worries, Trish," says Will as I approach. "We've only been here a few minutes."

"Oh, thank goodness." I smile and consider giving them a quick hug but can't quite bring myself to take the plunge.

"We bought you a ticket," Tilly says, holding one out to me.

Her smile is brighter than the sun.

"You did? Thanks, I can't wait," I say. "Haven't been to the zoo in years."

Tilly slips her hand in mine. "I come here all the time," she says proudly. "I can show you where to go."

"Fantastic!" I may be overdoing my attempt at enthusiasm.

Will raises his eyebrows. "Looks like you've got your own private tour guide there, Trish."

"Lucky me," I say as Tilly drags me towards the revolving gates leading inside. "I hope there are some otters – they're my favourite."

Tilly stops abruptly and turns to me wide-eyed. "They're my favourite, too," she gasps.

"Really?"

Tilly continues to stare at me as if I'm going to disappear in a puff of smoke.

"Trish," she says. "You're the best auntie ever."

It's a nice thing to hear.

"Come on." Tilly pulls me through the gate.

After two hours, we're all in need of a rest, even though we're only halfway through. I haven't wanted to say anything, but Tilly's limp has become more pronounced as the morning has gone on. She's no longer talking quite as fast and her face is less animated. When we reach the kiosk, I insist on buying us all hot chips and an ice cream, and we find a picnic table in the shade.

Will has been filling me about my family during snatches of conversation. Unlike me, he's kept in touch with his brother – our brother, I remind myself. Apparently, James has two young boys and runs a small trucking company. In Will's words, James is still a complete prick, yet Dad continues to believe the sun shines out of his arse.

"Dad took great delight in saying I'd be a failure," I mutter.

"Hey, you don't get dibs on that one, Trish. At least once a week Dad told me I was a total no-hoper and wouldn't amount to anything."

"I wonder what he'd think if he saw us now… Actually, I don't care."

Will hooks his arm in mine. "Neither do I."

After we've eaten, Tilly goes to play on the giant colourful dragon with secret tunnels within its body and I ask Will the one question that I've been trying not to.

"How's Mum?"

I wave at Tilly as she sits on one of the giant scales on the dragon's tail. Will takes a while to reply.

"She's the same, I guess."

We focus on Tilly, neither of us wanting to speak.

"She missed you," Will says eventually. "After you left."

"Yeah, sure," I scoff. "Bet she didn't even notice I was gone."

"She did. Every time I went home to visit, she'd ask after you. She was the one who told me where you lived."

It takes me a moment to digest. "How does she know?"

"Dunno." Will turns to me, his eyes blazing. "I blame Dad for how she is, Trish. Belittling her in front of us, always telling her how pathetic she is. What sort of husband does that? Why didn't he try to help her?"

My chest is tight and painful. "She *was* pathetic," I mutter. "She let him yell and carry on, and she never did anything to protect us, Will. Isn't that what a parent is supposed to do? Protect their child? I mean, look at Tilly – you'd do anything for her and you'd never let someone treat her the way Dad treated us."

"Mum was sick, Trish. She still is."

I laugh bitterly. "Don't defend her, Will, please."

Will stands and gathers the detritus of ice-cream wrappers and empty chip boxes. He walks to the rubbish bin, shoves everything in and wanders back. On the way, he calls to Tilly and says it's time to get moving soon. Flicking my thumb against my finger, I wait for Will to sit back down.

"Sorry," I mutter.

"Hell, don't be," says Will. "Mum was a bloody nightmare." He pauses and his eyes rest on Tilly. "Rachel was so good with her."

I'm about to ask who Rachel is and then remember it's the name of Tilly's mum.

Will goes on, "Once I found out about Tilly, Rachel and I got back together for a bit. She was always calling Mum, chatting about mundane things. It seemed mostly a one-sided conversation on Rachel's side and Mum never rang us, but it didn't seem to put Rachel off. She said she wanted to include Mum, make her feel a part of Tilly's life."

"She sounds like a saint."

Will nods. "In some ways she was. In others... not so much."

My stomach feels tight and uncomfortable and my legs are aching from sitting on the wooden bench seat. I stand up and do some light stretches, thinking about Rachel and wondering if we'd have got on had we met.

"How long were you back together for?"

"About eight months."

"What happened?"

"Why did we break up?" Will considers this for a while. "As much as we cared about each other, I think we both realized it wasn't enough. We were staying together for Tilly's sake, but we didn't actually *like* each other much, if that make sense."

I nod. I've occasionally wondered if I fell in love with Pete because I so desperately wanted to experience love. We often disappointed one another and had few things in common. Though we barely argued, it wasn't because we got on well. Instead, I ignored a lot of things he did or said that were hurtful or irritating because I wanted our relationship to work. I wanted to prove to myself and everyone else that I was "successful" at love. I turned "being in a loving relationship" into a win or fail situation. And I've always been focused on success.

"Yeah, it does." I clear my throat. "So, why do you think Rachel made such an effort with Mum?" I ask.

"She had a cousin with bipolar who committed suicide. The cousin was only twenty-three and Rachel was a couple of years younger at the time. It really affected her. She thought Mum had something similar."

"Bipolar?"

"Yeah."

"Aren't you supposed to be up and down with bipolar? You know, manic crazy one minute and really depressed the next? Mum was never manic – she was more like a permanent zombie."

"Remember those times when she'd suddenly get out of bed and spend like a week cooking up a storm, making far too much food for Sunday school or organizing a million pamphlets; she'd stay up most of the night."

"Because she wanted to be on God's good side," I say flatly. "She was obsessed with helping the church; it was the only time she showed any sign of life."

"What about that time we went to Nelson?"

The long-forgotten memory of our family trip to the top of the South Island when I was eight years old flashes through my head like a series of movie clips: fish and chips on the wharf, swimming in the shallow breakers (I was too scared to go in over my head), playing at the local playground, having a ride on a miniature train. How could I have forgotten it? Our one and only family holiday.

"Mum planned everything, and for some reason, Dad just sat back and let her – which, now I think about it, was about the craziest part of the whole experience," says Will. "Remember how Mum never stopped? She was always moving; pacing about on the beach watching us swim, telling us to put on more sunscreen, to walk faster or wait for the others to catch up. And she talked! She talked non-stop. I remember one night at dinner being mesmerized watching her chat away. I wondered if her body had been taken over by some alien being."

I recall that moment, too. I didn't want to swallow my food because for some reason, I decided the second I swallowed, Mum would clam up again.

"You think that was a manic episode?"

Will nods. "Yeah, I do."

"But she went to the doctor. Why didn't they diagnose it? Put her on something. Dad was always sending her there to try to 'sort herself out', as he called it."

"Yeah, she saw the military doctor, who also happened to be one of Dad's Friday night drinking buddies. I imagine Mum wasn't exactly comfortable discussing her problems with Dr Wilkins."

I freeze at the mention of those dreaded Friday nights. Dad would make me pour whisky and serve sandwiches and sausage rolls. He must have seen the way the other men leered at me – Dr Wilkins being by far the worst offender.

"Trish," calls Tilly, and I blink rapidly, searching the dragon for my niece.

She's waving at me from a small window where the dragon's eye should be. Welcoming the distraction, I race over and peer into the hole Tilly is crouched inside.

"Wow, that's a very small space. How did you get in?"

Tilly points to an opening behind her. "I don't think you'd fit, Auntie."

I laugh and relax my clenched jaw. "Do we get to see the otters next?"

Tilly nods. "Right after the penguins."

"Penguins!" I exclaim as Will comes to stand beside me. "I didn't know there were penguins here."

"Come on, Tills," says Will, smiling. "Let's go and show Trish."

As Tilly wriggles out of the dragon, my brother puts his arm around my shoulder and squeezes.

"Thanks for coming with us today, Trish. It's been great to spend some time with you."

I wonder if I'll ever get used to my brother showing me affection.

"Thanks for inviting me."

"Tilly and I are having a few people over for Christmas lunch tomorrow. If you don't have any plans, maybe you'd like to join us. It's pretty low-key. Steak and sausages on the barbeque, salads, bread rolls."

Tilly grins up at me and I want to say yes for her sake, but I can't. This whole family thing is going to take some getting used to.

"Thanks for the invite, only I have plans already. Maybe next year."

"Sure thing," says Will.

Tilly looks disappointed for less than a second before she grabs my hand and leads me to the penguins.

28

I'm lying on my bed sipping a peppermint tea and reading a magazine in an attempt to recover from my trip to the zoo. I feel physically and emotionally wiped out, and strangely calm. It's as if time has slowed and I don't have to be in a rush to do anything, be anywhere or be anyone. I'm putting it down to pregnancy hormones giving me a false sense of well-being.

When there's a knock at the front door, I try to maintain my sense of inner peace and slowly get to my feet.

"Hi, Scott," I say, opening the door.

He smiles and my heart immediately begins to race – so much for staying calm.

"Hey, Trish. You're looking well."

"Thanks."

I invite him in and we make awkward idle chit-chat in the kitchen while I pour him a glass of water.

"You sure you don't want a tea?" I ask again.

"Just the water thanks, Trish."

As I hand it over, my fingers brush against his and heat rushes to my face.

"You really didn't have to get anything for the baby," I say in a rush.

Is it just hot or have Scott's cheeks turned red, too?

"I'm not sure you'll like it," he says nervously, looking down at the small present in his hand. "In fact, I nearly decided not to give it to you because, well, here..." He shoves the present across the table.

I unwrap it tentatively and lift out the most exquisite caramel knitted cardigan and matching hat.

"They're gorgeous," I breathe.

Scott grins. "Well that's a relief. Not perfect, though – I dropped a stitch near the neckline."

I stare at Scott, my mouth open. "You made these!" I exclaim, turning them over in my hands. "You're incredible – very talented, I mean."

He shrugs. "It was a good challenge. I've never made something so small and fiddly before. And we did have a deal, remember? You showed me your garden, so..." He dips his head.

"I'll show you mine, if you show me yours?" I can't help but flirt with him a little.

Scott's smile turns into something a tad sexier – I'm sure Lily would call it a smoulder.

"Exactly," he murmurs.

"So, what are your plans for Christmas?" I ask lightly.

Scott shrugs. "Not much. Mum's invited me to a barbeque at her place with her boyfriend and their friends, but I'm not that keen to go."

"Why not?"

"Mainly 'cause they all get plastered and make complete dicks of themselves."

I laugh. "What about your sister? The one who gave you the sleeping potion."

"Good memory. She's gone to the Gold Coast in Australia for a holiday with her husband."

"Nice."

Scott wrinkles his nose. "Rather her than me. From what I've heard, it's always packed with tourists and stinking hot. How about you? Any plans for tomorrow?"

I nod and fill him in on my Christmas Day traditions.

"What a great thing to do," says Scott. "I might volunteer, too."

"They're always looking for more helpers."

I'm about to ask Scott if he'd like to come with me, when my phone rings. Scott frowns as I pick it up. The screen flashes "private number".

"Sorry," I mouth as I swipe and hold the phone to my ear.

"Hello, Trish. This is Dr Trafford."

Oh my God! The genetic testing results must have come in. I've been hounding my doctor's receptionist daily but figured they'd all have gone on holiday by now.

"Hi," I say. "You're still working?"

"It's officially my day off, but the results are finally in for the paternal DNA testing and I didn't want you to wait any longer than you already have. I'm sorry they took so long – there was some hold-up at the lab. I've forwarded the email through to you."

My body starts to shake. "OK, thanks. I'll take a look."

"Normally this would be news I'd deliver to you in person, but I know you're keen to get the results. I have a space on Thursday at 8:30 a.m. I'd like you to come in and see me to talk about it further."

"Yes, OK." I risk a quick look at Scott and he's eyeing me with obvious concern. "Thanks."

When I hang up, Scott pries my phone from my hand, pulls out a chair and helps me to sit down.

"You're as white as a sheet," he says.

I shake my head. "I'm being ridiculous. It's fine."

"You're going to struggle to convince me on that one."

I can't wait another second. I need to know the results. Lunging for my phone, I open my emails and click once, twice. I scan the document and when I see it there in clear bold print, I moan.

"Jesus, Trish, you're scaring me now." Scott puts a hand on my shoulder. "What's going on?"

I can't believe it. I knew there was a chance. Of course there was. But I was convinced… I let myself think… I look at Scott and say it out loud so I have to accept the truth.

"Elliot is the father."

Scott looks back, his expression neutral. "I have no idea who Elliot is, but I'm picking you were rooting for the other guy."

I nod, blinking back tears.

"Sorry it's not the news you wanted," he says quietly.

I close my eyes and there's an image of Elliot's angry face telling me he wants nothing to do with me or the baby. Then Pete flashes into my head: smiling broadly, his hand on my tummy as the baby gives him a nudge.

"I'll be fine," I say, my voice and body on autopilot. "It's not like I was expecting the father to be involved. I was fully prepared to do this on my own."

"Just because the biological father might not be on the scene, doesn't mean you have to be on your own, Trish."

I open my eyes and tilt my head to look up at him. "Sorry?"

He leans towards me, his eyes locked on mine, then he stops, glances away and stands bolt upright.

"You have friends and family to help out," he says gruffly.

For one wild and crazy moment, I thought Scott was about to get down on his knee and propose. These pregnancy hormones are seriously making me soft.

"Can I call someone for you?" Scott asks.

I stare at my stomach and acknowledge for the first time since I fell pregnant that this baby isn't all mine. It's fifty per cent someone else – fifty per cent Elliot, to be exact.

"I think I need a bit of time on my own to get used to the idea first."

Scott clears his throat. "I'll go."

"Thanks."

When Scott reaches the door, he pauses and turns back.

"Trish, we haven't known each other long, but I know you're gutsy and caring and... well, you'll be a great mum."

Before I can formulate a reply, he's gone.

My house is eerily quiet. I can't hear a thing apart from a faint buzz in my ears. It's like I've hit a giant pause button and if I move so much as a muscle, the button will be released.

So, Elliot is the father of my baby, I tell myself. I try to recall the colour of his eyes. Is he taller than average? Does he drink or smoke? I slept with the guy and saw him at work nearly every day and yet he's a stranger. What does he like to eat? What does he do in his spare time? Oh, God, what kind of family is he from? What if he has parents who want to be doting grandparents to this child? *My child*, I think, placing a protective hand on my stomach. If only I didn't have to tell Elliot. Why can't this baby have a mum and no dad? Obviously it has to have a dad, biologically speaking, but maybe I keep that information to myself – tell my child when the time is right, or maybe never.

I lower my forehead until it's resting on the table. Scott was right – I wanted Pete to be the father. Worse, I'd let myself believe he was. And Pete... I'm pretty sure he's convinced he's the father, too. A loud groan vibrates in my chest. My head pounds and I need to figure out a way to move on from here, or at least get up out of my chair. I thought I wanted to be on my own, but I don't. Snatching up my phone, I send an SOS.

29

"I have to run a check on this Elliot guy," exclaims Lily. "It's crazy, Trish. None of us have even met him."

"Yeah." Mags sits next to me on the couch, her arm around my shoulder. "At least with Pete we knew he was just a prick not some psycho."

"Mags," says Emma, frowning. "That's not helping."

I didn't have to wait long for my friends to turn up. Lily and Mags were banging on my door within fifteen minutes of sending the message, and Emma arrived not long after. The fact that they came running on Christmas Eve shows just how amazing my friends are.

I'm still numb, apart from a throbbing headache, but there's a tingling in my arms and legs, like the numbness might be wearing off.

"This is where you get to say I told you so, Em," I say, wriggling my fingers to try to get some feeling back.

"How do you mean?"

"Yesterday you were saying I shouldn't assume Pete was the dad."

Emma is silent for a few seconds. "I'm sorry, Trish. I know you really wanted it to be him."

"What?" Lily practically shouts. "He's an arsehole."

"Not recently," replies Emma, her voice carrying a warning. "He's been incredibly supportive. Even went to an antenatal class with Trish."

I moan, remembering Pete's enthusiasm.

"Hold up." Lily raises a hand. "What have I missed?"

I let Emma fill her in.

"He sounds like a changed man," says Mags.

"Almost too good to be true," says Lily sarcastically.

"Yeah, well, let's see how he responds when I tell him the results," I mutter.

Emma leans over to squeeze my hand. "Take a couple of days to get used to the idea, Trish. You don't have to rush into telling anyone."

"I just want to get it over with. Actually, what I really want is to delete the email from the doctor and pretend I don't know the truth."

"How important is it to tell the father, anyway?" says Lily.

"Very!" Emma and Mags state together.

"But surely women don't always reveal the sperm donor."

I should be used to Lily's bullet-to-the-chest comments, but every now and then one gets through.

"Elliot and Pete weren't just sperm donors. You make it sound like I *meant* to get pregnant."

Lily opens her mouth to say something, closes it and whispers, "Sorry."

That's seriously something, coming from her. I must look freaked out.

Emma gives my hand another squeeze. "Trish, I know it'll be tough, but Elliot and Pete both need to be told. You understand that, don't you?"

"I know, Em." Scrambling to my feet, I put my hands on my hips and stand up tall. I've dealt with shock and disappointment all of my life. Like Scott said when he left earlier, I'm gutsy. I can deal with this, like I've dealt with countless things before. "The sooner I tell them, the better."

"One of us could go with you?" offers Mags. "I don't mind."

I smile at the three concerned faces I know so well. "Thanks, guys. I'd better manage this part on my own."

Emma grimaces and flops back hard against the cushions. She sucks in her breath and holds it.

"Emma?" I ask, all of my worries gone in an instant.

"It's nothing," she whistles through her teeth.

"Like hell," says Lily, practically falling over herself to land in front of Emma. "What's up?"

Emma shakes her head and tries to smile through her grimace. "Give me a sec," she gasps.

We all wait, collectively holding our breaths.

Slowly, Emma's tense body starts to relax and she breathes out. "Phew, that was a big one."

"Jesus, you can't be in labour yet, Em," says Lily in panic.

"I'm not. Calm down. I'm sure it was just a Braxton Hicks. A practice run, getting me ready for the real thing."

"A what?" asks Mags, perplexed.

I remember my midwife mentioning them, but I've yet to experience one myself. If Emma's response is anything to go by, I'm not sure I want to.

"It's a tightening of the uterus. Your stomach literally goes rock hard and sometimes, when it's a biggie like that last one, it can feel pretty powerful," Emma says.

"Powerful, eh?" mocks Lily. "That's one way of describing it."

"Have you had one yet, Trish?" Mags asks.

I shake my head.

"Something to look forward to," Emma says, winking.

"Can't wait."

Suddenly, I start to laugh and the others crack up, too. Tears prick the corners of my eyes as I laugh and laugh with my friends, and it feels so good. I've lost all numbness, my headache has receded, and I feel alive and hopeful. It's such a strange experience for me; simply to be here in this moment and be happy, even when I know, in a hazy no-point-worrying way, I'm dealing with some major shit right now. Again, I wonder if pregnancy hormones are involved in this odd mood. It's so unlike me to be this positive.

"What's so funny?" asks a deep, familiar voice. Pete stands in the doorway, shifting his weight from one foot to the other. "You were all laughing so hard, you didn't even hear me knock."

We look at one another, our smiling faces frozen in place.

Mags finally clears her throat. "Hey, Pete," she says, her voice squeaking. "You gave me a fright."

"Sorry. The door was unlocked, so..." He trails off and looks at me, confused. "You still OK to have dinner out? I booked us a place."

My friends are watching my reaction, trying to gauge what they should do.

"Absolutely," I say firmly. "This lot were just leaving."

"Yeah." Lily grabs her keys and phone off the coffee

table. "Come on, Mags. I'll drop you home on my way to the supermarket. Darryl gave me a list, for crying out loud."

Mags stands. "A list of what?"

"Stuff he thinks we need."

"And you don't?" Emma asks, gathering her things.

"Well, we probably do, but I don't need a list to remind me. That's what your memory is for. Lists are for old people."

"I write lists all the time," says Mags, giving me a sly wink. "Good luck," she mouths.

They file past Pete and mutter fairly lukewarm goodbyes. I suspect none of them would be upset if he were offered another fancy job in Australia. Whatever trust and affection they had for him has long gone.

"The girls still hate me, then," says Pete ruefully as he comes to sit beside me and plants a light kiss on my cheek. "What was so funny, by the way?"

I'm light-headed and my legs feel jittery with nerves. "Just a pregnancy joke. Wasn't very funny, but..." I shrug as if that explains everything.

"Right." Pete glances down at my stomach. "How's junior getting on?"

Oh my God! Did he just call my baby junior? This is far worse than I thought. Pete's gone potty in the head. Never in a million Sundays would I have thought he'd use that word. The problem is, it's so nerdy and unexpected and, well, cute, that I have an urge to kiss him.

Shuffling back to gain some distance from Pete, I take a deep breath and decide to jump right in.

"I found out about—"

Pete raises a hand and interrupts. "Guess where I booked us for dinner."

My heart is thumping. How could he stop me like that? Already, I feel like I'm not going to be able to get the words out.

"Where?" I ask eventually.

Pete grins. "It's this little Japanese dumpling place someone recommended recently. I stopped in to check it out on my way here. A little tacky with all these funny wooden booths and flags flying everywhere, but they were surprisingly full, which is a good sign – only just managed to squeeze us in."

It has to be the restaurant Scott took me to. Which is almost laughable if it weren't so awful. At least I have a renewed sense of commitment. There's no way I can go out to dinner with Pete now.

"I found out the results of the DNA tests."

"Oh!" Pete grabs my hand and holds it against his chest. "Did I win?"

Did he win? Is that seriously what he just said? Should I be angry or horrified or amused?

"No," I say flatly. "Elliot is the father."

As my words sink in, his expression changes rapidly from excitement to horror to complete and utter shutdown.

"Shit," he whispers, letting his grip on my hand go limp.

I pull my hand away. "Sorry," I murmur. "If it's any consolation, I had hoped it was you."

Pete blinks once, twice, three times. "Well that's that, then," he says.

I study his face, hoping it'll change in some way, that he'll reach out for me, tell me he still wants to be involved, that he loves me, that this won't be the end.

Nothing alters. His face is blank, as if a curtain has been wrenched closed between us.

"Pete…" My voice dies. I have no idea what to say.

Slowly, Pete gets to his feet. "I think dinner is off," he says quietly. "Don't you?" Then without another word, he walks out of the room.

I stare at the empty doorway. "And there he goes," I say, my voice hollow.

The baby gives one giant kick in agreement.

30

ahoo, it's Christmas.

W   I open one eye and quickly close it again. I'm seriously considering changing up my routine, especially as I barely slept last night. Maybe I could spend Christmas Day in bed instead. Order some takeaways, watch a crap movie, eat a ton of ice cream. Surely I deserve a dispensation.

The problem is I need to pee and my pyjamas are soaked with sweat I'm so hot. Kicking off the covers, I try to keep my eyes closed in the hope I'll forget about my bursting bladder and doze, but my eyelids keep fluttering open of their own accord.

Accepting defeat, I stumble to the bathroom, empty my bladder and crawl back into bed. Sun is streaming through a crack between the curtains onto my bed. Sighing, I get up to try to eliminate the offending bright light, but once my hands are gripping the curtains, I can't help but poke my head between them, just to check on my garden. Then I discover it's a glorious day outside and that's it – I might as well get up.

Putting on a light cotton dress over my swimsuit, I decide to have breakfast before my swim, as baby and I are ravenous. I make my coffee, a bowl of fresh berries, and an oven-toasted ham and cheese croissant, arranging everything on a wooden tray and adding a few roses I've gathered from the garden for an extra flourish – it is Christmas Day, after all. Then I carry my tray outside and sit in the small patch of shade at one corner of the porch. It's already meltingly hot and barely past nine o'clock.

Being on my own is good, I say to myself eating a strawberry. Pete is gone (again), but I can deal with that – I've had practice. And I don't feel as heartbroken as I thought I would. A part of me is almost relieved. Also, I won't be on my own much longer. Soon, I'll have a child to care for.

There's a light breeze but even so, by the time I've finished breakfast, I'm dying to cool off in the sea. Throwing a towel around my shoulders, I slip on some sandals and walk to the beach.

When I arrive, I waste no time peeling off my dress and running into the water. Lying on my back, I close my eyes and feel the heat of the sun on my eyelids.

I stay in the water for ages, then eventually I towel off, walk slowly home and have a cold shower before heading to the City Mission, my elf hat firmly on my head.

"Trish! Check you out," yells Lucas, charging towards me. "Bloody hell, you're pregnant." He grips my shoulders and plants a wet kiss on my cheek. "Congratulations, sweetie."

Lucas has been running the Christmas lunch for as long as I've been volunteering and is the most enthusiastic person I've ever met. Everyone loves the guy, me included. He's happily married with seven kids and nine grandkids (at last count), most of whom are setting out cutlery, napkins, and Christmas crackers on the round tables in the cavernous hall. Soon, he'll greet every single person who comes through the door and will find them a seat, introduce them to their neighbour, make them feel visible and welcome.

"Who's the lucky guy?" asks Lucas, steering me towards a chair and insisting I sit.

"Some random," I say with a shrug. "We're not together."

Lucas flops in a chair beside me. "More fool him."

"Where do you want me?" I ask, eager to change topic.

"Well, I thought you might like to be in the kitchen with your friend. Nice bloke, by the way."

I frown. "Sorry?"

"Scott. He said you told him about us."

Scott is here... I can't decide if this is a good or bad thing.

"I... I didn't realize he was coming." I gulp loudly. "Put me where I can be the most useful."

Lucas raises his eyebrows and gives me a funny look. "I'd feel better if you were close to Scott. That way he can keep an eye on you, make sure you don't overdo it."

"It's not necessary—"

Lucas shakes his head, grinning. "I've seen the way you work, remember, Trish." He pulls me to my feet. "Come on, you can be in charge of dessert."

I follow Lucas into the kitchen and spy Scott near the back at a long stainless-steel workbench. He has his head down and is peeling potatoes.

Familiar faces come over to say hello and offer congratulations. Most of them are people I'd probably never associate with if it weren't for this one occasion each year when random people gather to help out. I love it – this melting pot of generous human beings.

Scott has seen me now and is giving me a nervous smile.

"Fancy seeing you here," I say, wandering over.

"Please don't think I'm stalking you, Trish. I only just decided to come and help at the last minute. Ever since you mentioned the lunch it's been on my mind and, well, I hope you're OK with me being here. If you'd rather, I can—"

I hold up my hand, laughing. "Stop, Scott. It's fine."

"Really?"

"Of course."

Lucas has been standing beside me throughout our exchange and he's looking back and forth between us, trying to figure out what's going on.

"Alrighty, then. Now you've got that sorted, Trish, I'd like you to organize Scott and the rest of these guys." Lucas points to various people nearby who look up and smile as they hear their names. "They're all relative newcomers, but you're an old pro. So I need thirty pavlovas with lashings of cream and strawberries."

I nod. "Sure thing, boss."

Lucas throws one arm around my shoulders and gives an enthusiastic squeeze. "OK, team," he says loudly, "I'm leaving you in the extremely capable hands of Trish. Once you have your dishes under control, most of you will need to help out front serving our special guests."

He races away and I turn to the group, who are looking at me expectantly. Eyeing the large cardboard trays laden with strawberries, I switch into work mode, clap my hands once and stand up straight,

"Right, first off, you'll have to tell me your names again.

Then we're going to get to work taking the green tops off these strawberries."

A couple of hours later, the dessert is ready. Pavlovas have been laid on platters and covered with whipped cream. Extra bowls of cream are in the fridge and the mountains of strawberries have been cleaned and trimmed. The hall is filled with people who would otherwise have gone without a special meal at Christmas and a loud din of excited chatter fills the air. The day is so hot and muggy that even with all the windows and doors open, the hall feels like a sauna.

Most of the guests look happy and relaxed, but there are a few staring into space with a dull, absent expression. The judgey part of me wonders if they're on drugs, while another part of me wants to go and sit with them, take their hand and ask them to tell me who or what they're missing.

In the corner of the hall is a giant Christmas tree covered in lights and tinsel. There's a tower of brightly-wrapped presents underneath, all of which have been donated by local families and businesses. A hoard of excited children hovers nearby, keeping an eye on the gifts as if they might suddenly disappear.

Scott and I have had a few short snatches of conversation, but mostly we've been too busy. A couple of times he held out a glass of water and insisted I pause for a drink, and I'm currently sitting on one of the benches lining the perimeter of the hall, because both Scott and Lucas demanded I take a break.

I didn't argue, as my feet are puffy and sore. Plus, my

stomach feels heavy and my lower back aches. Not to mention I'm dripping in sweat. The day has turned out to be harder than I thought, though I don't for a second regret coming.

Stretching my legs out, I glance over at Scott. He's at one of the serving tables doling out roast potatoes. His hair is tied up in a ponytail and is damp with sweat around the neckline. Someone gave him a red bandana with mini Santas on it and he's tied it around his head. It's a sexy look on him. Very sexy.

Glancing my way, he catches me watching him and smiles. I smile back, my stomach fluttering.

"Right, Trish," says Lucas, handing me a plate piled with chicken, stuffing, roast potatoes and salad. "Eat up."

I take the plate guiltily. "Some people haven't started eating yet," I protest.

"Nearly everyone has a meal and you need sustenance before you can help serve dessert."

Too hungry to argue, I balance the plate on my knees and eat.

After everyone has eaten what's quite likely their best meal of the year – including the dessert, which was devoured in record time – I head back into the kitchen to start scraping and stacking plates. A hand suddenly rests on my shoulder.

"I can take over, Trish," says Scott, his breath warm on my cheek.

I shake my head. "Have you eaten yet?"

"No, but—"

"You can take over once you've had food," I state firmly.

Heat is radiating not just from Scott's palm resting on my shoulder, but his whole body. I'm clearly not the only one who's finding things hot around here.

"Fine," Scott says reluctantly. "I'll be back shortly."

Less than ten minutes later, Scott returns, accompanied by Lucas.

"Right, Trish, step away from those dishes," Lucas states. "I've given Scott here strict instructions to drag you out of this oven. You've been amazing, as always, but it's time to rest, OK?"

I glare at Scott, guessing he was the one who got Lucas involved in this effort to have me evicted. But Scott's looking remarkably unruffled by the daggers I'm shooting in his direction.

"Let's go, Trish. I'm taking you down to the waterfront for a giant scoop of the world's best Italian gelato and we're going to sit on the wharf to cool off."

"What if I don't want to?"

Truth is, I'd love a gelato more than anything else in the world right now, but I'm not going to tell him that.

Scott grins and shrugs. "We can do this the hard way or the easy way. Either way, you're coming with me."

Lucas slaps Scott on the back, laughing. "Ah! You've met your match here, Trish, my girl. Now get on with you." He gives me a not-so-light shove towards the door.

The moment I'm out of the building, I stomp off down the road, Scott running to catch up.

"OK, slow down – you've made your point."

"What's my point, Scott?"

Scott clasps my arm lightly, forcing me to slow

"Trish, please accept that others actually care about you

and should be allowed to watch out for you. That's how relationships work."

"Really?" I snap.

"Yes, really." He crosses his arms and studies me with a frown. "Can we go and eat gelato now, please?"

I blow damp hair from my forehead with a loud sigh. "Yes. But, Scott, for future reference, I don't cope well with being told what to do."

"Yeah." Scott's frown is replaced by a gentle smile. "I'll keep that in mind."

My toes tingle and I have to look away from his searching brown eyes.

"That was one of the best Christmas Days I've ever had," announces Scott as we approach my car. "Which says something about my childhood, I suppose."

We've spent nearly two hours down at the waterfront eating ice cream and watching boats go by, the sea breeze wonderfully cool and reviving.

I laugh and rummage for my keys. "Don't even get me started on family Christmases."

"Actually, that was a subtle cue for you to open up about your family."

I narrow my eyes. "Easy, Scott."

He holds up his hands in surrender. "OK, I'm sorry."

Opening my door, I turn to Scott to say goodbye. Our conversation has been relaxed and easy. So much so, I'm reluctant to leave. I get the impression Scott's in no hurry, either. If I wasn't so dog-tired, I'd stay. There's also the fact I really, really need a shower.

"Thank you for the ice cream – I mean, gelato."

"You've very welcome. Thank you for allowing me to be a part of today. It was special."

His voice is stilted and his cheeks are flushed. Now, I suddenly feel awkward.

"I hardly *allowed* you to do anything. You just showed up."

"You know what I mean."

I think we're both stalling, not wanting to say goodbye.

"Look, Trish, I haven't wanted to bring it up because I figured you didn't want to talk about it, but…" He pauses. "Are you feeling any better about the DNA results? About the father, I mean."

Damn him. Why did he have to go and drag that up? I've spent all afternoon without giving the situation a second thought.

"I'm still working through it," I say gruffly, hoping he'll take the hint.

"Sure. Sorry."

"Well…" I shuffle my feet. "Bye, Scott."

"Bye, Trish." He leans in and kisses me on the cheek. "Take care," he murmurs.

For a few seconds I freeze, unable to move until Scott shifts away. Taking a shaky breath, I clamber into my car and take off without looking back.

31

Over the next few days, I stick to my routine: early morning jog, shower, work, home, movie or book, bed. I field a number of regular calls and messages of support from my friends and one polite text from Scott asking how I'm doing. I send him a breezy "I'm great," with a thumbs-up emoji.

Elliot avoids my desk completely, leaving me both relieved and pissed off. It's not until Thursday afternoon that I spy him coming out of Tash's office, his face red.

"Elliot," I call, rushing out from behind my desk. "Can I talk to you a sec?"

I feel like all eyes in the office turn towards us.

Elliot frowns. "I just got a complete roasting from Tash over something I had no control over, so this probably isn't the best time," he growls.

Where has the gentle guy I used to think was far too nice and agreeable gone?

"OK, well, can I catch up with you after work? Please," I add.

His eyes narrow. I suspect he realizes what this is about. My throat is so tight I want to choke.

"I can meet you at Five Frogs," he states, his face still blotchy and red. "But I can't stay long."

"Thanks," I say and quickly return to my desk.

Clicking my mouse, I pretend to be absorbed in the graph on my computer screen. When I finally risk a look around, everyone has returned to work.

I've been waiting at a table in the corner nursing a lime and soda for twenty minutes before Elliot enters the bar. He strides over and sits opposite.

"I'm assuming you got the results," he says, crossing his arms.

No idle chit-chat needed, then.

"Yes," I croak before clearing my throat. "According to the DNA tests, you're the biological father."

"Right."

I jolt at his abrupt and rapid response. From his expression, I could have announced I just bought a new vacuum cleaner. That is until I notice the red stain creeping up his neck and the prominent vein bulging from his clenched fist on the table. I'm now extremely glad we're in a noisy bar with others around.

"I thought you should know, but I don't expect anything from you," I say in a rush. "You didn't ask for this or want it."

"No," he snaps. "I didn't."

I stand up, wishing I could click my fingers and be at home.

"Thanks for meeting me," I say to the top of his head.

For a second I try to think of something else to say, but my mind is blank. "Bye."

When I get to the door, I turn to look at Elliot and he hasn't moved. Fair enough. The poor guy has a fair bit to get his head around: namely, he's going to be a dad.

Whether he acknowledges the fact or not remains to be seen.

I'm surprisingly calm on the drive home. The hard part was telling Elliot and now I have, I feel as if a weight has been lifted. I make myself a simple meal of rice and stir-fried vegetables with a fried egg on top. Then I curl up on the couch with a gardening magazine.

When my phone pings with a notification, I don't even contemplate checking it, but then as I turn the page, I have a sickening realization. I know what the notification is. It's a reminder telling me I have antenatal class tonight.

For at least twenty minutes – having made the decision not to go – I try to read, but I can't shake the feeling like I'm missing an important meeting and letting the side down. Correction: letting my baby down.

Sighing, I slam my magazine on the coffee table, put on some sandals, grab my bag and open the front door. A small scream escapes my lips as I come face to face with Elliot.

"Jesus," I breathe. "You scared me."

"Sorry."

He looks calmer now – less like he's about to turn into the Hulk.

"Can I talk to you?" he asks.

I hesitate. "I'd like to... It's just—"

"You're going somewhere?"

I nod. "Antenatal class started five minutes ago."

Elliot nods slowly.

"I can skip—"

"I'll come," Elliot interrupts, giving a half-hearted smile. "Better start understanding this whole baby thing a bit better."

I stare at him, my mouth open. "But…"

Elliot rubs a hand across his mouth. "Look, Trish, I'm still getting to grips with the news. And I'm trying to figure things out, but I'm the dad like you said." He pauses and stares at my swollen belly as if it's appeared out of nowhere. "I have to step up."

"I'm not expecting you to. I mean, this is… Why don't you come in and we can talk some more? I don't need to go to the class."

Elliot shakes his head. "No, Trish. Let's go. It'll be good for me."

I don't want Elliot to go to the bloody antenatal class. It's the last thing I want to happen. But how can I say no?

"OK," I say, stepping out and closing the front door.

Already I'm picturing the other members of the group. What will their reaction be when I turn up with dad number two?

32

Margot looks up as I push the door open.

"Trish. Glad you could make it."

"Sorry I'm late," I say, my cheeks on fire.

Elliot pushes the door open further and steps beside me.

"Hi," he says to the room. "I'm Elliot, the baby's father."

He speaks so loud and proud I want to punch his smug face and run away screaming. Elliot's obviously warmed to the idea that he's planted his seed.

The entire group is staring at us like we're going to perform a spectacular magic trick. If one of them mentions Pete, I'll bloody throttle them.

Margot stands up and walks over. "Lovely to meet you, Elliot." She shakes his hand. "Come and join us."

Everyone leaps up and crowds around to say hello. They're clearly overcompensating owing to the awkwardness of the situation. Finally, Elliot and I are able to sit in the circle of chairs and Margot resumes her talk on ways to induce labour. I try to listen, but Elliot won't stop shuffling in his chair, raising his hand to ask an endless stream of unbelievably dumb questions – does he even know where babies come out? To make it all so much worse, I keep receiving sneaky looks of sympathy from the sea of perfect-looking couples.

Seb isn't even trying to hide his fascination. He's leaning back, arms crossed, grinning at me like I've just flashed him my tits. I want to kill him with my bare hands. But not until I've throttled Elliot first. How can he have changed his tune so fast? One minute he wants nothing to do with me or my baby, the next he's asking what a cervix is.

I've got to stop being so worked up and angry. This isn't how I act. I don't let emotions get the better of me. I control them, no matter what.

The second the meeting ends, I hightail it to the car, Elliot trotting behind me. I wait, my hands gripping the wheel as he gets in the passenger seat and waves enthusiastically to Becky and Ben.

He turns to me with a wink. "Hot sex and a curry, eh?"

Without a word, I start the car and yank it out onto the road, narrowly missing a van parked in front. Elliot grips the door as I hurtle around a corner.

"I didn't mean anything by that, Trish. I don't expect to… I just thought it was funny that curry and sex can induce labour."

By the tremor in his voice, I think he's finally picked up on my less-than-happy mood.

"Was I embarrassing?" Elliot asks at last.

Where do I start? Before I can open my mouth, he carries on.

"There's just so much for me to learn, you know? I need to start catching up."

"There's no exam at the end, Elliot," I say, gritting my teeth. "You're not going to pass or fail."

"It's far bigger than that, Trish." His voice is filled with awe. "There's a freakin' baby."

When we get back to my place, I say goodbye to Elliot before we've even got out of the car. I want to make it clear I've no intention of inviting him inside.

He walks to his car slowly, glancing back at me several times as if I might suddenly call out to him, which I definitely won't. It's not until his car disappears down the street that I let out my breath.

That man – no, boy! – is the father of my child. Him with his pathetic excuse for a moustache and extra-long fingers (I noticed them for the first time tonight). As for his pigeon-toed walk... How could I have missed it? Maybe I'll have a boy and he'll be the spitting image of Elliot. Not that Elliot is unattractive. He has nice eyes, perfect eyebrows... he's broad across the shoulders and his skin is a lovely olive tone. But what's on the inside? What parts of his character, his personality, his background has yet to be revealed? Apart from the fact he clearly didn't focus in biology class when it came to female human anatomy.

I head inside and have a long glass of water – I've been insanely thirsty for the past two hours but unable to swallow a drop. Then I have a long shower, flick the kettle on and eat three chocolate biscuits while waiting for it to click off. After making a peppermint tea, I head to the couch and grab the remote. Time to watch something mindless and mind-numbing. Stretching my legs along the couch, I make myself comfortable and do my best to erase the agonizing – let's be honest – embarrassing antenatal meeting from my mind. Without warning, I start to giggle, remembering the faces of everyone there. Victoria practically had her jaw lying on the floor. And Ethan was unable to meet my eye. Wait till I tell my friends – they're going to find the whole story hilarious.

33

For the next week I field daily visits from Elliot. He turns up at my desk every morning and asks in a low, not-so-secretive voice how I'm doing. I tell him I'm fine and he leaves, which I can deal with. Just.

It's his lunchtime visits I come to dread. He asks me what I'm having for lunch and if I haven't yet decided, or if it's something that isn't up to scratch according to whatever website he's been reading, he insists on getting me something – either a salad with chicken (important for baby to have protein, he says) or a soup laden with vegetables. It takes all of my strength not to tell him to piss off and let me eat chips.

I'm struggling to get any work done and it comes as no surprise on Friday morning when Tash calls me into her office.

"How far along are you now, Trish?" she asks the second I've closed her office door.

"Six weeks to go," I say. "But I feel fine."

"I'd like you to finish up at the end of today," states Tash, closing a folder on her desk and placing it to one side. "I'll continue to pay your full salary until the end of the month when you were due to take maternity leave."

She hasn't looked at me at all while she's spoken and I refuse to reply until she at least lifts her head. Finally, she does.

"Why?" I ask.

She blinks a couple of times. "I think it's for the best, don't you?"

"No."

Sighing, Tash leans back in her chair, crosses her arms and indicates that I should sit in the chair opposite. I do so reluctantly and she continues.

"I understand from office gossip that Elliot is the father. It's none of my business who you sleep with, Trish, but when it starts disrupting things around here... well, I need to take action."

"How exactly are things being disrupted?" I ask quietly, trying to contain myself.

"Look, believe it or not, I'm doing this for your benefit. Elliot won't leave you alone, everyone is watching, and you must be finding it harder and harder to concentrate on work. Also, if I'm brutally honest, the only work you have left is dull as shit since you handed most of the juicy stuff to Mark."

How dare she! I'm so furious right now, I don't know if I want to yell and throw something or burst into tears.

Tash holds up a hand as if sensing I'm about to lose it.

"Before you tell me to go fuck myself, take a second to think about what I've said."

"I don't know how I managed to work with you," I growl.

"Trish, you're one of the best, if not *the* best employee I've had. Work has been your entire focus and I could give you any project or client no matter how challenging and be confident you'd nail it. But work can't be your sole focus now. The sooner you accept it, the happier you'll be. Trust me."

"How the hell would you know?" I mutter, not caring if she fires me on the spot.

"Because I've been where you are and I fought it – fought till the day I gave birth."

It's the first time I've ever seen Tash looking vulnerable. Her eyes are watery and her voice has changed pitch. One cheek is shaking and she keeps having to bite down on her lip.

"I never slowed down," she says. "And I paid the price."

I had no idea she was pregnant. "What happened?"

"I had severe hypertension. The symptoms were there but I ignored them: heart palpitations, sweaty, short of breath. I thought it was work stress." She takes a deep breath. "My son was born four weeks premature and he only managed to breathe for two minutes before he died of a stroke."

I put a hand over my mouth. "Oh, God," I mutter. "Tash, I'm so sorry."

She clears her throat and sits up straighter. "Take the time to slow down, Trish," she says, her voice now firm. "Your position will be kept for the requisite six months' maternity leave. If you don't come back, I'll advertise for someone else."

It's clear she wants me gone so she can be left alone with her pain.

I get to my feet. "I'm very sorry for your loss, Tash," I say to her bowed head. "I'll make sure I've got everything in order before I leave."

She nods without looking up and I return to my desk. All of my anger has gone, replaced by sadness. Now, I understand Tash's relentless drive and commitment to work, along with her ability to be a complete bitch. I can also see how my pregnancy would have brought the loss of her newborn back into focus.

Tash is right: work needs to take a back seat. What's wrong with allowing myself to slow down and enjoy the last few weeks of pregnancy? I wonder if there might be another reason Tash wants me gone from the office. It must be hard seeing me at work every day – for my stomach to be a constant reminder of the little boy she lost.

"I could get used to this." I lean back in my deckchair and enjoy the warmth of the sun on the skin of my exposed belly.

Emma sits beside me, her protruding white stomach also proudly on display. She came around with a container of freshly baked ginger slices (of which I've already devoured two) and a surprise present of two blue-and-green striped deckchairs. She spied them in her parents' garage when she was picking up her baby car seat that had been in storage. Her parents agreed they'd be a good addition to my back garden.

I loved them instantly and we thought it our duty to try to them out.

"I don't think I've ever seen you this relaxed," says Emma. "Being unemployed suits you."

I know she's teasing me, but just hearing the word "unemployed" makes me cringe and it's only been a day since I left work. Word got around, somehow, and though I was planning to slip away at five o'clock and simply not return, the rest of the office suddenly converged on my desk with flowers and a card. They wanted me to go to the pub for a drink, but I politely declined, citing pregnancy exhaustion as my foolproof excuse. I'm sure they were secretly relieved.

But this morning I woke up with the most wonderful sense of peace. It's been years since I haven't had work dominating my life. Now, I seem to have a big expanse of extra air and space that I'm able to fill up on.

"What time do you have to pick up Freddie?" I ask, adjusting my sun hat so it covers my face but still lets me breathe.

"One o'clock," she murmurs. "Do you think our babies have absorbed enough vitamin D yet?"

I was given a folder brimming with pamphlets and other baby paraphernalia from Margot at class a couple of nights ago (I went on my own this time after telling Elliot firmly he was not to come). One of the pamphlets went on about how the womb can absorb vitamin D directly from the sun. I have no idea if it's working, but I'm loving the feeling of warmth on my belly and my baby does too, judging by its acrobatics.

"Thank God my maple tree has grown enough to screen off the neighbour's kitchen window," I say. "He'd be calling the police, complaining of indecent exposure."

We both laugh. I'm exaggerating, but he's a fairly intimidating old guy. Plus, it was kind of creepy the way I'd occasionally catch him standing at his window staring at me in the garden while he sipped his cup of tea. Well, I assume he was staring at me. Maybe he has shocking eyesight and was looking at some random blurry shapes. I'm trying not to be so quick to judge people after my talk with Tash. Lily thinks my boss' sob story in no way makes up for her poor treatment of me, but that's Lily through and through. There's black and there's white, and that's it as far as she's concerned. I'm various shades of grey, especially when it comes to trying to figure out other people.

"Scott popped into the café yesterday," Emma says casually.

"What?" I sit up and my hat falls onto the grass. "Why?"

Emma shrugs, her eyes still closed against the sun. "For something to eat, I guess. I was busy in the kitchen but spied him as he was about to leave."

"Oh." I lie back down, feeling disappointed but not wanting to show it.

"I dashed out to say hi and he asked after you," says Emma. "Why didn't you tell us he was with you when you found out the DNA results?"

"I forgot, I guess."

Emma's quiet and I think she's going to leave the conversation alone, when she pipes up again.

"He said you both helped out at the City Mission on Christmas Day. Did that slip your memory, too?"

I wrinkle my lips. "Yeah, must have." I'm attempting nonchalance, but I'm not sure I've achieved it.

"Sure," Emma says. "Keep telling yourself you don't care about the guy and it's bound to sink in eventually, Trish."

I consider denying it and getting all up in arms, but I'm too relaxed and chilled. Plus, there's more than a kernel of truth to Emma's words. I've thought about texting Scott several times. He seems to come into my mind every time

I'm in my garden, or when I walk into the baby's room and see the cardigan and hat he knitted sitting on the dresser. I should have put them away in a drawer by now, but they're just so beautiful and, well… a cute guy knitted them for me. It's bordering on a miracle.

I don't message Scott *because* I like him. Very much. And because I'm pregnant with another man's child and I now have stretch marks beginning to appear around my belly button (my stomach looks like a bloody balloon). What possible chance is there for me to develop a relationship with him? None. Zip. Zero.

"You're not going to be pregnant forever," says Emma, as if she's been privy to my thoughts. "Eventually, you'll have your body back and feel sexy again."

"Is that what happened with you?"

"Well, I got maybe ninety per cent of my body back. The other ten per cent went to shit."

We grin at each other.

"Thanks. I can always count on you to keep it real, Em."

"Anytime." She groans and slowly gets up. "I'd better get moving before I fall asleep." She pulls her top down over her bulge, takes a step, then winces and puts a hand on her lower back.

"You OK?"

"Yeah. I've just had a sore back for the past couple of days. It comes and goes."

I sit up, frowning. "You could be in labour. Margot was talking about it at the last class. Sometimes you get pains in your back instead of your stomach."

Emma's eyes widen. "Oh, crap. I hadn't thought of that."

"Isn't your due date soon?"

Emma nods, her hand still rubbing her back. "Ten days."

"So it's possible, right?"

Emma shakes her head. "Freddie was on time."

"The baby doesn't know that."

Emma rolls her eyes. "Thanks."

"Come on." I stand up to lead her inside. "Let's at least ring Finn and put him on alert."

"No. He'll start to get all nervous and panicky. I'll ring Mum after I've collected Freddie. Ask her to come over."

I purse my lips. "Are you all right to drive to school?"

"Of course I—" She breaks off and bends over.

A wet patch appears on the leg of her grey maternity three-quarter trousers and travels slowly downwards. A trickle of clear liquid runs over her bare foot and onto the grass.

"Shit," Emma murmurs.

"Please tell me that's your waters breaking."

She slowly straightens and nods, her face pale. "I think I'd better call Finn."

By the time Emma's phoned Finn and asked her mum to collect Freddie from school, she's breathing hard. I offer to call the midwife and she simply nods then gets down on her hands and knees on the kitchen floor and starts to groan. I rub her lower back as I make the call.

"Sounds like she's pretty far along," says Leanne. "Best I meet her at the hospital. Tell her to go straight there."

I hang up and run around gathering a few things. Then I return to the kitchen to find Emma standing.

"Let's go," she states, heading towards my front door. "I

at least want to get to the car before the next contraction hits."

We make it as far as the letter box, where Emma moans and I once again help her to drop onto her hands and knees.

"Press hard, Trish, on my back," she pants.

I press my palm firmly into her lower back.

"More!" Emma snaps.

Using both hands, I press down as hard as I can. "I'm worried I'm going to break something."

"No, it's good. It's helping," gasps Emma.

A car hurtles along the road and pulls up in front of my house. Finn leaps out and races over.

"Em," he says, crouching to wipe the hair from her face. "Let's get you to the hospital, gorgeous."

He appears calm, but when he glances up at me, there's panic in his eyes.

Between us, we get Emma into the passenger seat of Finn's car.

"Do you want me to come with you?" I ask, helping her with the seat belt.

"I'll be fine. See you on the other side." Emma's smile is weak but genuine.

"Good luck," I murmur, giving her hand a squeeze.

I watch them drive off and feel a deep ache in my chest. Women give birth all the time. Their bodies are designed for the purpose. Emma will be all right. The baby will be perfect. Nothing will go wrong.

I look across the road at a man walking his beagle. I watch a sparrow disappear into the hedge next door. A car drives past, the driver looking bored. It's just another day for most people. The ache in my chest intensifies and I turn to walk inside. My hand shakes as it closes the front door. I'm scared for my friend, and for myself.

I sleep fitfully that night, waking every hour or so to check my phone. At 3 a.m., a message finally arrives from Finn:

> Hey, Trish. Emma had a baby boy about ten minutes ago. Both mum and baby Leo are fine. She'll call you later. Finn

"Leo," I mouth. Better cross that one off my list. Not that I have a list. I've been looking at names – endless streams of them – but nothing is screaming "pick me". Who cares if I don't have a name yet? Emma and her baby are OK. It's all that matters.

Snuggling back under my covers, I curl into a foetal position, close my eyes and drift into proper sleep at last.

Waking late, I lie in bed for at least twenty minutes before getting up. I consider going for a light jog or a walk, but I'm feeling too lazy. Normally, I'd be ravaged with guilt if I didn't immediately leap out of bed and do some form of exercise, but I'm blissfully guilt-free. It's a pleasant change.

After I've eaten some banana on toast and given the house a quick vacuum, I give Mags a call.

"Want to go visit Em this morning?" I ask. "I could pick you up?"

"Absolutely," says Mags. "Is she up for a visit, though, after her ordeal?"

I frown. Why is Mags describing the birth as an ordeal? I have a sneaky suspicion Finn might have been thin on the ground with details in his text.

"What exactly do you mean by ordeal?"

Mags is silent.

"Spill," I demand.

"They didn't want you to worry," she says nervously. "Emma was going to phone you this morning."

"Well she hasn't phoned, so you can tell me instead."

"I don't know the exact details, but apparently the baby was the wrong way around and got stuck. Emma ended up having an emergency caesarean."

A chill runs through my body. "Oh no."

"The main thing is they're OK."

"I suppose."

"Chin up, Trish. It doesn't mean you're going to have any problems. If anything, it's probably reduced the odds, hasn't it?"

"No."

Mags sighs and I can tell she's frustrated. While Mags may be the kindest, most thoughtful person I know, her tolerance for anyone who isn't upbeat and positive is a little low. She believes negativity is infectious – if one person is down, they'll bring others down with them. This may be true to a point, but what if everyone was happy and positive all the time? It would be downright freaky. Everyone has their moments in the deep end – some are just lucky they don't drown.

I'm not sure I'm ready to go to the hospital now.

"Maybe we should hold off going to visit. Wait till we hear from Emma."

"Good idea." Mags yelps, giggles and starts talking in a muffled voice. "Sorry," she says, coming back on the line. "Phoebe was tickling me."

I roll my eyes and say a quick goodbye. One day soon I'm going to demand Mags brings this new woman of hers out into the open. It's about time we got to know her.

The next few days pass in a contented haze. I visit Emma every afternoon and cuddle baby Leo as we chat. We avoid discussing the caesarean – it's clear neither of us want to talk about it yet. Seeing Emma's glowing face is enough for me to know that I can get through a caesarean or anything else that might be thrown my way. I can't wait to hold my baby and I'm almost (I repeat, almost) excited about going into labour.

Most of my time is either spent at the garden centre, in the garden or floating in the sea to cool down. I've gone a little crazy with pots – I can't stop buying them and filling them with lettuces and herbs. They're starting to crowd my back deck, but I love how they look and smell – especially the lemon verbena. I've taken to pulling off a sprig and putting it in my morning cup of Earl Grey tea so I can inhale the aroma as I drink. I've also dug out two woody and scraggly lavender plants and replaced them with camellias. Then underplanted them with carpet thyme.

Elliot seems to have backed off, which is an unexpected though very welcome development. He's sent me a couple of short text messages asking how I'm doing, but otherwise he's been surprisingly distant. Not that I'm complaining. I'm assuming at some point we'll have to sit down and talk things through. I don't even want to think about the possibility of him asking for custody rights. Probably I should be speaking to a lawyer – the old Trish would have already had a document written and signed by all relevant parties by now. But I can't seem to muster that old Trish anymore. This one is far easier and kinder to live with.

I'm surprised when it gets to Thursday afternoon and I realize I'm looking forward to the evening's antenatal class. At our previous meeting, Margot organized for the soon-to-be mums to join a WhatsApp group chat and I've been enjoying the light banter and discussions. I've even joined in on occasion. They're not such a bad lot. And it's nice knowing there are others going through this pregnancy thing along with me.

Which is why when Mags turns up out of the blue and insists she come to the class, I'm not exactly thrilled.

"I'm happy going on my own. In some ways it's easier than having another person there."

"You can never have too much support, Trish."

"I don't know."

I'm stalling. She'll be crestfallen if I say no. Mags loves helping others. Especially those she thinks are vulnerable. It's the reason she has so many cats. Mags volunteers to be a foster home for displaced or stray cats and, of course, has ended up keeping the ones that couldn't be rehomed. Her small house permanently smells of cat wee, which is why we rarely go over there. Also, Lily isn't exactly a cat person – she lives in terror of a cat landing on her lap. I have to admit, my desire to have a cat has diminished since Mags accumulated her feline friends.

After brief consideration, I decide the risk of offending my friend is too great.

"Sure," I say, feigning enthusiasm. "I'd love you to come."

So I turn up with yet another person to class and the first thing Mags does – before she's even completed the obligatory introductions – is announce that she's my friend for life (so lovely), and she is going to love me no matter what (strange, but OK, I'll go with it). Then she says, her cheeks flushed, her eyes wide and watery, that she's gay and the happiest she's ever been. After which she sits down, puts a hand on my knee, leans in and kisses me on the cheek.

I'd forgotten how much of a sharer Mags can be, especially when she's nervous.

Of course, *I* know she has a girlfriend and that our relationship is platonic, but do the rest of the room? Hell, no. They're now all staring at me as they try to factor in the possibility of two dads (they've been too polite to ask about Elliot and Pete) and a second mum.

Even Margot is speechless. She keeps looking from Mags to me and back to Mags as if we're going to start making out.

Priya stands up and walks over. Her stomach is so much bigger than last week and her walk has turned into a wide-legged waddle.

"Welcome, Mags," she says, smiling and leaning down to give my friend a hug.

Then it's my turn. She pulls me into her stomach, her arms around my shoulders (hugging doesn't work well when one is sitting and the other standing, especially when heavily pregnant). It feels far too intimate as my head pushes against her firm basketball belly.

"So happy for you, Trish," she whispers in my ear.

"Thanks," I mutter, willing her to let me go.

But she doesn't. Instead, she pulls me even tighter and gives me a sloppy kiss on the forehead.

I should have come to the meeting on my own.

34

It's mid-morning and I'm still lying in bed reading. I considered getting up to go for a speed walk (running is no longer an option), but I had a restless night and after finally falling into a deep sleep around 4 a.m., I'm in no hurry to go anywhere. Until four months ago, I was a back sleeper. Now, I have to lie on my side and within minutes, my shoulder begins to cramp (why has my mattress suddenly got so hard?), my hip feels numb, and the skin on my swollen stomach feels stretched and sore.

The midwife suggested I use pillows to help, and I've tried stuffing one between my legs and under my belly but with limited relief. All I want to do is lie on my stomach or my back, but both are off limits. In fact, after the midwife told me that lying on my back could cause reduced blood flow to the foetus, I've been paranoid I'll accidently deprive my baby of oxygen. I've resorted to stuffing pillows behind me to reduce the chance of inadvertently rolling onto my back in my sleep.

Now I'm propped up in bed, a cup of tea and a piece of shortbread on the bedside table, and a view of my garden through the open window. The baby has been giving me the odd nudge to let me know things are OK and I'm not thinking about how I'm going to get through the day, for a change. In this moment I feel brighter, as if the sun has come out from behind a cloud.

My phone buzzes and I'm tempted to let it ring, but when I check who's calling I realize I haven't spoken to my brother since our trip to the zoo.

"Hey, Will."

"Trish, how are you?"

"Really good."

"Great."

There's nervousness in his voice.

"Everything all right?" I ask, worried about Tilly.

"Actually, ah… I got a call from Mum yesterday. Dad died from a heart attack on Monday."

My body freezes. "Oh."

"Yeah. Exactly."

I don't know what to make of the news or how I'm supposed to feel about it. Maybe I'm in shock.

"The funeral's tomorrow," says Will. "I wondered… well, would you come with me? I figure I should go, even though we weren't exactly on speaking terms. I don't want Tilly there, so I've arranged for her to go to a friend's place after school." He hesitates and speaks again. "Mum said we could stay the night with her, but…" He trails off.

"There's no way I'm staying in that house," I blurt.

Will is silent.

"Honestly, Will. I'm not sure I'm up for the whole family reunion thing."

"He was our dad, Trish. I think you should come, otherwise you might regret it later."

He has a point. As much as I wish I'd grown up with a

different set of parents, they were still the ones I got lumped with. Every now and again, Mum and Dad showed signs of affection, possibly even love for their children, like when they bought me that purple bike, or when Dad let me stay with Grammy Rose. I need to hold on to those moments.

"OK," I whisper.

"You'll come?"

"Yes. But I'm not staying. We'd have to go down there and back in a day. What time's the funeral?"

"Two in the afternoon."

"So if it's a three-hour drive, let's say three and a half in case the traffic's bad, we could leave there at 5 p.m. and be back by nine at the latest."

"Fine by me. I'll pick you up. I imagine being stuck behind the wheel for that distance while you're heavily pregnant wouldn't be much fun."

I'm about to argue because I like to drive. More accurately: I like to be the one in control so I'm not reliant on others. That's how I've always been and my friends don't even ask anymore – they just assume if we go somewhere, I'm the driver. But why put myself through the discomfort of driving when I don't have to?

"Thanks," I say finally. "What time?"

"How about we leave at nine so we can have a couple of stops on the way to stretch the legs?"

"Good. I'll see you then."

"Trish?"

"Yeah."

"We'll stick together, OK? You and me, we'll look out for each other. Deal?"

My heart contracts. I learnt growing up I could never rely

on my family. They weren't going to help me cope with the school bully or study for a test or ask me how my day was. I was a member of a unit, not a family: a group of people who existed side by side with no connection. Till now.

"Deal," I say with a choke.

"See you tomorrow," Will says quickly and hangs up.

My father's dead. And tomorrow I'll see my mother for the first time in years. What's she going to say when she sees me? What's everyone at the funeral going to say? They'll be whispering about me, staring. The errant daughter, pregnant out of wedlock with no father on the scene. I suppose my brother James will be there. Another person I'd hoped never to see again.

Ten minutes ago, I was feeling fairly happy with my life. Now, I want to dive under the covers and hide. Permanently.

Stop it, I tell myself. I can get through the funeral. I can deal with those people. I'm proud of the life I've built for myself. My house, my garden, my friends, my career. Soon, I'll bring a child into this world and he or she is going to be loved and nurtured, listened to and encouraged. I'm going to hug my child every single day. They're going to feel loved and seen. I'm not a product of my parents. I'm my own person in spite of my parents. So yes, I'll go to Dad's funeral out of familial responsibility. But not out of respect for him – he lost that years ago. And not for Mum. She deserves nothing from me at all.

35

"We should probably get out of the car," says Will. "Suppose."

Since we pulled into the church car park ten minutes ago, neither of us has spoken. After a morning of comfortable, easy-going chatter during the drive down, we can no longer pretend we're fine.

I stare through the windscreen at the church where I spent so many uncomfortable, distressing hours.

"I hated this place," says Will. "Still do."

"Yeah. Doesn't fill me with warm fuzzies, either."

"I remember Dad once had a big rant at me here," says Will, glaring at the church. "He told me I was slouching and I wasn't giving the minister enough attention and respect. Dad actually accused me of looking too happy in church. Can you believe it? He said I smiled too much." Will sighs and gives a rueful shake of his head. "I was four years old, Trish. Not unsurprisingly, I never smiled in church again."

"I can't believe you found anything to smile about in the first place." It's good to hear Will talk this way – maybe I can be brave enough to talk about our parents, too. "I used to play a game in my head," I say quietly, my heart thumping. This is the first time I've talked about the realities of my childhood with anyone. "When we were filing out of church, I'd look around at the other families and imagine I belonged to them instead. I literally pictured myself walking over, taking another mum or dad's hand and leaving with them."

"I used to go home after church, shut myself in my bedroom and cry."

I'm dumbfounded. "Really?"

He nods. "For years."

"You were so stony-faced, like nothing affected you at all."

Will laughs. "Trish, I learnt early on it was better never to show any emotion around Dad. My bedroom was the only place in the house where I didn't feel like I was being watched and judged and could let it all out."

"At least you didn't have to deal with Mum," I whisper.

Will bites the tip of his thumb and assesses me. "It must have been tough. Sorry I didn't help more. I thought about it. I mean, I could see you found it hard. But if I'm honest, I hated seeing Mum in that state. I just wanted to avoid her as much as I could."

I shrug. "Dad probably wouldn't have let you anyway. He thought it was my duty as the daughter to take care of Mum, and to take over running the household when needed."

"Which was basically all the time."

"Yeah. That's how it felt."

"What was she like? When you took in her meals and helped her to shower and dress, did she talk to you? Tell you what was wrong?"

"She was catatonic mostly," I say, my voice flat. "Barely even registered my presence."

"What about when she was up and about? Did she ever mention her 'episodes', as Dad called them?"

"Never. One day I'd be hanging out the washing, cooking a meal, vacuuming the house, doing my homework at midnight. The next, I'd get home from school and she'd be cleaning the oven and acting like everything was fine."

"Do you think they ever loved each other?"

"Mum and Dad? No. Or if they did, it was before we came along."

Will opens his door. "It's not a nice thing to say on the day of our father's funeral, but I wonder if she'll be happier now he's gone."

"I wouldn't count on it, Will," I say, climbing out of the car.

We walk side by side to the church door and make our way into the dimly lit foyer. Our brother James stands rigidly in a suit at the entrance. He automatically holds out an order of service, then clocks who we are and his hand drops to his side.

"Hello," he says, his voice deep and gruff.

His expression is just as Dad's used to be. Serious, no-nonsense. No hint of emotion. He's put on weight and has few more frown lines and a little less hair at the temple but is otherwise unchanged.

"James," says Will, his voice tight. "Remember us?"

"Hello, William, Patricia." His gaze barely lands on me before he looks away. "I wasn't sure you'd come."

I clear my throat, determined to speak. "I wasn't sure either," I say firmly.

Then I hold out my hand and wait for James to hand me the order of service. Without thanking him, I walk down the aisle and take a seat in the third row from the back. The church is half full at most, which surprises me. I thought there would be a mass of military types filling every corner.

A few people to turn to look at me and I recognize their faces. Ghosts from my past. People I knew but never knew. Acquaintances of my parents, work colleagues of Dad's. I drop my head to avoid their stares and shuffle over so Will can sit beside me.

"If Dad were here, he'd be accusing you of making a spectacle of yourself, showing up pregnant," Will whispers.

I raise my eyebrows. "Do you think I give a shit?" I whisper.

Will smiles. "Nope. And nor should you."

James appears in the aisle beside us. "Family are seated in the front row," he mutters.

"We're comfortable with right here," Will says loudly.

More faces turn towards us.

I've spied the back of Mum's head. I can tell it's her by the way she sits: timidly, as if she's afraid of taking up too much space.

James glares at us, his cheeks glowing, then he marches to the front row and sits beside a woman I presume is his wife.

The service is mercifully short. We stand to sing a hymn, the minister gives a short drone about Dad being an upstanding, hard-working citizen. A guy in full military attire and a chest full of medals talks about Dad's services to the army and James reads a small section of the Bible. Mum doesn't move for the entire twenty minutes. No one does. Even in death, Dad has everyone well-trained, or at least nervous about his disapproval.

Will and I stand as James leads the procession of guests out of the church and I manage a quick assessment of his wife as she follows him. Even though I was at their wedding, I barely remember her. Clare is short, trim, immaculately dressed and wears the same wary expression I recall seeing on anyone's face when they stood within arm's distance of Dad. Following them are two young boys with their heads down, their hands clasped behind their backs.

Will leans towards me and whispers in my ear. "Our nephews, Jonathan and Benedict."

I've heard him but can't respond, because Mum's behind the boys and she's stopped walking and is staring at me.

"Trish," she whispers, her eyes wide.

Then her eyes flit to Will.

"Hi, Mum," says Will.

He steps forwards and puts his arms around her for a fraction of a second before letting her go. He hasn't given her time to hug him back, even if she wanted.

I stay rooted to the spot. Mum catches sight of my stomach, audibly gasps and turns away to cough. She hacks away till the person behind her, who I recognize as a cousin, pats Mum on the back at the same time as she propels her forward and out of the church.

I fix my eyes at the back of Will's head as everyone else streams out behind Mum, staring at me as they go past.

The air outside is fresh and reviving after the stale humidity inside. I inhale deeply and follow Will off to one side. We silently observe everyone gathering to murmur his or her condolences to James and Mum. No one approaches us and I have to work hard to resist smiling. I'm no longer a part of this false and empty world anymore. I got away and made a life for myself. I escaped.

My heart flips when I spy James' two boys hovering by the church gate. They look watchful, as if they're under threat. I'd like to go to them, crouch down and introduce myself. But if I do, I'd be crossing a line. A line I'm not ready or willing to cross.

Will squeezes my arm. "How are you holding up?" he asks quietly. "Ready to escape?"

I nod.

"I'm going to talk to Mum briefly," Will says, chewing on his thumb. "Is that OK?"

I shrug. "Go for it."

"Do you want to come with me?"

I smile weakly. "No, thanks."

Will slowly makes his way through the crowd and taps Mum on the shoulder. Her back is to me as they talk. After less than a minute, she grabs Will's arm, leans in and kisses him on the cheek. Then she turns and looks at me. There are tears in her eyes and her face is so twisted with emotion, I turn away and head towards the car.

Mum doesn't chase after me or call out my name. Which shouldn't hurt because I don't want to speak to her. I want to leave this reminder of my past and go home. There's nothing for me here. There never was.

36

"I can't believe your dad died and you never told us," says Lily, leaning back in one of my newly acquired deckchairs and flicking off her sandals.

We're soaking up the sun, waiting for the oven timer to tell us our mince and cheese pie is ready. Lily rang to say she was coming for a visit and would bring lunch. She thought it was a hilarious joke bringing a meat pie. In reference to Elliot, of course – or "pie guy" as she calls him. If he hadn't bought me a pie all those months ago, I wouldn't be pregnant in the first place. What a thought.

"We weren't exactly close."

I speak with my eyes closed and hands pressed on my taut and painful stomach. I've been having Braxton Hicks contractions all morning and I'm starting to think this baby wants out sooner rather than later. I've also been experiencing an alarming sensation like someone is scratching at my cervix with a fingernail. The midwife assures me this is normal, but bloody hell, it's not the nicest pregnancy experience to date.

"So, two weeks till D-Day. Anything you want to do before you're burdened with the responsibility of a child for the rest of your life?" Lily jabs me lightly on the leg.

"I can always count on you to help me feel happy and prepared for what lies ahead, Lils," I say, grinning.

The oven timer starts to beep and Lily leaps to her feet. "Don't move."

I listen to her bang and crash around the kitchen for a few minutes before I open my eyes, lift my head, then slowly and inelegantly stagger to my feet. There are a few weeds poking their cheeky green leaves out of the soil beneath the hydrangeas, but there's no way I can crouch to remove them. Not if I want to make it back up to standing again.

"I feel like a stranded whale," I call, heading towards the kitchen. "And I'm putting on about a kilo a day."

"Ah, the joys of pregnancy," calls Lily.

When I get to the kitchen, she pulls out a chair and demands I sit. Then she places a plate containing a large wedge of pie and a token salad consisting of about three lettuce leaves and a couple of cucumber slices before me.

"Voila!" she says, flinging out her arm. "Your gourmet meal."

"Thanks, Lil."

We eat and chat, and for a few fleeting seconds here and there, I manage to forget the fact I'm heavily pregnant. I've spent the week getting ready both mentally and physically for the imminent birth of my baby. My hospital bag is packed, the baby seat is beside the front door and I have about ten frozen meals packed into my tiny freezer. A part of me wants the baby to come now and another wants it to stay inside forever.

"Darryl asked me to marry him again," says Lily matter-of-factly before shoving a mouthful of pie in her mouth.

"Wow! He was brave. What did you say?"

Lily swallows and raises her eyebrows.

"Holy crap," I say, my knife and fork clattering on the table. "You said yes."

Lily shakes her head in disgust. "I have no idea what came over me, Trish."

I push back my chair, stand up and throw my arms around my friend's head because I can't really bend down. Her face presses against my stomach.

"All right, all right," she says. "Let's not freak the kid out before it's even born. Also, I think my face is against the little blighter's butt."

Laughing, I release my friend and pat my stomach. "I think you're right. That feels like my baby's bottom."

Lily screws up her face. "Lovely."

"So, you're going to do it then? Marry Darryl," I ask.

"I guess."

"Wow. Who would have thought? The beast is finally tamed."

"Are you insinuating I'm the beast?" Lily looks at me with mock indignation.

"I wouldn't want it any other way." I kiss Lily lightly on her head. "Congratulations, Lily. I think you made a good decision."

"Really?"

"Absolutely. Darryl's one of the good ones."

Wincing as another Braxton Hicks picks up steam, I sit heavily and inhale deeply, in and out, waiting for the tightness to pass. Lily shovels a mouthful of pie in her mouth and chews slowly. She's acting cool, but her anxious eyes keep darting in my direction then back to her plate.

"Are you sure that's normal?" she finally asks.

I nod and my body sags as the contraction ends.

"You're not, like, in labour, are you?"

Lily's face tells me this would be a truly horrific turn of events.

"No. Well, I don't think so."

"Great," Lily says, rolling her eyes. "Just what I need."

I dig into my pie. "So," I say, chewing. "Have you set a date?"

"For what?"

"Your wedding!"

Lily screws up her nose. "Oh, right. Nah, not yet. Maybe we could just stay engaged and never get married."

"That sounds more like it." I giggle and Lily sticks out her tongue.

"This is a big step, Trish. Huge."

She's right. This is big for Lily. And I wouldn't be surprised if the engagement is off again by the end of the week. Then on. Then off. It could well be years before Lily finally lets herself commit.

"I know, Lils. It's right up there with having a baby."

Lily nods vigorously. "Exactly! Do you ever feel like we're just acting like grown-ups, Trish, instead of actually being them?"

I nod. "All the time. I'm pretty sure the biggest part of being a so-called grown-up is faking it till you make it. It should be a thing. Adult Imposter Syndrome."

"Uh-huh. We could write a book about it."

After we finish our lunch and Lily heads back to work, I decide to work off the pie with a walk. It's funny how little

I miss running. Pounding the streets, trying to notch up a certain number of kilometres in a limited amount of time. Running was about the end result. It was a means to an end and that end was worth it if it meant I stayed fit, didn't gain weight and kept my mental demons at bay.

Walking is about breathing in the air, checking out what's growing in people's gardens, smiling at the dog running in crazy happy circles in the park. When I walk, stray thoughts come and go and instead of dwelling on them, I just let them sit in my brain until they decide to move on.

Even my muscles react differently. When I'm running, my legs and arms, even my neck, are tense. But when I walk, my body stretches out and relaxes. Maybe it's the pregnancy hormones making me feel more flexible and less wound up. Which is fine by me. The stretchier I am when forcing a baby through my vagina, the better.

I stop walking as another Braxton Hicks kicks in. It wasn't that long since the last one. The tightness passes quickly this time, perhaps because I'm focusing on the sparrow dancing around at my feet.

"Trish!"

I turn and spy Scott jogging towards me, sweaty and, well, sexy as hell.

Heat rises to my face. "Hey," I say, instantly wishing I wasn't the size and shape of a baby elephant.

"You look ready to pop," he says, coming to a stop. "It can't be long now."

"Three weeks."

Scott lifts up the edge of his T-shirt and wipes his brow. Of course, this exposes his well-defined abdominals, plus the narrow line of dark hair from his belly button to his...

"How are you?" I blurt, averting my eyes to a spot behind his head.

"I'm good. Been thinking about you, actually."

There's a moment of awkward silence.

"Don't let me stop you," I say. "If you want to keep running."

Scott shakes his head. "It's fine. I was about to run out of steam anyway. Are you heading anywhere or just out for a walk?"

"Just walking."

"Mind if I join you?"

I hesitate. "Ah, sure."

We continue along the footpath.

"I've been wanting to apologize for being short with you on Christmas Day," I say. "When you asked me about the baby's father."

"It's fine. I figured you were dealing with stuff. How did the potential dads take the news about the DNA results, if you don't mind me asking?"

"Not that well."

"Bastards," he mutters.

I smile. "It's fine. I'm happy neither of them are involved."

"So they aren't... I mean, you're not..." Scott trails off.

"Pete has disappeared – I expect never to be seen again. And Elliot, the biological father, is... Actually, I don't know what he's up to. He's been staying distant. Which, again, is fine by me."

A middle-aged man on a fancy road bike and head-to-toe Lycra flies towards us and Scott grabs my hand to pull me out of his way.

"Slow down," he yells as the man shoots past. Scott squeezes my hand. "Idiot. You OK?"

I glance at our joined hands and up at his face. The sun is bright behind him and his face is mostly in shadow.

"Yes," I croak.

My legs are shaky and I'm not sure if it's fright from the near miss with the man on the bike or the way Scott is looking at me.

He clears his throat and lets my hand go. "Actually, I should probably head home and do some work."

"Sure."

"Will you be around tomorrow? I knitted a blanket for the baby and thought I could swing round in the morning to drop it off."

Oh my God, who is this guy?

"You didn't need to do that."

"I know. I saw the pattern and it was just too cute, so I had to give it a go. It's got a hood with little bunny ears on one corner, which sounds cringe but it's... Actually, the whole fact that I knit is cringe anyway—"

"Stop being so hard on yourself. You should own it – the whole knitting thing."

"You don't think it makes me too... I don't know... weird?"

I laugh. "No, I don't. Well, only a bit."

Scott grimaces. "Thanks."

I push his arm. "I was joking."

We smile at each other and I should look away, but I don't.

"Well..." Scott looks at his feet. "I should go. Does ten o'clock sound OK?"

Another Braxton Hicks is ramping up and I need him to go before it gets more intense.

"Sure, see you then."

My hands rest on my hard-as-rock belly as he runs away.

"It's gorgeous," I breathe, stroking the cream blanket. "And the bunny ears are adorable."

Scott looks anxious. "I nearly chickened out of giving it to you."

"Why?"

He shrugs. "I don't know. It's like I'm putting myself out there somehow. Making myself vulnerable."

I'm reminded of the first time we met on the plane when Scott talked about auras. He's the most open person when it comes to talking about emotions that I've ever met. Which makes me more than a little scared, though not necessarily in a bad way.

"My dad died a couple of weeks ago," I say, surprising myself.

"I'm sorry, Trish. That's very sad."

I continue to stroke the blanket. "We weren't close. I hadn't seen him in years."

"But he was still your dad."

"I guess." I'm regretting my outburst. I'm not ready to talk about my parents with anyone. "Would you like a tea or coffee?" I ask, folding the blanket carefully.

"Sure, if you're making one for yourself."

I place the blanket on the chest of drawers and he follows me into the kitchen.

"So, do you have any plans for the afternoon?" asks Scott.

I flick on the kettle. "Sort of."

Scott pulls out a chair and sits at the table. "What does that mean?"

"Well, my antenatal group is having a final get-together barbeque before we start birthing babies, but I can't decide if I'll go."

"Why?"

Ignoring his question, I hold up a mug. "Tea or coffee?"

"Whatever you're having."

I smile wryly. "I'm having raspberry leaf tea because it's supposedly meant to help induce labour."

Scott's eyes widen in horror. "Might pass on that one. I'll have an ordinary tea, thanks."

I busy myself with making the tea.

"So, you didn't say why you're on the fence about the barbeque," Scott states.

"They're nice people, but I'm pretty sure they're going to surround me and ask a million questions."

"About what?"

I fill Scott in on the disturbing news that I've taken three different people to antenatal class already. He laughs till he cries, which I guess is fair enough.

"You're going to be mobbed, Trish," he says, wiping his tears. "Their imaginations will be running wild."

"How so?"

Scott shrugs. "They might think you're part of some weird cult. Or maybe you're taking co-parenting to the extreme – two gay dads and two gay mums."

His smile is contagious.

"That's hardly encouraging me to go." I indicate towards the back door. "Should we sit outside?"

"Absolutely."

We retire to the porch and I do my best to sit up straight and not look like I'm uncomfortably eight and a half months pregnant.

"Did you go to your dad's funeral?" Scott asks.

I nod and fix my gaze on the rosemary. I swear I only trimmed it a couple of weeks ago, but it's getting scraggly again.

"How was it?"

"Fine."

I'm on edge, concerned Scott's going to probe further, but he falls silent. It's not an accusing silence, or a threatening one. It's calming. I take a couple of deep breaths, sip my unpleasant-tasting raspberry leaf tea and study him out of the corner of my eye. He's cupping his mug in both hands and has his legs stretched out in front, crossed at the ankles. His faded denim shorts have a small rip on the thigh and a couple of dark leg hairs are poking through. I have a sudden desire to place my hand over that hole and rest it there. When I tear my eyes and thoughts away from his shorts and risk a quick glance at his face, Scott's looking at me. For a moment the silence continues, our eyes locked together.

"It's beautiful," Scott whispers.

"What is?"

"This moment."

Blinking, I look away.

Scott clears his throat. "So, I've been meaning to ask, Trish. Do you know if you're having a boy or a girl?"

How does he manage to remain so relaxed? My heart is thumping so hard, I'm sure Scott must hear it.

"No. It's a surprise."

"What do you think you're having?"

I shrug. "Initially, I thought I was having a boy, then a girl, and now I'm convinced it's got to be a boy again."

"Why is that?"

"Because I keep getting booted in the ribs by big powerful feet." As if my unborn baby has heard me, I receive a hard, sharp kick. "Oww, just like that," I exclaim.

Scott's shakes his head. "I can't imagine what it must be like to have a fully formed human being in there. Isn't nature incredible?"

There he goes again: so unafraid to speak openly. I reach for one of his hands, place it on the top of my belly and press.

"Feel that?"

Scott's eyes widen and he nods.

"It's a foot or a knee." I press his hand into the bony lump and the lump responds with a violent jab.

"Jesus," Scott says loudly. "I see what you mean. That's a football star right there."

I lift my hand and wait for Scott to take his hand off my belly, but it stays there.

"Do you think they'll kick again?" he asks eagerly.

My baby responds with another solid nudge.

"Wow! that's incredible."

Grinning, he looks up at me. But when he catches my expression, his smile disappears and he quickly pulls his hand away.

"Sorry," he mutters.

"It's fine," I say quickly. "Honest."

I can hardly explain that for a split second there, I allowed myself to imagine he was the father and we were having a special soon-to-be mum and dad bonding moment. Then I reminded myself of the true facts and I wanted to throw something.

Scott takes a couple of quick gulps of his tea and stands. "I should let you get on."

I shuffle forwards, readying myself to launch my body out of the chair.

"Don't get up." Scott holds out a palm. "I can see myself out."

I slump back, weighted with disappointment. I don't want him to go and I wish I didn't feel this way.

"OK," I whisper.

Instead of leaving, Scott frowns at the pot of basil nearby.

"How about I come with you to the barbeque?" he blurts.

I freeze. "What?"

"You came to the wedding in Tokyo with me, maybe I could come to the barbeque and, I don't know, stop them from bombarding you with questions."

"You don't think if I turn up with yet another guy, it won't cause even more speculation?"

Scott shrugs. "Probably, but if we stick together, none of them would dare to ask anything in case they offend. Actually, we could have some fun with it."

"How?"

"I don't know. We could pretend we're engaged, or we could say we just met, or... I know – why don't we say we just met on a dating website and it's our first date?"

Smiling, I shake my head. "You're crazy."

Scott sits back down beside me and grasps both of my hands.

"Look, I wasn't going to say anything because I know the timing is way off, but there's something between us, Trish. I know you can feel it." He hesitates. "Or maybe that's just wishful thinking by me."

"Scott, I'm about to give birth to another man's baby."

"I know, I know, but you aren't in a relationship – at least I don't think you are."

"I'm not."

"So, if we put the pregnancy aside for a second and focus on the fact I like you and would love to spend more time with you…"

I jerk my hands away and lean back.

Scott sighs. "I went too far, didn't I?"

I take a deep breath in and let it out. Normally, I run a mile in awkward moments like this, but I don't want to keep blocking out my emotions. I'm tired of being the ball-breaker, take-no-prisoners, cope-on-my-own Trish.

"You're right, Scott. There is something between us. I like you and if circumstances were different—"

He leans forwards and his lips press onto mine, stopping me from speaking. I resist for barely a second before I'm kissing him back. My hand reaches behind his head, grips his hair and pulls him closer. He groans slightly and kisses me harder. Eventually, we pull back.

"You were saying?" Scott says.

I close my eyes. This can't be happening. I'm about to give birth. I can't get into a relationship – not now. I feel Scott's fingers brush my cheek and tuck a strand of hair behind my ear.

"Trish?" he says. "You OK?"

"Not really," I say, my eyes still closed. "This complicates things."

"How?"

I open my eyes and give him my best stink eye before dropping my gaze to my stomach. "It's pretty obvious, isn't it?"

"Look, I appreciate this is perhaps not the best time to be making a move on you…"

I bite my lip to stop myself from laughing. He's too damn perfect for his own good.

"All right, all right," says Scott. "Hassle me, why don't you."

"No, it's—"

I break off. A Braxton Hicks comes on so fast, I catch my breath. I was hoping after a constant run of them yesterday, I'd be off the hook.

"What's wrong?"

I want to say it's fine, but this contraction isn't like the others. It's far more intense and painful, and there's a strange sensation in my nether region: a weighted, tingling pressure, like my insides want to burst out of my vagina.

"Shit." I gasp.

Scott leaps to his feet. "What's going on, Trish?"

My eyes prick with tears. "N-Nothing," I stammer. "I just—"

Leaning forwards, I drop off my chair onto my knees and put my hands on the warm wooden boards of the deck. I pant through the pain.

Scott kneels beside me and rubs my back. "You're OK," he murmurs. "Breathe, Trish."

"I think I might be in labour," I hiss.

"What should I do?"

The contraction is beginning to ease. Slowly, I sit back on my haunches. "It's gone now."

I'm embarrassed he's seeing me like this. Any attraction he may have felt towards me will have been wiped out by the vision of me on my hands and knees panting like a dog.

Slowly, I get to my feet. "Would you mind leaving now, Scott?" I ask. "Something's come up."

Scott laughs softly. "See, that's why I think you're amazing."

I walk past him and into the kitchen. "I mean it," I call as I hear him following.

"I'll go as soon as someone else arrives, Trish. I'm not leaving you here on your own."

I pick up my phone and roll my eyes. "I'm calling my midwife now and I'm quite capable of managing this, Scott."

He crosses his arms and lifts his eyebrows. "Doesn't mean you have to," he states.

I call my midwife and she answers on the second ring. "Hi, Trish. Everything OK?"

"I'm fine, thanks. I think I could be in labour, though."

Leanne listens as I explain.

"It sounds like you may have been in labour for some time. Is there someone there with you?"

I glance at Scott. "Yes."

"OK, so if you could ask them to time your contractions – how far apart they are, how long they last. It helps to give me an idea how quickly you're progressing."

"All right."

"I'm with a patient now, but once I've finished, I'll pop by and see you."

"OK."

Hanging up, I'm about to call Emma, when another contraction causes me to double over, my hands on my knees. Scott rubs my back again.

"You need to time it," I gasp. "How long it is and how long between each contraction."

Scott pulls his phone out of his pocket and hits the timer.

Neither of us speak as the contraction builds in intensity, then fades. Scott leads me to a chair.

"What do you need, Trish? Who can I call?"

I reach for my phone, my hand shaking. This is it. I can't believe it. Oh, God, I'm not ready.

Scott eases my phone out of my shaking hand. "Trish, let me help. I'll call Lily, OK?"

I nod. Emma. Lily. Mags. I don't care which one. That's not true. I want them all here. They're my squad. My family. I can't do this without them.

Scott talks to Lily and his voice barely registers. Everything around me has faded. It's just me and my baby, held together by my trembling body.

A glass of water is placed in my hand. "Take a sip," Scott says. He assists as I lift the glass to my lips and let a trickle of water down my throat. "Lily's on her way. She's ringing the others, too."

"Too late to have second thoughts now," I say.

Scott drags a chair beside me, sits and clasps my hand.

"You've got this, Trish. Soon you'll be holding your baby in your arms."

"I've got to get the critter out first."

Scott doesn't respond, which is fair enough. The poor bugger's probably freaking out. I should tell him to go, but truth is, I don't want to be on my own. Not now.

"I don't have a girl's name yet," I murmur.

"What's your boy's name, if I'm allowed to know?"

"Felix."

"Nice."

"I should have a girl's name too, just in case."

"There's no rush. Maybe you need to look at the baby first and then the name will come to you."

"Maybe."

I scramble to my feet. I'm restless all of a sudden. Like I need to be doing something – vacuuming the house or tidying. I feel as keyed up as I used to before presenting to clients.

Scott watches me pace around the kitchen. "Ah, Trish, I'm sort of out of my depth here. What should I do?"

I stop to put my hands on my hips and glare at him. "How the hell should I know? This is new to me, too."

Rather than take offence at my snappiness he smiles.

"Good point. OK, well, we'll figure it out as we go."

"I need the bathroom," I mutter before racing down the hallway and slamming the bathroom door.

I'm so desperate to pee, I'm worried I'm going to wet my pants. Groaning, I pull up my dress (a black stretchy cotton number that I've been wearing almost continuously for the past month because it's so comfy) and with difficulty, manoeuvre my knickers down to my knees. I lower myself onto the toilet seat. As I let the urine dribble out, my baby's head presses heavily on my vagina. It's an alarming sensation to put it mildly. I quickly block the thought of what's to come. Having to share my body with another human being has been no picnic and I'm ready to get the baby out. I just wish there was another way.

I stagger to my feet, sort my clothing, flush the toilet and wash my hands. When I open the bathroom door, Scott is directly in front of me, his face pale and serious.

"Everything OK?" he asks.

I nod and smile in reassurance as the poor guy clearly needs it, but my smile converts to a grimace as another contraction hits.

"Bloody hell," I exclaim, putting my hand against the wall.

Scott knows without asking that I need to be on my hands and knees. He helps me down to the carpet, rubs my lower back and checks his phone.

"Six minutes since the last one," he says.

I'm trying to remember the breathing techniques Margot taught us at the antenatal class I went to with Mags, but for the life of me I can't recall a thing.

There's a pounding on my front door.

"Trish," calls Lily.

"It's unlocked," Scott yells.

The door slams open and Lily comes hurtling through.

"Fuck!" she says, running over and crouching beside me. She gently lifts my curtain of blonde hair – already damp with sweat – from my face and drapes it down my back. "I love you, Trish," she murmurs, "but I'm not prepared to watch a baby covered in bodily fluids exit your vagina and I'm confident Scott feels the same way, so you need to keep the little so-and-so inside till we get you to the hospital, OK?"

All I can do by way of reply is groan loudly, my fingernails clinging to the carpet.

Scott stops rubbing my back.

"Keep going," I shout, and his rub vigorously resumes.

Lily puts a hand over mine and squeezes. She doesn't stop squeezing until the contraction releases me and I slump sideways onto my hip.

"That was fun," I mutter, giving them both a small smile.

"Looked like it," mutters Lily.

She has the most terrified expression on her face I've ever seen.

"I need to stand."

They both help me to my feet and I'm about to suggest they both sit down and take a few deep breaths, when I hear a stampede of feet and Mags and Emma fly through the door.

"Trish," Mags exclaims, tears in her eyes. She throws her arms around me. "This is it! You're actually having a baby."

"What did you think was growing in her belly for the past few months?" asks Lily. "A bloody tapeworm?"

Scott snorts and covers his mouth. "Sorry."

Mags lets go of me and I look at Emma.

"You all right?" Emma asks softly.

I nod and swallow over the sudden lump in my throat.

She gives me a small smile, then kisses me on the cheek. "You got this," she whispers.

I take a deep breath and slowly let it out. "So," I say, glancing around at all the faces staring at me. "This is awkward."

Scott clears his throat. "I'll go," he says. "Since the cavalry has arrived."

He's read my mind. Now my friends are here, I need Scott gone before things deteriorate and I start leaking fluids or screaming or something worse I haven't even read about yet.

"Thanks," I say. "For everything."

"No problem." He fills Emma in on the time between contractions before giving me a quick peck on the cheek. "Good luck," he says before disappearing out of the door.

"Bye, Scott," calls Lily. "Thanks for calling me."

The second he's gone, three sets of eyes turn to me and raise their eyebrows in unison.

"What?"

Lily rolls her eyes. "Trish, as soon as you pop this sprog, we'll be demanding full details on Mr Dark and Dashing. You've clearly been keeping him on the down-low."

"What was he even doing here?" demands Mags. "Are you sleeping with him?"

"No!"

Mags slaps her hand to her chest. "Thank God! That would just be too weird."

"It wouldn't be that weird," says Emma. "Well, OK, maybe a bit."

"Hello," I shout. "In labour here." Already, the oncoming contraction is making me shake.

"Oh, shit. Sorry," says Lily. "Do you want to get back on the floor?"

I shake my head. "Mags," I hiss through clenched teeth. "What were those bloody breathing ex—" I'm physically incapable of finishing my sentence. Instead, I lean heavily against Mags and groan.

"Trish, honey, you're doing great," says Emma, patting my back lightly.

Too lightly. I wish Scott's firm hand were there instead. I stagger to my room, crawl onto the bed and curl up on my side.

Mags kneels beside my head. "OK, Trish, let's try one of those breathing exercises."

I nod and fix my eyes on her face.

"Breathe in deeply and exhale slowly, evenly in and out, in and out."

She demonstrates and I try to follow, but my breathing remains fast and shallow.

"I can't," I gasp.

Someone has removed my sandals and is rubbing the soles of my feet. I can't decide if I like it or if it's the most annoying thing in the world. The contraction eases and I allow my tense body to relax.

"Well done, Trish," says Emma. "Now, have you called the midwife?"

"Yes, she's coming soon."

"Good, then let's sort your bag for the hospital."

I point to my wardrobe. "It's in there."

Emma opens the wardrobe door and pulls out a small blue suitcase. "This it?"

I nod. "The car seat is in the hall," I mutter. "I should have put it in the car already."

Lily leaps to her feet. "I'm on it," she calls.

We know without speaking how relieved Lily is to have an excuse to escape the room.

Less than five seconds pass before Lily returns, her eyes wide and hysterical.

"The midwife's here," she says breathlessly. "I saw her pull up."

"Are you going to let her in or just stand there?" asks Mags.

"Oh, oh, yes." Lily dashes out again and I manage a small laugh.

"I think she's going to need a sedative," says Emma.

Leanne strides in with a big bag over her shoulder and I immediately feel better.

"Trish, how are you?" she asks, sitting next to me on the bed and instantly putting a couple of fingers on my wrist to feel my pulse.

"Fantastic," I mutter.

She pulls a stethoscope out of her bag. Emma and Mags stand still as statues as Leanne gently pulls up my dress and listens to the baby's heartbeat.

"Sounds good," she says, then she winks. "Ready for the next contraction?"

I immediately feel tightening of my uterus. How did she know?

"Not really," I bleat.

"As this one builds, I want you to focus on relaxing your other muscles, Trish. Start at the top and work your way down: your forehead, your cheeks, your jaw, your neck, your shoulders, your legs. Accept that your uterus is giving you hell and allow it space by relaxing everything else as best you can."

I close my eyes and allow the pain in my stomach to build. I don't try to fight it. Instead, I accept this is what my body is meant to do. I do as Leanne suggests and concentrate on getting other parts of my body to relax. By the time I've got to my legs, the contraction has passed.

"OK, I'm going to check your cervix and see how dilated you are before the next contraction."

"We'll wait outside," Emma says, pulling Mags out of the door.

With Leanne's help, I remove my underwear, lie on my back and bend my knees, my feet on the mattress. I stare at the ceiling and hold my breath as she shoves her fingers inside me while simultaneously squeezing the life out of my lower pelvic region. It's not the nicest experience, but at least she's quick about it.

Leanne sits up and removes her glove. "You're seven centimetres and the baby is fully engaged, Trish. We need to get you to the hospital now unless you want a home birth."

I shake my head vigorously. "No way."

"OK, then. Let's go." Leanne helps me back into my clothes then opens the door to inform my friends of the situation.

Emma comes in with a cold wet flannel and wipes my face – it's the best face wipe in the history of face wipes.

"Wow, Trish," she gushes. "Seven centimetres is impressive."

She makes it sound like I got an A in an exam.

"Thanks."

"Right, let's get Trish to the car before the next contraction," states Leanne.

I'm helped off the bed and into the front passenger seat of my car. Lily takes the wheel, and Emma and Mags squeeze into the back next to the empty baby seat.

"See you on the ward," says Leanne through my open window.

My hands shake as I stretch the seat belt around my large belly. "Go fast, Lils," I demand, one hand on the dash, the other resting on my baby.

My friend needs little encouragement. At one point, as Lily runs an orange light and comes within inches of being hit by a van, Mags screams. I don't care. If anything, I wish Lily would go faster. My eyes are glued to the road ahead and I'm willing my body to hold on.

We screech into the drop-off zone at the hospital in record time and Emma has leapt out and is opening my door as the next contraction hits. I swear, and groan, and probably terrify a few people walking past on the footpath, but I honestly don't give a shit. I don't give a shit about anything except getting this baby out.

While Lily goes to park, Mags takes my arm, Emma grabs my suitcase, and I try not to waddle as we go through the main entrance and enter the lift along with a couple of men in suits, a nurse in scrubs and a patient with a tube up his nose. They all shuffle as far away from me as possible as we ride the lift to the delivery suite. Not that I blame them. I imagine I don't have the friendliest of expressions on my face right now.

Thankfully, we're welcomed onto the ward by a smiling nurse, and I've been shown to a room and changed into the ugly hospital-issue gown before another contraction hits. It feels different to the others and rather than groaning, I find myself growling deeply, like a dog under attack.

Leanne appears at my side. "Sounds like you're getting ready to push, Trish, but you need to wait a little longer yet."

"I want pain relief," I gasp. "Lots of it."

Leanne smiles calmly. "I'm afraid it's too late for an epidural, Trish."

I hope she can read from my face how much I hate her right now.

Emma comes around the other side of the bed and starts to stroke my head. "Trish, hang in there. You're so strong. Just keep going a little longer."

My eyes start to water. "I can't, Em." I choke. "I can't do this."

Mags grips my hand. "Yes, you can, Trish. You can do bloody anything."

The contraction goes on and on. Just when I think it's easing off, it comes back with more intensity. My body is shaking and sweating and all I want to do is...

"I need to push," I yell. "Now."

The midwife is poking between my legs. She lifts her head to meet my gaze and nods.

"OK, Trish, you're fully dilated. When I say, start to push."

Emma is wiping my face with a cold cloth and Mags is squeezing my hand, but not as much as I'm crushing hers.

With a guttural noise I can't quite believe is coming from me, I begin to push. There's a sharp burning sensation down below. It's agonizing, but I don't care. I don't care how much pain I'm in – I need to get this baby out.

"OK, Trish," says Leanne. "I can see your baby's head. You're doing so well. Get ready to push again. One, two, three... push," Leanne says.

I growl. Surely this is it – the baby will slip out the way it does on TV. But it doesn't. I push and I push for what feels like hours, but I don't make any progress.

"It's not coming out," I moan. "I can't do this."

Emma frowns then dashes from the room. Seconds later she's back with Lily.

"All right, Trish." Lily stabs a finger in my direction, her face ghostly pale. "This is the last place I want to be because a) you're trying to push a baby out of your vag, and b) I can't handle seeing my friend in pain, so here's what we're going to do. We're going to get this over with *right now*."

The fire and energy in Lily's voice is infectious. I feel pumped and about as pissed off as she looks.

"OK!" I yell.

"All right." Lily perches on the bed beside me. "All I've got to go on is those shit movies where the woman giving birth screams her head off, so let's do it. Let's all scream so loud, the nurses out there sipping their coffee will hit the panic button."

I nod. Emma leans in and wipes the sweat off my face, and Mags grips my hand.

"Ready, girls," Lily says loudly. She looks at me and winks. "One, two, three…"

I take a deep breath, glare at my belly and push. Lily starts to scream, followed by Emma, Mags and then me. At first, it's a polite scream. But once I start, it feels so good, I get louder and harsher. Lily, Emma and Mags match my volume and my ears reverberate with the noise. The sound is a source of power, filling me with strength. For a few seconds, my vision is lost to the pain as I feel my baby move.

"The head's out, Trish," Leanne yells. "One last push!"

I clamp my mouth closed and my friends do the same. The sudden silence is eerie and irreverent. I close my eyes, give one more push and my baby is born. I can see its perfect, wrinkled body in Leanne's arms.

"Congratulations, Trish. You have a baby girl," she says, lifting the baby closer towards me. "Would you like to cut the umbilical cord?"

I shake my head and watch as the midwife does the honours. Tears fill my eyes as my little girl is placed on my chest. I cup her bottom and tiny head. Her eyes are wide open and she doesn't make a sound. She simply stares calmly up at me, as if to say "Hi, Mum. I know who you are and I'm confident you'll take great care of me." I stare back, mesmerized and immediately afraid. I should say something or smile, but I can't.

"Trish," Lily whispers.

I glance up at my friend and her face is red and blotchy, her cheeks wet with tears.

"She's amazing," Lily murmurs. "Just like her mum."

My heart beats loud and fast. I can't let them see how terrified I am. I have to act normal. I've just had a baby – I'm supposed to be overcome with joy. I focus on the tiny, curled fingers of my daughter. Her weird fingernails are like pieces of cling film – too thin and fragile to be called nails. I will myself to look back at the face of my baby: to meet her unsettling gaze again. But when I eventually do, her eyes are closed.

She probably feels let down by her mother already.

As I have done so often in my life, I force myself to smile, lift my head and look around the room. My friends grin back.

"Welcome to motherhood," says Emma.

"Does she have a name?" asks Mags.

Scott's suggestion that I'd take one look at the baby and know what to call her was incorrect. I haven't got a clue. This baby is more a stranger to me now than when it was growing inside me.

"No. Not yet."

"Right." Leanne starts to lift the baby off me. "I'm going to weigh her and give her a quick look over, then you can have her back. Do you have a blanket you'd like me to wrap her in?"

Nodding, I point to my bag. Emma opens it and pulls out the blanket Scott knitted. I'm not sure how it got in there.

"No," I say firmly. "Not that one."

She rummages around and pulls out another fluffy cotton one covered in brown bunny rabbits. "This?" she asks.

Biting my lip, I nod.

A few minutes later, Leanne hands my baby to Lily.

"If you could hold her, I'll help Trish deliver the placenta."

Lily's eyes widen in panic for a second, then soften. Her entire body seems to relax and mould to the shape in her arms.

"Watch out, Darryl," murmurs Mags.

Lily ignores her, which is the worst response I could have asked for. Even Lily, who goes out of her way to avoid the merest whisper of cluckiness, has the mother gene. The gene I suspect I didn't inherit because my mother didn't have it to pass down. Oh, God, what have I done?

Leanne is frowning at me.

Once again, I force myself to smile. "What happens now?"

She considers me for a second, her face serious. "Actually, I was going to suggest your friends leave us to the next bit.

You may not want them around while we get the placenta out. Also, you have a small tear, so I'll need to get the registrar to stitch you up."

"Oh, we can stay," says Emma.

"No," I say, already wishing my friends were out of the room. "You guys go. I'd rather there wasn't an audience."

"You sure?" asks Mags.

"Absolutely."

Lily comes over and leans down to give me the baby.

"Do you think you could keep holding her?" I mutter. "Just till I'm sorted here."

There's a long moment of uncomfortable silence and I know everyone is judging me. What mother wants her child taken away from her seconds after birth?

"Good idea," announces Leanne. "Now, Trish, delivering the placenta is like delivering a baby, only less intense. You still need to push it out."

Is she serious? No one told me about this part.

"I think that's my cue to leave," says Lily, cuddling the baby to her chest. "You sure I should take her?"

I nod without looking at anyone and my three friends leave the room, Lily last of all. There's a sharp twinge in my chest as the door closes behind them.

"Right, Trish, I'm going to press on your uterus while you push out the placenta. Ready?"

"Ready," I say flatly.

Less than half an hour later, I have four stitches in the increasingly painful, swollen area between my legs and I'm finally able to cover up with a sheet. Leanne has popped out to let my friends know I'm doing fine and to check on the baby again, leaving me alone at last.

Resting my head against the pillow, I turn to look out of the window. The maternity ward is on the sixth floor and although it's getting dark, I can just make out the sea in the distance. I'd love to go to the beach right now. Float in the water on my back. Feel weightless and free.

Leanne returns and pulls up a chair beside my head. She leans back and crosses her arms.

"How are you feeling?" she asks.

I drag my eyes away from the window and look at my hands clasped together on top of the sheet. "Wrung out."

"Totally understandable. In fact, new mothers go through all sorts of crazy emotions after they give birth."

I'm silent, too scared to look at her.

"Trish, not enough people talk about the fact that the birthing process can be brutal. Some women go into a form of shock. They beat themselves up because they think they should be full of love for their new baby and they're not, because they're still trying to process what they've been through."

I look at Leanne now. She sits so calmly and her expression tells me that nothing I say could disappoint or surprise her. It's like she understands everything I'm going through and it's OK.

"Thanks," I whisper.

"I want you to focus on getting through the next few hours, Trish, that's all. Don't think about the future or worry if you're getting it right or wrong."

I nod.

"Right, let's get you into that shower."

I slowly sit up and swing my legs to the side, wincing as my tender parts press into the mattress. Leanne helps me to stand and I shuffle towards the bathroom. There's a high-pitched newborn's cry coming from outside my room. What if it's my baby crying out for me?

"She'll wait for you, Trish. She just wants her first feed." Leanne gives a wry grimace. "Breastfeeding can be a challenge in itself, so have your shower and take a second to recover. You'll only be a few minutes." Striding into the bathroom, Leanne turns on the shower and hands me a towel. "I thought you might like to be on your own for this. Call out if you need any help." She walks out, leaving the door ajar.

I avoid looking in the mirror and peel off my gown. Stepping into the shower, the hot water washes over my face and body and I start to feel a glimmer of light, of hope in my chest. Reaching for the soap, I look down at my swollen belly. You'd be mistaken for thinking a baby was still in there. But there isn't, because I actually bloody gave birth. And I have a daughter. A beautiful, healthy little girl.

I quickly lather soap over my body and rinse it off, desperate to see my baby and hold her in my arms.

Before long, I'm lying in bed wearing my favourite pyjamas while an infant with an impressive head of dark hair (where on earth did that come from?) suckles at my breast. It took a few attempts to get her mouth to latch on to my nipple, but now she's on, I don't think she's going to let go in a hurry.

Emma and Lily have left and the midwife is sorting out some paperwork at the nurse's station. Mags is hovering by the window, watching over us both like a sheepdog. Any time I so much as move, she jerks and comes running. Truth is, I'd like her to go home so I can get some rest and spend some time alone getting to know my daughter.

"Honestly, Mags, you should go, too. As soon as this little one falls asleep, I'll be trying to do the same."

"You sure?"

"Absolutely."

"It doesn't feel right leaving you alone."

"I won't be. I can push that button anytime I need help."

"You know what I mean."

"Actually, Mags, I've just realized I'm not going to be alone for a long time." I glance down at my baby. "I've got this one to keep me company."

Mags strokes the top of the baby's head. "True."

Suddenly, I know what I'm going to call my daughter. Gazing at her tiny features and plump rosebud lips, I can't believe how right the name is – as if it were made for her.

"Rose," I murmur.

"Sorry?" says Mags.

"Her name is Rose," I say, smiling.

"That's perfect. I know how much you love roses."

"Actually, I'm naming her after my grandmother. Grammy Rose."

"Wow, you've never mentioned her before. Were you close?"

"Yes," I say quietly. "We were."

Rose flutters her eyes open briefly before she gently releases my nipple and drops off to sleep.

37

I'm discharged home the following morning and the next few days are a blur of feeding Rose for hours on end, between snatching moments to eat and sleep. Lily comes over every morning before work either to hold Rose or watch her sleep while I have a long shower – the only time in the day when I can focus solely on myself. Then the midwife pops in to check on us both mid-morning. Mags brings me something for lunch (usually from Emma's café) and Emma tries to come over in the evening after both of her boys are in bed; though, understandably, she sometimes doesn't make it out of the door.

Tomorrow, Elliot is coming to meet his daughter. What if he takes one look at Rose and decides he wants to exert his rights as the father and demand some sort of custody? Rationally, I know my baby can't be taken from me, especially as she's almost permanently attached to my breast, but I still worry.

"Do you want me to be here?" asks Mags. "When Elliot comes over."

I shake my head. "No, I'm sure it'll be fine."

"You don't look sure."

I hear Rose's cry and take a quick sip of my tea. I only put her down in her bassinet ten minutes ago.

Mags leaps to her feet. "I'll get her," she says, practically running from the kitchen.

Smiling, I take a large bite of chocolate brownie. Breastfeeding is hungry work.

"How was your visit from Will?" Mags asks, walking back in with Rose nestled in her arms.

Rose looks like she can't decide if she wants to wake up or not and I reckon I've got a few more minutes before she demands another go at the milk machine.

"Great. Tilly came, too. She was so excited to hold her little cousin."

"I bet."

I open my mouth to say more but close it again. I was about to mention a part of my conversation with Will I'm doing my best to forget. Apparently, Mum's been ringing him every few days since Dad's funeral asking if she can come and visit me. Mum hasn't made any attempt to see me since I left home. Also, why go through Will? She could have asked for my phone number and called me. Why the sudden interest now? It's not like Mum's going to be a doting grandmother – or doting mother, for that matter.

"Phoebe and I broke up," says Mags, smiling goofily at Rose as she gently rocks her.

"Oh no, I'm sorry."

Mags shrugs. "It's OK. If I'm honest, we didn't actually get on that well once I got over the infatuated stage."

"She seemed to make you happy."

Mags frowns. "Actually, I think it was finally being myself that made me happy. Now that I've embraced the fact I'm gay, and my friends and family are being so supportive, I feel like I'm comfortable being in my own skin at last. I know who I am, if that makes sense."

"Totally."

We smile at each other.

"Love you," I say, blowing my friend a kiss.

Rose has her eyes closed, but she's started to do that thing with her lips where she's searching for milk. I wolf down the rest of my brownie, knowing I'm on borrowed time.

"Has Scott been to visit?" Mags asks in a tone she's trying to make sound casual and we both know is anything but.

"No. Why?"

"Just thought he might have been. You never did tell us what was going on there."

"Because there's nothing to tell. He's a friend, Mags."

Mags snorts. "Trish, that's a load of bollocks and we both know it."

Rose has her eyes open now and her face is screwed up ready to cry. Mags hurriedly hands her to me and I get Rose latched on, wincing as she begins to suck at my painful nipples.

"Can I get you anything?" Mags asks, consternation on her face.

"A new body," I mutter, and for a moment the darkness I felt last night returns.

I push it away, as if I'm forcing a large, heavy object from the room. I can't afford to have one of those episodes. Not now.

*

But after Mags leaves, the heaviness descends again. It sits like a weight in my chest and I have to muster all the energy I have to change Rose's nappy and coax her back to sleep. The second I lay her in her bassinet, I crawl into bed, pull the covers over my head and let the blackness return.

The night is relentless. Rose must pick up on my mood, because she won't settle. Even when I try to breastfeed her, she wriggles in distress. She'll only take a couple of sucks before she cries and arches her back. Even once I finally manage to rock her to sleep, she only sleeps fitfully for about twenty minutes before she's awake and crying again. I find myself wanting to scream at her, throw her onto the bed and walk away. I hate myself. Every single part of me.

At 6 a.m., as the sky finally lightens into day, I carry Rose outside and pace slowly round and around my garden. Rose finally starts to relax in my arms and I'm so afraid she'll cry again, that I begin to talk. Surely, if I fill the silence with noise, she won't be able to.

I talk about the plants in the garden. I tell Rose about the jasmine growing along the fence and how badly it needs a trim. I tell her about the hibiscus and how much it likes the warm, sunny corner, and the Japanese maple I planted because I love the way the leaves change colour with the seasons. I tell her the names of all the varieties of roses I have growing and which ones have the best scent. I talk for more than an hour until I'm hoarse. Then I lie on the grass, still damp with morning dew, curl up on my side, with Rose pressed to my chest, and close my eyes.

Lily finds me there half an hour later. I wake to her gently shaking my shoulder and whispering my name. Blinking my eyes open, I stare at her face, inches from mine.

"Bad night?" she asks softly.

I can only nod, tears in my eyes. I want to tell her about the blackness hovering around the edges of my vision. The weight I'm carrying deep inside that I'm afraid is going to spread until I can't stand up anymore. But how do I explain?

Carefully, Lily extracts the deeply asleep infant from my arms.

"I'm going to put her in her bassinet and come straight back," she mutters.

I roll onto my back and look up at the fat white clouds. My mind is blank. Empty.

Lily returns and helps me to my feet. She supports me like an old lady as I stumble into the house. After pressing me into a kitchen chair, she pours me a glass of water. I try to raise it to my lips, but my hands are shaking. Without speaking, Lily holds the glass for me and I drink.

"You look like complete shit," she states, grabbing a banana out of the fruit bowl and peeling it.

She breaks off a chunk and holds it in front of my mouth with a stern expression as if she's trying to feed a fussy toddler. I open, chew and swallow, without tasting a thing.

Lily pulls out her phone. "I'm calling in reinforcements."

The rest of the day is colourless. People come and go, giving me strange looks I don't understand. My friends, the midwife, Will. When Elliot arrives and I watch the father of my child holding his baby for the first time, it brings nothing but calm resignation. When he leaves without the baby in his arms, I experience a fleeting moment of relief, nothing more. I have no idea what he said to me, or what I said back. I have no idea what anyone is saying to me. I'm on an island and no one can reach me. Not even my own daughter. One minute she's latched on to me, the next she's gone. Either way, nothing inside me alters.

Then I'm being led to a car and somehow I'm back in hospital again. A nurse puts a pill into my hand, tells me to swallow. I do as she says, lie on my back and stare up at nothing. Finally, I sleep.

I wake in agony. My breasts are rock-hard and painfully full of milk. In a panic, I sit up and find Rose asleep in a cot beside me.

"I gave her some of mine," murmurs Emma. "I hope that's OK."

She's curled up under a blanket on the puffy chair beside the window. It's dark outside.

"Some what?" I ask.

Emma studies me for a few seconds. "Milk," she says finally. "I gave her some of my milk. They tried her on a bottle, but she wasn't having a bar of it."

I blink a few times, trying to understand. "You breastfed my baby?" I say uncertainly.

"Yes."

I stare at Emma, wondering how to make sense of what she said, where I am.

"Why?" I say at last. "Why didn't you wake me?"

Emma sits forwards and now her face is no longer in shadow, I can see the tears dribbling down her cheeks.

"The doctor's recommended you sleep as long as possible.

They said…" She takes a deep, shaky breath. "They said you were too fragile to be woken."

I frown. "Em, that's ridiculous. What am I even doing here?"

She wipes her cheeks and comes to sit on the edge of the bed. "Leanne thinks you may have post-natal depression. Apparently, it's more common in people who already suffer from a depressive disorder."

"I'm not depressed," I state. "I just have down days sometimes."

"Trish, yesterday wasn't just a down day, and you know it."

I glance back at Rose, willing her to wake. My breasts are leaking just thinking about feeding her. I press my palm against the edge of my breast, hoping it'll somehow ease the pressure.

"God, my boobs hurt."

Emma nods. "I'll get the nurse so you can express." She hurries from the room.

I stare at Rose and have this strange sensation she's not my baby. There's been a mistake. A mix-up. This baby looks like Rose but she isn't – she's an imposter.

Emma returns with a nurse, who drags behind her a contraption on squeaking wheels. She shows me how it works and before long, I'm being milked by a machine making a loud humming sound. I'm surprised the noise doesn't wake Rose, but she's oblivious. The relief as my breasts start to deflate is indescribably good.

"That should be enough," says the nurse, who introduced herself as Jodi. "We want to leave plenty for little Rosie here."

My eyes widen. Why would she do that? Change my baby's name. It's Rose. No one has called her Rosie and if I have my way, no one ever will.

"Rose," I say firmly. "Not Rosie."

The nurse apologizes, though she looks in no way sorry, before dragging the breast pump machine behind her out of the room.

Emma is looking at me funny. It's as if she's nervous, afraid of me even.

"Your mum's here," she blurts.

"What?"

"She's waiting in the corridor. Your brother called her."

"Why?"

"He was worried about you."

"Why would he call Mum?"

Emma perches on the bed and squeezes my arm. "I think you should talk to her, Trish. Please."

"I don't want to see her. I've got enough to deal with."

"I've just spent an hour talking with her and I think you should hear what she has to say."

"I don't even know why she bothered coming. She doesn't care about me, Em. She never has."

"I don't know what she was like as a mum, Trish, because you never talked about it, but I still think you should listen to her. And for the record, I think she does care, very much."

Frowning, I stare at Rose. I still feel strangely disconnected from her. Disconnected from Emma, too. It's like I'm going through the motions of being in this room, without fully being here.

"OK," I whisper.

"Thanks." Emma squeezes my hand. "I'll go and get her."

I watch Emma leave then stare out of the window, my mind blank.

"Hello, Patricia."

I startle, hearing Mum call me by my full name.

"Hi," I mutter. "Long time no see."

Ignoring my comment, Mum shuffles closer. Her hair used to be the same blonde as mine. Now, it's mostly grey and it's grown out past her shoulders. Dad hated it whenever Mum's hair got too long. He thought it made her look flighty.

"Congratulations," Mum says, standing next to Rose's cot and gazing down at her. "She's beautiful."

I stay silent.

Sighing, Mum steps closer again. For a second I think she's going to lean down and give me a hug or something equally as ridiculous, but she crosses her arms instead.

"I've been sick for many years, Trish. Since before you were born, though I had no idea until recently what was wrong with me."

I roll my eyes. "Sick with what?"

Mum has her gaze fixed on the floor. "Depression. Bipolar tendencies. Anxiety. Not the types of condition your father would have approved of."

I scoff. "Is that your way of excusing yourself from the fact you were a useless mother?"

Mum slowly looks up at me and I wish I could take back my words.

"I was sick, Trish. I still am, though medication and counselling are helping. And it's not an excuse. I should have been stronger for you and the boys. I should have been a better mother. I have so much regret and guilt I can hardly get myself out of bed in the morning."

Rose is waking up. She's jerking her arms about and her eyelids are fluttering.

"I'm not like you," I say firmly. "If that's what you're implying. I'm not depressed and I'm definitely not checking out on my responsibilities."

"I agree. You're not like me. You're a million times better in every way. What you've done with your life, honestly, it's staggering, Patricia. You've had a successful career, travelled the world, bought your own house. You have wonderful friends and now a gorgeous baby. You're so much stronger than me. You always have been."

"I became independent at a young age," I say sarcastically.

"Yes. You did." Suddenly, Mum uncrosses her arms and grabs my hand. "Why are you in hospital?"

"Excuse me?" I try to pull my hand away, but her grip is vice-like.

"Tell me why you're here. People don't end up in hospital for no reason."

Glaring, I yank my hand free. How dare she interrogate me like this.

"I don't know," I snap.

"You're an intelligent woman, Trish. I think you know but you don't want to say it out loud."

"Mum, you haven't seen me in years. How can you even presume to know anything about me?"

"I know you're strong, determined, and that you hide your emotions for fear of being thought of as weak. Weak like me."

I shake my head and clench my jaw. I will *not* cry in front of this person. I won't.

Rose begins to whimper and I lurch out of bed, shove past Mum and pick up my baby. Pretending my mother is no longer in the room, I unhook my maternity bra and press Rose to my breast. I stroke her head as I watch her drink.

"Your Grammy Rose, she tried to help me," says Mum. "Several times she arranged for me to see her doctor so I could explain how hard I was finding everything, but I couldn't do it. I couldn't talk because I was scared and embarrassed. I didn't want anyone, even a doctor, to see how sad and pathetic I was."

I act as if I haven't heard a word Mum's said.

"When I ended up in hospital after what your father called my 'breakdown', you went to stay with your gran, remember?"

I give a fraction of a nod. As if I'd ever forget the one time in my childhood when I felt truly happy and safe.

"She loved having you live with her. She asked if you could stay longer, but your father wanted you home. He…" Mum takes a deep, shuddering breath. "He wanted you home to take care for me, your brothers, the household. But you were still a child. It wasn't fair, Trish. I should have insisted you stay with your grandmother, who loved you and cared for you the way you deserved."

Rose is a watery blur as I blink over and over, willing myself to hold it together. My throat is too sore to speak, not that I have anything to say.

"Emma tells me you named Rose after her. She'd have

loved that, Trish. I... I wish I hadn't... I wish she'd been in our lives more."

I refuse to react to Mum's anguished voice.

She perches on the bed and reaches up to stroke my hair back off my face gently.

"Trish, honey, why are you here?"

My tears can't be contained as they slip down my cheeks. "Because it's hard to keep fighting it," I say with a choke.

Mum pulls my head onto her shoulder and begins to cry. "I'm sorry," she gasps. "I'm so endlessly sorry I haven't been there for you. But I can help, Trish, if you'll let me."

"I'm n-not depressed," I stammer. "I refuse to be."

Mum rubs my back in small circular motions, the way I suddenly recall her doing when I was five years old and lying in bed feeling miserable after having had my tonsils removed. I'd completely forgotten about that moment until now.

"Whatever this is you're feeling right now," Mum says, "you need to be vulnerable and brave enough to talk about it. You can't keep fighting it on your own. Especially now, when you have a daughter who needs you."

"*I* needed you," I whisper into Mum's shoulder.

Her familiar scent is comforting and unsettling in equal measure. It's another part of my mother I had no idea was locked away inside me.

"As much as I wish I could, I can't change what happened, but you can speak to the right people, get treatment, be there for Rose the way I wasn't for you."

Sniffing, I wipe my face with my arm. Rose has fallen asleep with her lips still holding tightly to my nipple. Her tiny fist grips a strand of my hair and she's frowning as if to say she's holding on to me no matter what.

A streak of sunlight is cutting across the bed, turning her little bare feet a bright golden yellow.

"OK," I murmur, giving Mum a shaky smile. "I'll try."

38

The next day, Lily takes me home. There's a bunch of flowers on the table from Elliot with a note saying he'll come and see me soon, and a lasagne in the fridge from Emma. Mags has cleaned the house, emptied the rubbish and made up the spare bed in my office. I've agreed to let Mum come and stay for a few days, and I can't decide if I'm stark raving mad or excited. I'm definitely nervous.

"Thanks, Lil," I say, transferring a sleeping Rose from her car seat to the bassinet. "I'll see you tonight."

She's going back to work, then coming over later to help me eat the lasagne, but also because I may have begged her to be here so I don't have to be on my own with Mum all evening.

Once Lily leaves, I step out into my garden, place the baby monitor on the porch step, then stretch my arms up and back, trying to release the tension in my shoulders. I retrieve my secateurs and straw hat from the small shed, and slowly start to deadhead my roses, the sun warm and reassuring on my back. I don't want to get ahead of myself, but colours appear brighter today and my head feels clearer.

I'm so absorbed I don't hear Will until he's standing right beside me.

"Jesus," I exclaim, my heart leaping from my chest. "You scared the hell out of me."

"Sorry," he says quickly. "I knocked and knocked, then I came round the side of the house to see if you were out here. Stunning day, isn't it?"

He gives me a quick hug – something he does every time he sees me now as if he's making up for lost time. Not that I mind.

"Were you stopping in to check up on me?" I smile to let him know I'm not offended.

Will grins. "Actually, yes and no. I found out some exciting news and wanted to share it with you, plus I wanted to check how you were doing."

"Well as you can see, I'm fine."

Will raises his eyebrows. "You're not just putting on the Trish bravado, then?"

Maybe I had fewer people fooled than I thought. "No, I'm not."

"Good. So can I tell you my big news?"

"Of course."

We sit down side by side on the bottom porch step.

"You know how I ended up being taken on full-time by that landscaping company I was doing contract work for?"

I nod, remembering how relieved Will was to be offered a more stable income.

"Well, I'm buying the business."

"What?"

"The guy who's been running the business wants to

move South to be closer to his wife's parents now they're expecting a second baby. He's selling. To me." Will puffs out his chest proudly.

"That's fantastic." I throw my arms around him. "I'm very happy for you, Will."

"Thanks. No more clean and clear for me. Now, I'll be in charge of the fun stuff, like design and maintenance. Actually, I wondered if maybe you might be interested in helping me out?"

"Me?"

"I haven't a clue what's involved in running a business. You're the brains in that department. Plus, I expect you know more about plants than me. Maybe you'd consider... I don't know... joining me?"

"How do you mean?"

"Well, we could be business partners – or not," he says quickly. "I'm not asking because I need you to be involved financially or anything. I'd just... well, I thought it might be something you could be interested in, but there's no pressure and I wouldn't be taking over for a few months yet." His cheeks are flushed and he shuffles his feet, clearly embarrassed.

"Will." I put a hand on his shoulder. "Congratulations. It's wonderful news. And thank you for asking me to be involved. Can I have some time to think about it?"

"Of course."

A faint cry comes from the baby monitor.

"I'd better get Rose," I say, hurrying into the house. "Stay for a cuppa?"

"Sure," says Will, following me inside. "I'll put the kettle on."

*

Mum arrives with a large suitcase shortly after Will leaves. I show her to her room and try to act relaxed, even though we're both nervous as hell.

"Sorry it's a little cramped," I say, holding Rose on one shoulder and patting her back, waiting for her post-feed burp.

"It's perfectly fine," says Mum, avoiding my eye.

"OK, well, I'll leave you to settle in."

"I thought I'd go to the supermarket for a few things."

I stop in the hallway and take a deep breath. This is going to be harder than I thought.

"Maybe you could write me a list of things you need," says Mum, poking her head out of her room.

I focus on keeping my voice relaxed. "I was going to go in the morning."

"Well, now I can save you the trouble."

This does not bode well. I warned Mum before she moved in that I wouldn't cope with her trying to do things for me.

"You're moving in as backup," I'd explained. "Temporary backup."

"Trish," Mum says, reading my face. "I'd like to get a few things for myself. I'm going to the supermarket anyway, so if there are certain items you'd like me to get, I can. That's all."

Maybe I'm overreacting. I've always been in charge of every part of my life. I've had to be. And I'm not ready to relinquish that control, especially to Mum. She's let me down so many times, I'm not about to allow her back in that easily.

"I'm going in the morning anyway," I say firmly. "It'll be my first outing with Rose."

Mum looks like she's about to argue but changes her mind. "OK." She shrugs. "But I was hoping I might cook tonight, if that's all right with you?"

"Emma made a lasagne, remember? Lily's joining us."

"Oh, right, I'd forgotten."

Ignoring her crestfallen face, I head into Rose's room to change her nappy.

Once Mum leaves for the supermarket and I've got Rose down for a sleep, I can't resist the patch of sun on my bed. It's beckoning me to lie down. I decide to rest, just for a few minutes before I put a load of washing on. Within seconds, I feel myself drifting off.

When I open my eyes, the first thing I see is Scott sitting in the feeding chair, knitting. His face is lowered and he's concentrating on his work, knitting needles clacking together. The wool is a deep burgundy red and it's coming from a flax bag at his feet. I lie still, watching.

His thick dark hair is up in a ponytail, as it was on the plane the first time we met. He's grown a short beard and it makes him look like he should be on the cover of some *National Geographic* magazine. A mountaineer or wildlife photographer. Instead, he's knitting – not exactly an extreme sport.

Scott pauses and glances over at me. When his dark eyes meet mine, I catch my breath.

"Hi," he says softly. "Your mum let me in. I hope it's OK. I didn't want to wake you."

"It's fine," I murmur. "I wondered when I was going to see you."

His eyes widen. "I wanted to come see you earlier, but I

figured you'd be busy." He glances towards Rose's bassinet. "She's incredible, by the way."

I slowly push myself up to a seated position. "She turned out all right, I suppose."

Scott laughs and I feel better than I have done in days.

"That's a nice blanket she's wrapped up in," he says lightly.

Now it's my turn to laugh. "Thanks. Some guy knitted it for me."

"A guy?" Scott looks horrified. "What a freak."

"Oh no, it's a surprisingly attractive trait in a male."

My cheeks flush as I realize I've gone too far. What the hell am I doing? This is not the time to flirt.

Scott puts his knitting down and leans forwards, his elbows resting on his knees. "Trish, you're surprisingly attractive when you blush."

Of course, that comment just makes me blush even more.

"So…" Scott leans back and clears his throat. "Your mother has moved in."

I raise my eyebrows. "Indeed."

"Interesting."

I shake my head. "Interesting doesn't even begin to describe it."

I then proceed to give Scott an abridged account of the past few days. When I mention my unexpected re-admission to hospital, his face turns sombre.

"I'm sorry you went through that," he says. "But I'm glad you're taking your mental health seriously. It's just as important as taking care of your physical health, though most people find it easier to go to the gym than talk to a psychiatrist."

I'd forgotten how earnest and unafraid Scott is when it comes to talking about the stuff most guys shy away from. But then, I'm fast understanding Scott isn't like most guys.

"Yeah, well, let's just say I'd rather go to the gym any day than talk about my emotions with some shrink."

Mum pokes her head in the door and gives me an awkward fake smile.

"Everything OK in here?" she says.

"Yes."

"I hope you don't mind me letting Scott in. He said he was a friend and since I'm new around here—"

"Mum, it's fine."

Mum looks at Scott and back to me. "That's good. I'll…" She glances at Rose and back to Scott. "I'll leave you to it, then."

The second she disappears, Scott leans forwards again.

"Trish, does she think I'm the dad?"

"What? No, of course not."

"Are you sure?"

I frown. Maybe Mum's a little behind on the genetic make-up of my child.

"Actually, I don't know. I've not really filled her in on the details."

"That might explain the evil stare just now. Either that or she's against men with ponytails."

"Men with ponytails who knit."

We both burst out laughing, which unfortunately gives Rose one hell of a fright and she lets out a cry of alarm. I leap out of bed and pick her up. She immediately settles in my arms and stares up at me with her knowing blue eyes.

Scott comes to stand beside me and leans in to look down at my daughter.

"You must just want to stare at her all day long," he whispers.

I nod, my heart racing. Where his shoulder presses against mine, my skin prickles.

"It's certainly an occupational hazard," I add.

Rose looks as if she's returning Scott's smile, but I know what's about to come.

"Get ready," I say

"What?"

Explosive noises erupt from Rose's bottom and the smell of newborn poo attacks my nostrils.

"Well, that's one way to say hello," says Scott, stepping back.

I carry Rose to the changing table and lay her down. "I understand if you want to leave the room for this. Pretty sure it's a leaker." Lifting her legs, I notice a yellow stain already seeping through her bodysuit.

Scott sits back on the nursing chair and reaches for his knitting. "I might just finish this row."

Shaking my head, I clean up the mess and change Rose into a completely new outfit, including the caramel cardigan Scott knitted.

I hold her out towards him. "Any chance you can hold her while I rinse her clothes?"

Scott puts his knitting aside and reaches for Rose without hesitation. "Thought you'd never ask," he says calmly.

Once again, the man surprises me and my stomach does a little somersault when he confidently props Rose on his knee, both his hands supporting her head, and starts to chat to my baby as if she's a friend he's bumped into on the street.

"Hello, Rose. You're looking particularly lovely today. And what have you been up to?"

Rose gurgles in response and I gather her soiled clothes and leave them to enjoy their conversation.

I make it as far as the laundry door before Mum appears.

"Oh, I'll sort those for you, Trish," she says, snatching the clothes from my arms. "It sounds like you're having a lovely time."

"Mum," I snap as she dumps the clothes in the bucket and turns on the tap. "I'm perfectly capable."

Mum spins around, tears in her eyes. "Trish, I…" She straightens and clears her throat. "I realize you're more than capable of washing these things, but I've just been listening to my daughter laugh for the first time in forever and selfishly, I want to keep hearing her laugh, so please, let me clean up baby poo."

Yet again, I wonder what possessed me to allow my recently estranged mother to move into my house. I'm torn between wanting to scream at her and give her a giant hug.

"OK," I say, choosing to do neither. "Thanks."

When I return to my room, Scott's humming a tune and Rose is staring at him, mesmerized. I know how she feels.

"Is that from the musical *Les Mis*?" I ask.

Scott grins sheepishly. "'Do You Hear the People Sing'. It's a classic. And before you ask – yes, I like musicals. I knit and I like musicals."

I whistle softly. "Wait till Lily hears."

Scott gets to his feet and tucks Rose confidently on his shoulder. She begins to snuffle and bob her head around. Hungry yet again.

"You look very much like you've done this baby thing before," I say. "Anything else I should know about you?"

"Only that I'm a sad sap. I didn't know what to do with myself once my wife left me, so I went to live with my extremely tolerant friend Chris in Melbourne. He and his partner had only recently had their first baby and I was part hindrance, part nanny, depending on the situation. After six weeks, they suggested I come back home and sort out my shit. A polite way of saying they'd had enough of me."

Rose is getting more and more frustrated with the lack of lactating breast in her immediate vicinity and Scott hands her over. I sit in the feeding chair and hesitate as I unhook my maternity bra. Sure, breastfeeding is a completely natural thing and I should be able to feed Rose in front of Scott, but...

"I've got something in the car for you," says Scott a little too cheerfully. "I'll go grab it."

He retrieves his knitting bag and shoots out of the room.

"Subtle, Scott," I say, smiling.

I've finished feeding Rose and am burping her on my knee when he eventually reappears.

"Did you get lost?" I smirk.

He smirks back. "I figured you didn't want an audience, so I sat in the car for a few minutes and knitted another couple of rows."

"What are you making, by the way?"

"A jumper for Chris' baby. The one in Melbourne. Well, he's not a baby anymore. He turned three last week."

Emma lets out some wind followed by a dribble of curdled milk. Without me asking, Scott strides to the changing table, pulls a muslin cloth off the pile on the bottom shelf and crouches to dab at the milk trickling down Rose's chin onto my hand.

"You're starting to freak me out," I say.

"Sorry?"

"You just... you don't act like most guys, which is a good thing, but also, kind of... strange."

Scott finishes dabbing and stands up. "I'm going to take that as a compliment, even though I'm not sure it's meant to be one."

I take the cloth from his hand, throw it over my shoulder and place Rose facing over the same shoulder, my hand on her bottom. I've received too many baby sicks on my clothes to count and I know Rose isn't done with bringing up milk yet.

"So, I put your present on the back porch," says Scott. "You can look at it later if you want."

"I can't believe you got something else, Scott. You've already been so generous." I get to my feet. "But I'm intrigued, so let's go see."

"It's not exactly original," he says, following me through the kitchen and out of the back door.

On the porch sits a black pot with a white bow tied around it containing a rose bush studded with delicate white buds.

"A rose for Rose," mutters Scott.

I swallow hard. "It's beautiful."

"The lady at the garden centre said it has an incredible scent and it's called 'Madame Hardy', which I liked because, well... because you're tough and well, hardy sounds pretty awful when I say it out loud."

Laughing, I lean over and kiss Scott on the cheek, his beard tickling my lips. "Thank you, Scott. I'm going to take it as a compliment."

"Phew."

Mum appears at the back door. "You have another visitor, Trish," she says nervously.

I wonder if she thinks I'm going to snap her head off again.

"Who is it?"

"Elliot someone."

Scott's eyes narrow. "Thought he wasn't on the scene."

"Not exactly." Rose is starting to grizzle and I shift her to a new position. "I'm still trying to figure out the role Elliot wants to play in all this."

Scott frowns and nods. "I should get out of the way."

"Scott—"

He holds up a hand. "Truth is, Trish, it's probably best I don't see the guy. Maybe I could come back tomorrow and plant the rose bush?"

"That would be great," I say, wishing Elliot hadn't shown up and Scott could stay.

Instead, I jiggle Rose in the hope she'll stop fussing, and watch him stride away.

"Hey, Trish," says Elliot, stepping outside. "Is that guy who just gave me a dirty look on his way out the new boyfriend?"

"What are you doing here?" I snap.

Rose is in full-blown grumpy mode now.

Elliot looks at his daughter like she's an alien with six heads. "Is she OK?"

My good mood is rapidly disappearing. "Would you like to hold her?" I ask, shoving Rose in his face. "You are the father, after all."

Startled, Elliot backs away. "I wouldn't even know where to start. Actually, I wanted to talk to you about... our situation."

"I told you, I don't expect you to be involved."

"I know, but I feel responsible and it would be weird just to disappear knowing I've got a daughter out there."

Mum suddenly appears and without a word, takes Rose out of my arms.

"I'll give her some time with her nappy off on the mat," Mum says. "She can have a good kick and see if that helps."

My mouth hangs open, but before I can argue, Mum's gone with Rose in her arms. I'll deal with her later, but for now...

"So, what are you suggesting we do, Elliot?" I say, crossing my arms.

"I have a girlfriend now – Saskia. We've... Well, I've been seeing her for a while and she's special, you know?"

"I'm happy for you."

Which is true. I'm glad he's moved on, that he won't attempt to try to rekindle something with me – not that there was a spark to begin with.

"The thing is," says Elliot, "Saskia was a little put out when I told her about Rose and I want to reassure her that she's the most important thing in my life. I want to..."

Elliot takes a deep breath and blows it out. "We've only been together a couple of months, but I want to ask her to marry me. Only before I do, I think we need to sort things out here with Rose."

He looks so young and earnest I want to laugh. I'm also slightly horrified this man-boy is the father of my child.

"Sounds sensible."

"I mean, let's be honest. I don't even know how to hold a baby and you and I, we never had a relationship, not a proper one, so I thought maybe I could be excused of father duties."

"Right. That's being very blunt."

"I'll visit from time t-to time," stammers Elliot, "and as she gets older, she might want to hang out with me or even come and stay, but I'd rather not be *involved*, if that makes sense. Apart from financially. I'll help out there of course."

"Sounds like a good plan to me."

"Really?"

"Absolutely."

Grinning, Elliot plants a wet kiss on my cheek. "You can always call me if you need something, OK?"

"I'm sure we'll be fine, but thanks."

Elliot looks at me fully for the first time since he arrived.

"Do you think it makes me a bad person?" he asks quietly.

I take some time to consider my answer. Does it make him a bad person for not wanting to stick around and be a dad to Rose?

"Some might feel that way, but I don't. My biggest fear since Rose was born was that you'd want to have some kind of ownership of her. I think we need to do what works for both of us."

Elliot nods. "Yeah. I told Mum and Dad about Rose and they freaked. They keep insisting I do the right thing, whatever that is. Apparently, I'm being irresponsible."

"If you ask me, you're taking responsibility by being open and honest. Like I said at the start, I'm not expecting anything from you. I want to do this parenting thing on my own. That way, I get to make all the decisions," I say, winking.

Elliot throws his arms around me. "That sounds more like the old Trish."

Smiling, we pull apart.

"All right, cool, so I'll maybe give you a call in a week or so, see how Rose is doing," says Elliot.

"Fine."

"Maybe I could bring Saskia round sometime, too."

I can hear Rose crying somewhere in the house and I need to go to her. It's such a powerful urge, I feel nauseous.

"Sure, Elliot." I skirt past him into the house. "I need to check on Rose. Are you OK to see yourself out?"

I don't wait for his reply as I hurry down the hall towards my daughter.

39

"I'm taking Rose in to work shortly," I state, keeping my back to Mum as I slice of a hunk of cheese. I'm addicted to cheese and apple at the moment. After banana on toast, it's the best combination ever. "They've been asking me to bring her in for ages."

That's not entirely true, although one of the girls did comment on a photo I put on Facebook asking when they'd get to meet her. And surprisingly I received an email from Tash a few weeks ago suggesting I pop in for a visit. I suspect she wants to check I'll be coming back to work.

The main reason I've decided to go in to work is to get away. Mum has only been living here for three days and I'm already looking for an excuse to leave the house. She's not doing or saying things wrong as such – if anything, she's trying too hard. But I'm not dealing with her being in my life and she knows it.

"That's lovely," Mum says neutrally. "I'll do a vac while you're out."

"You don't need to."

Mum presses her lips together. I know I sound harsh, but I can't help it. I slice through my apple, the knife banging hard on the chopping board.

"Trish," Mum says. "I don't think this is working out."

Ignoring her, I press a piece of apple and cheese together and take a big bite.

"I was asking too much," continues Mum. "I can't expect you to welcome me with open arms after everything I've put you through."

Swallowing, I look her square in the face. "I didn't think it would be so difficult."

Mum nods. "I know."

I want to say more. I want to tell Mum I'm angry with her. That she has no right to hold my daughter in her arms and act like a doting grandmother. I also want to tell her that every night I pinch myself because I'd given up on having a parent who cared. I want to say that having her here is both terrifying and extraordinary.

But I can't. I can't say anything.

Mum blinks rapidly, fighting back tears. "I'll go, but can I still call you in the next day or two, see how you're getting on?"

Hugging Mum would be too much. Instead, I place a hand over hers and squeeze.

"Of course, Mum. That would be lovely."

Sniffing, Mum gives me a watery smile. "Thank you for giving me a chance, Trish. Really."

"Small steps," I say softly.

"Small steps," Mum agrees.

It's strange walking back into the office. This used to be the only place I felt I belonged. At work, I was confident in myself and my abilities. Now, it feels so foreign and I'm such a different version of myself, I find it hard to believe I ever slaved away hour upon hour within these walls.

I've barely made it past the reception desk before I'm mobbed. The females coo and carry on, gushing over how amazing I look and how cute Rose is. They're right – she looks completely adorable asleep in the front pack in her little yellow jumpsuit (a gift from Mags). The males in the office hover uncertainly at the edges, a few brave souls coming in for a closer look.

My nemesis, Mark, is one of the few in the office who stays behind his desk. Correction. The little prick has taken over my desk. He used to sit by the emergency exit door. Now, he's not only taken over my portfolios, but he's also nabbed the most prized desk in the place – one I worked my butt off to gain. Mark is leaning back in his chair (I bet it's my old chair) grinning at me like there's nothing wrong. A fool who didn't know better would think he was pleased to see me. The wanker.

As soon as I can break free from the clucky masses, I stride over and do my best to stare down my opponent.

"Made yourself comfortable," I state. "How's Omnus going?"

I happen to know from a work colleague that the Japanese company has been less than impressed with his work so far.

Mark doesn't look in the least put out. Instead, he laughs. "No one could do the job as well as you, Trish, but I'm doing my best."

I narrow my eyes. What game is he playing at?

Tash appears at the open door of her office. She crosses her arms and assesses me with a frown.

"Trish," she says gruffly.

"Hi, Tash," I say, walking closer.

She glances at Rose briefly and I see a glint of pain in her eyes before they harden.

"Since you're here, let's talk."

Tash dips her head and I follow her into her office. It's unchanged, though sparser than I remember. There's not a single personal effect, I realize. No picture frame, no souvenir, no magazine, book or object unrelated to work.

"I'm glad you came in," says Tash in her no-nonsense work voice.

When she closes the door and points me towards a chair, it sets off alarm bells. Tash only closes her door when she has something unpleasant to say.

"I have a proposition I'd like to put forward regarding your future employment."

No beating around the bush, then. Not that I should be surprised.

"I'm entitled to the full six months' maternity leave," I say firmly.

I figure Tash is going to try to talk me into coming back sooner. I've been keeping tabs on the company enough to know they're struggling.

Tash glances at Rose once again. "I understand," she says, her voice less confident. "In fact, if you decide you need more time, please come and talk to me."

I'm stunned into silence. Did she really just say that?

"The thing is, Trish, I've decided to take a sabbatical." Tash picks up a pen and fixes her eyes on it as she taps it lightly against her desk. "I'm going to go travelling," she says firmly. "See the sights of Europe."

"Wow, that's great." It's the craziest thing I've heard out of her mouth. In fact, if she hadn't said it to my face, I wouldn't have believed it. Trish lives to work. Anything else is trivial. "Where did that come from?"

Tash continues to tap her pen, avoiding my eye.

"I just need to," she says, as if no other explanation is required. "Anyway, I'm not rushing off. First, I have to find a suitable replacement while I'm gone. Someone I can trust."

"What about Mark?" I snap.

Tash pauses from the incessant pen-tapping and looks up. "He's a twat, Trish, as we both know."

I bite my lip to stop myself from smiling. "So where do I come in?"

"Well, obviously I want you to take over my role. No one else has the same level of skills."

"I'm glad you noticed."

"It would need to be full-time," says Tash, her gaze straying to Rose again. "Not easy with a young baby and no husband to help."

I can't help but laugh. "Tell it like it is," I say. "Please."

"It's a good opportunity for you. Putting a CEO role on your CV is like gold. Doors would open, Trish."

From Tash's tone, I can't decide if she thinks I should be leaping for joy or running for the door. Is she testing me somehow? Challenging me to decide if I want to have a corporate career or give it up?

"Consider it," says Tash, standing and opening her office door. "Get back to me by next week if you're interested in discussing things further."

"Thank you," I say, heading through the door. Pausing

next to Tash, I lower my voice so no one can hear. "Regardless of what I do, I hope you go travelling and find what you're looking for."

Then I'm out of the office and back on the hot, noisy street. All I can think about is getting home, kicking off my uncomfortable shoes and feeding Rose. My boobs are about to burst.

40

"Leo is so fat," exclaims Emma.

"He's chubby," I say, taking a bite of the bacon and egg pie she brought over.

Emma snorts. "Next to Rose, he looks like the Michelin man."

Our babies are lying on their tummies, side by side on a rug I laid out on the grass under the maple tree. They're naked, apart from the sun hats we've popped on their heads.

"Leo is going to be six months tomorrow," says Emma, shaking her head. "Where did the time go? Actually, I take that back – I know exactly where it went."

"I know what you mean. The last few months have been the longest of my life and yet they've disappeared in a flash."

"How are you feeling?" Emma asks. "You know…"

"I'm good. The sessions with the psychologist have really helped. I still have the odd moment when I feel down, but usually it's because I had no sleep the night before and I haven't been taking proper care of myself. Now I recognize the signs and make sure I do the things I know will stop my low mood from developing into something worse."

"Such as?"

I shrug. "Warm bath, a long walk, a healthy meal and an early night, hanging out with friends and family. The simple stuff."

"Speaking of family, how are things with your mum?"

"Not bad. I talk to her most weeks and her last visit was fairly successful. She's gone on a two-week camper van trip around the South Island with Will and Tilly. They look like they're having a great time, according to Will's Instagram posts, anyway."

"What about Scott?" Emma asks, raising her eyebrows briefly.

I take another bite of cake, chew and swallow. What about Scott? How do I respond to that question? I think about him all the time. When he comes to visit, I never want him to leave. Rose smiles at him more than anyone else. He's not the type of person I imagined I'd ever fall for and yet...

"He popped in yesterday," I say lightly. "Stayed for dinner."

"And?"

I shrug. "And nothing."

I'm embarrassed remembering yesterday. Rose was asleep and Scott and I were sitting on the porch drinking tea. All of a sudden, I couldn't take it anymore, so I leant over to kiss him on the lips, but he turned his head away and I kissed his ear. To make it worse, he just stood up and started talking about some stupid rugby game and how he'd never really considered himself a rugby man before. I just sat there, my cheeks glowing, and I knew then I was hopeless. Hopelessly in love with a guy who wasn't interested in a mildly depressed mother.

Emma looks like she wants to say something but is holding herself back.

"Maybe he's giving you space while you sort out the whole motherhood thing."

I laugh bitterly. "There's space and then there's wide open plains stretching as far as the eye can see."

Emma stands and turns Leo over to start dressing him. "He was keen on you, Trish. We could all see it."

I thought Scott was keen on me, too. Until he wasn't. He's different now: friendly, without a hint of anything more. Crouching beside Emma, I carefully flip Rose onto her back and slip on a nappy.

"Enough fresh air time for you, little one," I say, blowing a raspberry on her tummy.

She giggles and all thoughts of Scott disappear. The love I feel for my daughter is so big and powerful, I struggle to remember how distant and unfeeling I felt towards her after she was born. My greatest fear is that I'll somehow end up in that dark place again.

Emma staggers to her feet. "Oomph! I swear Leo weighs the same as Freddie."

"That's harsh," I say, laughing.

"I'd better dash," says Emma, slinging her bag on her shoulder. "See you on Saturday."

Darryl has organized a surprise birthday party for Lily – a picnic at the reserve next to the beach, complete with a marquee and three-piece band. He's invited just about everyone Lily knows and we didn't have the heart to tell him Lily is likely to go berserk. It's far too thoughtful and grown-up for her liking. But maybe she's not the same Lily she used to be. Maybe she's changed. I know I have.

"I turned down Tash's offer," I say, following Emma through the house and out to her car, Rose tucked on my hip.

Emma grins. "Excellent news."

"And I told Will I'd help him out with the landscape business, see where it leads."

Emma finishes strapping Leo into his car seat and gives me a hug. "Thank God for that."

I know my friends have been doing their best to stay neutral, but I'd have been blind if I hadn't seen how much they wanted me to turn my back on the big corporate career and do something that might bring me a little joy as opposed to a great deal of stress.

"It was a no-brainer, really," I say. "Once I got past the dent-to-my-ego part."

"Success and intelligence aren't tied to a fancy job title and hefty pay packet," Emma says, not for the first time.

"I know."

Watching Emma drive away, I breathe in the smell of freshly cut grass. The sky is a dazzling clear blue and I decide it's far too nice an afternoon to be cleaning the house – the job I'd set myself once Rose was asleep. Instead, I settle Rose in her push chair and head for the park.

Only a few paces from home, I hear my name being called.

Scott waves and dashes across the street with his "I'm being friendly but that's all" smile. I attempt to smile in return, but I can't. He stops next to me, clocks my scowl and his expression turns serious.

"Mind if I join you?" he says, shoving his hands in his pockets.

I have an urge to yell, "Yes, I do mind."

Instead, I give a brief nod and start walking, Scott matching pace beside me.

"Lovely day," he says, his voice tight.

Here we go again, playing friends. Only I'm so tired of it and it's too hard having to pretend.

Stopping abruptly, I face Scott. "OK, this isn't working."

Scott looks as if I've slapped him.

"What?"

"You being so nice and friendly."

He looks so hurt I wish I'd never opened my mouth. But I have to say how I feel about him, even if it sends him packing.

"I like you, Scott. A lot. And it's hard to be around you. It's hard because…" I take a deep breath and stare at the ground. "Because I want more and you don't," I whisper.

Scott is silent for so long, I figure he's trying to work out the nicest way to let me down.

"Remember when I came to your room at the hotel," he says at last. "To take you to Harry's wedding and I had that pin I put in your hair?"

I don't reply.

"It fell out of your hair while we were dancing and I put it in my pocket. I was going to give it back to you, but I… I kept it. It's on my bedside table and every morning, I wake and think about how this incredibly beautiful woman agreed to go to a wedding with a stranger to help him feel better."

I look up and glare at Scott's gorgeous dark brown eyes. "Please don't try to tell me what a good person I am. That I'll find someone who—"

Scott grabs my hand. "I don't want you to find someone else," he says. "I'm trying to tell you I've been crazy about you since the moment I stuck that pin in your hair."

"But you've been acting like... Yesterday when I kissed you..." I break off, my heart thumping.

Scott sighs. "I was giving you space, Trish. You have a newborn baby, you're trying to form a new relationship with your mum and you've been dealing with your mental health. I thought... It would have been so selfish of me if I'd tried to make a move, even though you're all I think about."

"Does that mean you're... that there's a chance?"

"Oh, God, I hope so, Trish."

Tears fill my eyes. "Are you sure you want to get involved with someone who never used to cry and now seems to burst into tears for no reason at all?"

Scott slides a hand around my waist. "If that someone is you, then yes."

As we lean towards each other, I inhale a subtle whiff of lavender. There's a glowing sensation deep in my chest, warm and bright like the sun. I wonder if it's emanating out of me like a golden aura.

"Could I please kiss you now?" asks Scott, his mouth inches from mine.

I press my lips to his in reply.

Acknowledgements

I started writing this novel at the beginning of 2020 – talk about a bumpy year! Like everyone, I could not have predicted the extraordinary times to follow.

Since then I've had many ups and downs as I've tried to care for family, manage a business, and find space in my head to write.

My heart-felt thank you to my three children, Grace, Sophie and George, and my husband, Mike. We have spent a lot of time together during the various lockdowns of the past two years here in New Zealand and I couldn't have asked for better company. Your support for my writing has been the one constant I could rely on in these unpredictable times.

To all my precious family and friends, thank you, thank you, thank you, for your love and kindness (and for buying my books and reading them even when I know they're not the type of book you would normally consider!).

Thank you to Hannah Todd for reading the first draft of this novel and providing insightful advice and feedback. Your enthusiasm for my writing has been tremendously encouraging, especially when I've been afflicted with self-doubt.

A bucket-load of thanks to my wonderful editor Martina Arzu, Claire Dean for her brilliant copyediting skills, and the rest of the team at Aria and Head of Zeus. I still get a thrill every time I hear from you because I can't believe I'm an actual published author with an actual publisher in the UK – a place I can't wait to visit again now our borders are finally opening.

Thanks to the team at Bloomsbury Australia, and to Ross and Melanie here in New Zealand who have gone above and beyond to support this local author – you are both superstars!

To my incredible staff Brea and Rachel at my favourite bookshop in the world (okay I may be biased), I am lucky and grateful beyond words. Thank you for being champion booksellers and for making The Booklover Bookshop the special place it is today. To all our loyal customers, thank you for your endless support.

To my fellow booksellers who have survived the past two years of Covid chaos, I raise my glass to you because it has been incredibly tough. At the risk of inciting further heated discussions, I believe providing books to our community is and should be an essential service – books bring more solace and comfort to those isolated and anxious than a pair of rollerskates or a six-pack of beer ever could!

As F. Scott Fitzgerald famously wrote: "That is part of the beauty of all literature. You discover that your longings are universal longings, that you're not lonely and isolated from anyone. You belong."

To my readers, you belong to a very special group. Without you I wouldn't be typing this right now. Without you, books and bookshops would cease to exist. Thank you from the bottom of my heart for choosing to be a reader and most especially for choosing to read this book.

About the Author

OLIVIA SPOONER lives in New Zealand with her husband, three children, a big hairy dog and an overweight cat. Olivia's previous novel *A Way Back to Happy* tells the story of Emma, Trish's friend. Olivia loved writing about Emma, Trish, Mags, and Lily so much she decided to tell Trish's story next. Olivia is the proud owner of an independent bookshop, where she happily shares her love of books with everyone who walks through the door. When not surrounded by books or creating stories, Olivia is most likely to be found at the beach or simply out walking – the more remote the location, the better. She loves a good meal and to the disbelief of her children, adores a massaged kale and avocado salad. And chocolate. Just not together.